CAN'T STOP THE FEELING

SINCLAIR SISTERS 2

JANET ELIZABETH HENDERSON

First published in 2019 by Janet Elizabeth Henderson

This edition 2020

This edition ISBN: 978-0-473-50627-8

Author's Website: http://www.janetelizabethhenderson.com

Text design by Vellum

Cover design by Janet Elizabeth Henderson

Editing by Liz Dempsey

Dear Reader,

First in 2014, and then to an even greater degree in 2018, the Mackintosh building of The Glasgow School of Art was gutted by fire. It no longer stands on the spot it occupied for over a hundred years, leaving the artists who honed their crafts within its walls heartbroken at its loss. I know, because I am one of them.

For four years, I was fortunate enough to walk the halls of the Mac. I sat in its lecture theatre, on seats that were so hard your bum was numb for hours afterwards. I showed my work in exhibitions held in the studios and corridors. I spent hours in the library, daydreaming under the Art Nouveau detailing and napping in the soft afternoon light that flooded the room. Most importantly, I worked in the studios, knowing that generations of artists had done so before me.

The Glasgow School of Art's Mackintosh building wasn't just a place to study—it was loved. It had its own personality —from the recurring Rennie Mackintosh motifs throughout the building to the worn stone steps that wound up to the studios above. That is why in this book, the art school can still be found in pristine condition. In the world inside my head, the building is still in one piece, and a new generation of artists walks it halls dreaming of fame.

So, please forgive me for taking poetic licence with history, but to me, the Mac still lives on, and I couldn't bear to write of a world where it doesn't.

With much love,
   Janet x

PROLOGUE

Eighteen months earlier, Kintyre Mansion, Scotland

The sound of breaking glass woke Donna Sinclair from a deep sleep. She lay as still as possible, straining to hear what had caused the noise. As usual, the mansion was eerily quiet. In the three months she'd been living in the housekeeper's accommodation at the top of the building, she'd become accustomed to the creaks and echoing noises in the old house. Although, she still didn't feel comfortable in the place, or in her role as housekeeper—a job she hadn't applied for but had been given because she happened to turn up on the day her boss fired the last one.

She sighed at the thought of her invisible boss. She hadn't seen hide nor hair of Duncan Stewart since the day he'd hired her—even though they both lived in the same building. Since his young wife died the year before, Duncan had retreated from the world, leaving his housekeeper to deal with it for him. His grief was a spectre hanging over the mansion. Although, some days she thought it might be the lingering spirit of Fiona Stewart.

Aren't you going to investigate? Donna wasn't surprised by the voice only she could hear. She looked over to find a life-size drawing of Hermione Granger standing beside her dresser. *You* are *the housekeeper after all.*

"Go away," Donna said. "You're a kid. What do you know?" She paused as something else occurred to her. "And you aren't real." She probably should have led with the last part.

Hermione was undeterred. *Isn't it your job to take care of the mansion?*

"It isn't part of my job description to put myself in danger." And yes, she was aware she was talking to an imaginary person. It happened a lot more often than she would ever admit. She had a tendency to sketch in the pages of the books she read, and those sketches had a habit of coming to life when she least wanted them to.

Stop being such a coward, Hermione said. *You're giving girls everywhere a bad name.*

She should never have started re-reading *Harry Potter* before she fell asleep. If she'd been reading *Lord of the Rings,* Frodo would have appeared and told her to stay under her bed until the problem passed.

Another smash drew her attention to the front of the house. It didn't sound like a window breaking, more like dishes being thrown against a wall. Part of her, the cowardly part, hoped Duncan would deal with the situation but considering his hermit nature, it seemed unlikely.

Donna! Someone could be breaking in. You need to deal with it.

"Fine," she grumbled.

After climbing out of bed and tugging on her old terry cotton robe, she grabbed her phone from the nightstand next to her bed and hurried for the door.

Don't worry, Hermione said. *I have my wand. I'll back you up.*

"What a relief," Donna muttered as she hurried down the stairs into the empty building beneath her. "Go away. I can't deal with you right now."

How rude! Hermione disappeared. Thankfully.

The sound of something else smashing made her trip on the stairs, and as she reached for the bannister to steady herself, she heard a voice—an angry, pain-filled wail that echoed through the mansion.

"Damn you to hell for leaving me, Fiona!"

Duncan.

She flew down the stairs. Rushing towards the sound of a man losing control. Donna didn't spare a thought for the danger involved in confronting him while he was enraged, all she could think of was getting to him. Of helping him. Somehow.

"Forever!" Another crash punctuated his roar. "You promised forever."

She rushed through the corridors to the main entrance, wishing she wasn't the only staff member who lived on-site. Wishing someone was there to help her calm Duncan and save him from himself.

"You lied!" he bellowed. "Forever didn't happen."

She ran across the marble entryway and yanked the front door open. A missile flew at her head. She ducked—just in time—and a half-full bottle of whisky smashed on the marble floor behind her.

Duncan stood in the middle of the driveway, at the bottom of the steps leading up to the mansion. His rumpled blue plaid shirt was buttoned up crookedly, his jeans had stains and his feet were bare. An overgrown beard hid his jaw, and tangled hair fell into his eyes. He looked more like a man who'd been living on the streets for months than the owner of Kintyre's mansion house.

"Liar!" He roared as he lifted his fists to the sky. "Liar!"

Agony came off him with such force that Donna half expected to find a storm raging overhead. There should have been lightning and an answering roar of thunder, but instead, all she could see were the stars.

He staggered back a step before bending over to reach for another bottle. It seemed that in the weeks since she'd last seen him, her boss had been working his way through the liquor cabinet.

A spear of guilt made her stomach clench. She should have checked on him. She'd been selfish, thinking only of her own comfort, when he'd been suffering alone. As far as she could see, there was no one else around to keep an eye on him. Three months and there had been no visits to the mansion. No calls from family. Nothing. She wasn't sure if he'd driven everyone away, or if his life had revolved around his wife to such an extent that there'd been no room for anyone else. It didn't matter what caused his isolation. Right now, there was no one to step in and stop the man from killing himself with his grief.

No one but her.

"Duncan!" She raced towards him, down the stone steps and into the night. Aware that it probably wasn't the smartest thing she'd ever done. He was massive, enraged and blind drunk. But he was also in pain, and she couldn't bear it. "Stop, Duncan, please," she called.

What she planned to do once she got to him, she didn't know. But, to her surprise, he froze. The intensity of his dark gaze made her stumble. He blinked. Once. Twice. And then frowned.

"Fiona?" The confused whisper broke her heart.

"Oh, Duncan, no." She approached him slowly, her hand out, as though he were a savage beast.

"Fiona!" It was a desperate cry.

He staggered the distance between them and fell to his knees on the harsh gravel. Strong arms snaked around her hips as he rubbed his face against her stomach.

"You came back." The wonder and love in his voice brought tears to her eyes. "I knew you wouldn't leave me. You said forever. You promised. And you always keep your promises." He pressed a gentle kiss to her stomach. "Ah, Fiona, I've missed you, lass.

A tear slid down Donna's cheek, and she found it difficult to get the words out through her tightening throat. "Duncan, Fiona's gone," she said gently. "I'm Donna, your housekeeper."

He was buried too deep in his drunken delusion to hear her. "I can't do this without you." He pressed his forehead to her. "Don't leave me again. I cannae bear it."

Another tear escaped, and she found herself reaching out with trembling hands to stroke the hair of the broken man who clung to her. To offer what little comfort she could when words were lost to him.

His breathing hitched at her touch. "How I love you. There's only you for me. Only you."

Her heart clenched, and she desperately wished that she had the power to bring his wife back for him. She wanted to reach through time and undo the injustices of the past. She wanted to give him hope. But there was none to give.

"Shh," she whispered as she stroked his unruly hair. "It's okay. It's going to be okay."

"They want me to lecture," he whispered. "To stand up in front of all those students and talk about my work. I can't do it. I can't talk about it, and I can't paint again. It would be better if everybody forgot about me. I'm washed up, lass. There are no more ideas for paintings in my head. And why would there be? What would I paint without you? Everything is so damn hard without you. Don't leave me again. Never again. You promised."

He let out a sigh of pure longing. "I think I've missed your lips most of all." He leaned back to look up at her with eyes that saw another. His fingers traced the curve of her mouth. "I've missed the way they look when you smile at me, and the way they purse in anger when I annoy you—which is often. I've missed the feel of them, satin against my skin. And the colour, a ripe peach in summer. I've just missed *you*, Fi. All of you."

He pressed his forehead against her. "I want to be with you so bad it's agony. Why did you leave me behind? And why didn't I have the guts to follow when I should have?"

"Hush now," she cooed as tears streamed down her cheeks, "it's going to be okay."

He took a shuddering breath. "I can't smile without you, Fi. I've forgotten how."

There was nothing else she could say. They stayed like that for what seemed like hours until Donna was shivering from the cold nipping at her bones. She couldn't let go of him. She knew she was a poor substitute for the woman he longed for, but in that moment, she was all he had to hold on to.

At last, Duncan's vice-like hold relaxed, and with one long, contented sigh, he slid to the ground in front of her. For a second, she feared he'd given up on life entirely, but his pulse was steady and strong. It was only the whisky and the emotion catching up with him.

There was no way Donna would leave him lying in the driveway. Even if her nature could allow it, the early morning temperature could still slip below zero. The calendar might tell them it was late summer, but Scotland hadn't received the memo. There was only one thing she could do, she reached into the pocket of her robe and pulled out her phone.

"Agnes," she said when her sister answered. "I need help."

"He snapped, didn't he?" Aggie said. "I knew it was only a matter of time. Hide the weapons. I'll call the cops."

"He hasn't snapped." Well, not in the way Aggie meant anyway. "He drank too much, and he's passed out in the driveway."

"Oh." Her sister almost sounded disappointed.

"I need you to get hold of Keir and his brother. I'll have to carry him into the house, and I can't do it on my own."

"You should leave him there to teach him a lesson." Aggie might be telling her off, but Donna could hear the rustling as she got dressed, ready to come to her aid.

"He's had enough hard lessons these past few months. He's grieving, not partying. He's been trying to drown his sorrows." For months, by the looks—and the smell—of it.

Agnes sighed. "I'll get the boys. We'll be there soon."

Grateful, Donna hung up and waited for them, spending the time clearing up the broken bottles and mopping the whisky from the reception hall floor. She would have liked to have been dressed in more than her robe when help arrived, but she didn't dare leave Duncan alone in case he drowned in his vomit. Not that there was any sign of him waking up enough to empty his stomach. He was still out cold, lying on the frozen ground, beside the overgrown rose bushes that lined the drive.

Headlights announced the arrival of her helpers, and a minute later, Mairi's ex-boyfriend climbed out of his truck. Keir had recently returned to town and bought the building that housed Arness' only garage. It also held the flat where Mairi and Agnes lived. The purchase had been a calculated move on his part. Keir had come home to win Mairi back—so far, it wasn't going well.

"So, this is the famous artist." Keir crouched down to get a look at Duncan. "Poor bastard."

"Thanks for coming out."

He smiled up at her. "You can thank me by telling your stubborn sister how awesome I am."

Donna winced, grateful Mairi was spending the night with Isobel and the kids, and hadn't been there when she'd called Agnes. Mairi would have lost her mind if she'd known Keir had been roped in to help. "I'm not sure that would do you any good."

"No, knowing Mairi, I don't think it would. Never mind. What do you need us to do?"

"I need to get him inside and into his bed. I can't leave him here."

He looked over his shoulder at his brother, who'd climbed out of the truck with Agnes. "Get his legs, Sean."

Together, the four of them managed to get Duncan into the house, up the stairs and onto his bed.

"This place stinks," Agnes said as she picked up empty beer bottles and plates of half-eaten food. "We need rubbish bags, heavy duty cleaning solution and a vacuum cleaner." She stared at the carpet in disgust. "Although, maybe we should just set fire to the room and be done with it."

"The cleaning stuff is in the cupboard off the kitchen," Donna said. "It's marked scullery."

"Of course it is." Rubbish in hand, Agnes turned towards the door.

"I'll help you." Sean followed her.

"He can't go on like this. You know that, right?" Keir said, his eyes on her fingers as they brushed Duncan's hair from his forehead.

She made a mental note to make a barber's appointment

for him, then wondered how she'd get him there once she'd booked him in.

"I know, I should have checked up on him before now. Don't worry, I won't leave him alone again."

She'd been so busy settling into the mansion, and getting to grips with her job, that she hadn't spared a thought for her grieving boss. All communication about her duties as house-keeper had come from his lawyer. Now, she wished she'd taken the time to find out what Duncan had been doing while she settled in.

Keir's face softened as he looked at her. "You've always had the biggest heart out of you and your sisters, but he isn't some stray animal you can rescue and nurse back to health. He's a full-grown man who's had his heart ripped out. The chances of you getting hurt are pretty bloody high."

She'd already figured that out all on her own. "I'll be careful."

"No, you won't. You're too damn soft." He gave her a knowing smile. "If you need help, shout out. If he scares you, get out of here. You can always call in the professionals to deal with him. Okay?"

Duncan would hate dealing with a stranger. He might be a mess, but he was a proud mess.

"Promise me," Keir said when she didn't answer. "Mairi might hate my guts right now, but I still care about her, and her sisters. I don't want you getting hurt."

"I promise. If I can't help him, I'll call someone who can."

On the bed, her boss stirred, and his hand snapped out to curl around her wrist. Keir took a step forwards to intervene, but Donna shook her head to stop him.

"What is it?" she said softly.

"The roses." His voice was hoarse, his eyes unfocused as he stared at her. "Did I damage the roses?"

"No. The roses are fine."

As he sank back into the bed, his grip loosened, and his hand fell to his side. "Fiona loves the roses," he muttered before he passed out again.

Keir gave him a pitying look. "Come on. We'll help clean up before we leave. In his state, he wouldn't notice if we drove a tank through here. You might want to get rid of the booze while we do it."

"Good thinking." Donna adjusted the pillow under Duncan's head. "I hate seeing him this broken. He looks so strong on the outside." His need called to her.

"Sweetheart," Keir said softly. "Don't go falling for this man."

As she nodded, Donna wondered if Keir's advice might be a little too late in coming.

CHAPTER 1

Present day, Kintyre Mansion, Scotland

It had been two long, painful weeks since Duncan had ordered Donna to fire their second cook—this time for whistling while he worked. Although, Donna thought the lord of the manor had been more annoyed by *what* the man had been whistling than by the noise itself. Apparently, ABBA wasn't 'proper music,' according to her boss. When she'd explained to him that he might want to put up with the whistling because decent cooks were hard to come by, he'd upped her salary and told her she could do the job until she found a replacement.

Although Donna appreciated the extra cash, as her bank account was being drained dry paying off all the poor people Duncan fired, having her cook was a decision they'd both come to regret. Because Donna was famous for three things —her talent for killing plants, her non-existent cooking skills and her inability to say no. It was her non-existent cooking skills that were slowly killing them off. If it wasn't a ready meal or a sandwich, then whatever she produced was inedible, and the frustration of trying to make it otherwise was driving her insane. If the new cook didn't start the next day, as promised, she was going to snap and beat her boss to death with a spatula.

"What the hell is that racket?" Duncan stormed into the kitchen, because Duncan stormed everywhere. It was his default mode.

"What does it sound like?" Donna was standing on a chair, on top of the table, reaching for the smoke alarm over her head. If she stood on tiptoe, she just might make it.

"Are you trying to break your neck?" he growled at her.

"Shh," she hissed. "I've nearly got it."

Her fingertips skimmed the alarm, but she couldn't get a grip. She stretched further. And lost her balance. Her arms windmilled. She squealed. And fell from the chair.

Straight into two strong arms.

Her fingers curled into the soft cotton of one of his many blue tartan shirts, and she held on tight. If he hadn't been there, she would have broken something for sure. Possibly her neck.

"That was the stupidest thing I've seen in quite some time," he said as he effortlessly cradled her against his chest. His broad, strong, muscular chest.

Ever since he'd stopped drinking, he'd been spending his time in the first-floor gym. All those hours working up a sweat had bulked him up, and he showed no sign of strain from holding her. He felt solid, strong—sexy. Her cheeks flushed at the thought. These were things she tried very hard not to notice about her boss. Along with the way his shoulders seemed to grow with every hour he spent working out, the way his jaw always had a hint of stubble on it, and how his eyes were so intensely black when he looked at her that she still hadn't figured out their colour. Aye, things like that. Those were the things she didn't dare notice. Instead, what she *forced* herself to notice, was that he was still very much in love with his dead wife.

"Put me down," she said, a bit more forcefully than she'd intended.

With a reprimanding glare, he put her on her feet. While she steadied herself, he jumped up onto the table and removed the alarm. Of course, he didn't need the chair for extra height. Sometimes being short sucked.

At last, blessed silence filled the house as Duncan frowned down at her. "Why didn't you get the handyman to remove it?" He put the alarm box on the table and righted the chair that had toppled along with her.

"Because you fired him months ago and I haven't found a replacement yet. Help me open these windows. We need to get the smoke out."

"What happened?" He swung the back door wide open.

"What does it look like?" She pointed to the stove. "I was making breakfast."

"Is that what you call it?"

Her eye twitched, and her fingers itched to reach for the knife block. "Nothing's stopping you from feeding yourself."

"I don't have a talent for cooking."

"And I do?"

Wisely, he didn't answer. Instead, he stared at the smoking frying pan. "What were you trying to make?"

"Fish."

"For breakfast?"

"There wasn't any cereal."

She looked at the charcoal lump and dared him to say

anything more. How was she supposed to know that the heat should have been on low? She thought everything that went in a frying pan got cooked on high. Isn't that what frying was all about? High heat? Cook it fast?

"Aren't you a vegetarian?" he said.

"Sometimes," she snapped. Was this the time for an inquisition? Really?

"Did you put oil in the pan first?"

"Why would I put oil in it? It's non-stick." Although, it had to be a cheap pan, as the Teflon coating had peeled from the sides and was curling up around the fish.

"Even I know you always oil a pan."

"Well, maybe you should be the one cooking then."

Duncan ran a hand through his hair, drawing her attention to the fact it was overgrown again. It fell over his forehead in a tousled mess that made her think of cool sheets and warm nights. She shook her head to clear it. That wasn't what she'd intended to think. She wasn't even sure where the thought had come from. No, all she'd meant to think was that it was time for another trip to the barber. Something he would no doubt complain about. It generally took a crowbar to get him out of the mansion. She was sure his self-imprisonment was part of the reason he was so bad-tempered—he was going stir crazy and taking them all down with him.

"Maybe you should offer the new cook more money to get her here today," he said.

The tension building in her chest felt like it was going to explode through the top of her head, and those knives looked more attractive every second. It had taken her days of negotiation to get Grace Blain to come cook at the mansion. She hadn't cooked for anyone since she and her husband had closed their restaurant. Donna had begged the woman to come out of retirement, promising her a salary she hadn't even cleared with Duncan. If it wasn't for the fact she'd known Donna her whole life and felt some affection for her, she doubted Grace would have been swayed for all the money in the world.

"Are you okay?" Duncan took a step towards her, caught sight of her face and wisely retreated. "Do you need to sit down?"

"What I need," she said evenly, squeezing the words from between clenched teeth. "Is a boss who doesn't keep firing the staff. Do you realise how hard it is to find people who want to work in the mansion?"

"Maybe if you hired people who didn't annoy the hell out of me, they would stay longer, and you wouldn't have to find replacements."

"This is *my* fault?"

He took another step back. "I didn't say that." His phone rang, and a look of relief swept over his face. "I need to take this."

"Since when? You never answer your phone." She dragged a fan out of the pantry and turned it on.

"Since now," he said. "Duncan here."

Donna unashamedly listened in. If he wanted privacy, he could storm back out again. She mentally went over the contents of the freezer. It was pointless. Unless there was a ready meal in there that she'd missed, there wasn't anything else she could cook. She'd picked the fish because she thought it would be easy. Damn fish had lulled her into a false sense of security. Now the house stank, and she was still starving.

There was no other option but to go into Campbeltown to eat. While she was there, she could bring back some Chinese food to reheat for dinner. She would have had it delivered hot, and at the right time, but Duncan had screwed that up too. They'd been put on a town-wide food delivery ban after he got into a fight with the pizza guy over a cold pie. The pizza guy was in his forties, built like a truck and hadn't appreciated being taken to task. She wasn't sure who'd swung the first punch, but she had been the one who'd turned the hose on them and broken up the fight.

This was her life. She hosed down her boss, the famous artist, to get him off the beer-bellied pizza guy. Really, the only way to go from here was up.

"No, I don't want to do a lecture for your students," Duncan snapped, bringing her attention back to him. "I've told you this before, Zoe." A pause. "No, I won't be in a better mood next month." He swiped the screen and then slammed his phone down on the kitchen table, no doubt damaging the screen.

He could order his own damn replacement this time.

"I thought you were dealing with this crap," he said.

"And by *crap*, you mean?"

"The begging emails and phone calls. So-and-so wants a lecturer, that one wants a new exhibition, this one wants to interview me about my work. I've had it up to here with all these stupid demands." He held up a hand to jaw height.

"How dare they show an interest in you or your work? What on earth are they thinking? Don't they know that artists don't want attention? The cheek of it."

He pinned her with a look. "I could do without the sarcasm."

"I could do with a boss who doesn't fire people for stupid reasons."

"Are you about done?"

He folded his arms again, drawing her attention to biceps she really didn't want to notice. Suddenly, she couldn't stop from seeing the way his shoulders filled his shirt and the way his thighs strained against the denim of his jeans. She was losing her mind. It had to be from food deprivation. Starvation. That's what it was. Because it couldn't be attraction. She'd trained herself not to be attracted to him because she had the good sense to realise that any attraction she felt would only lead to heartbreak. Unfortunately, sometimes her sensible brain and her horny body weren't on the same page.

"Yes." She waved a hand. "Carry on."

"I thought we agreed that you would tell these people I'm done with the art world and that all requests were going through you now."

"How can I stop people from calling you on your personal number, Duncan? I deal with your email and the mansion phone, but the iPhone is yours. If they want to call you on that to ask about your work, there's nothing I can do about it."

"I need to change my number. That phase of my life is over."

"You might change your mind," she pointed out. "You might start painting again. It would be stupid to burn bridges now when you could need them later." Although, she knew he hadn't even set foot in his studio in the past two years, and it didn't look like that would change any time soon.

"Tell them to back off," he said with a steely glare. "And get me a new number." He looked at the trashed phone. "And a new phone, this one's screen is cracked."

"Fine." Honestly, she was too hungry to argue.

"Good. I need you to fire the gardener as well."

She pinched the bridge of her nose. "Please tell me he wasn't whistling?"

"No." Duncan's face darkened. "He butchered Fiona's roses."

"Oh." The wind went out of her sails. "I'm so sorry. I told him not to touch the rose bushes."

The roses were a living memorial—left to grow wild—the

way Duncan's young wife had never had a chance to. In the two and a half years since Fiona's death, no one had touched the roses, although their unkempt appearance was at odds with the pristine symmetry of the Georgian mansion and grounds.

"I want him gone," Duncan said.

Donna reached for what little patience she had left, aware that his ire meant he was upset, and he just didn't know how else to express it. "We've talked about this. More than once. There are other ways to deal with staff who annoy you. You don't have to go straight to firing people."

It would also be cheaper for her if he didn't. Every time she had to let someone go, she ended up writing a severance cheque from her own bank account because she couldn't cope with upsetting them.

"I said I would consider other options, but not in this case. The gardener has overstayed his welcome here."

For once, she could understand why he was firing someone. But she didn't have to like it. "I'll deal with it," she said.

She grabbed her overstuffed messenger bag from the counter and slung it over her shoulder, making sure the copy of *The Hobbit* she'd been sketching in was tucked safely inside. The last thing she wanted was for a world-famous artist to see her amateur doodles.

"Where are you going?" Duncan demanded.

"Town."

"What about the gardener?"

"I'll deal with him as soon as I get back. But if I don't eat soon, I may kill someone."

He considered her. "You mean me, don't you?"

She thought it wise not to answer.

He frowned as he looked her up and down as though seeing her for the first time. Donna felt self-conscious. With her curves, she wasn't exactly a poster child for hunger. In fact, most men thought she could stand to lose a few pounds, and they weren't shy about telling her either.

"Did I specify a uniform when I hired you?"

She looked down at her clothes but couldn't see what had snagged his attention. She was dressed for work: in smart trousers and a shirt. Today, the trousers were grey, and the shirt was black. She might be the world's worst housekeeper, and she might have no authority over the staff, but she wasn't going to let that stop her from looking the part—damn it.

"You want me to wear a uniform?" Her voice rose to a screech at the thought of wearing a French maid outfit.

"No. I was wondering if I'd specified one because you seem to dress like we've got a dress code."

"All you specified when you hired me was that I wasn't to have any parties."

"Huh." He rubbed his chin. "That was it?"

It was clear he had no recollection of hiring her. Mainly because it'd happened during his alcohol-sodden days.

"That was it," she confirmed. "You opened the door, told me you'd fired the housekeeper and the job was mine. Then you left."

"Well"—he folded his arms—"I'm telling you now. There's no uniform with the job. Wear what you like."

She tucked a strand of her dirty blonde hair, which wouldn't curl but wouldn't lie straight either, behind her ear and considered her boss. "I do wear what I like."

"What I mean is you can wear more *relaxed* clothes, if you want. I want you to be comfortable here. This isn't just your job. It's your home too."

"And it only took you two years to notice," she muttered before smiling at him. "Thanks. I'll take that into consideration." She headed for the door.

"Don't forget to fire the gardener. I want it done today."

She tugged open the door, and in her haste to get away

from her annoying boss, promptly fell down the steps and into the garden. Humiliated, she jumped to her feet, dusted herself off and shouted, "I'm all right." Before running for her car, which she kept parked at the back of the house.

Food. That's what she needed. And caffeine. Everything would look better with both firmly in her stomach.

CHAPTER 2

Duncan watched his housekeeper trip down the back steps. She righted herself before he could rush to the rescue and then hurried away before he could say anything more to her. The woman was as graceful as a ballet dancer until she got flustered. It was one of her more endearing quirks. And she had many quirks. He might not have been paying attention to her in the first year or so after she started working at the mansion, but she'd become increasingly fascinating to him over the past few months. From watching her, he got the feeling that there was a whole lot more to Donna Sinclair than she let people see.

As he followed her out of the back door and watched her disappear in a cloud of dust, he heard whistling and turned to find the gardener, Bill, wheeling a barrow from the front of the house. He hated whistling. But he hated what this guy had done to his wife's roses even more.

The sight of the stalky stubs, where flowers once bloomed, had made his fingers itch to reach for the whisky. It had been eighteen months since he'd last tasted a good dram. And he instinctively knew it would be many more before he could trust himself to taste it again. He'd come to that realisation the morning he'd woken with a vague recollection of what had transpired the night before, to find that strangers had cleaned up around him. It had been the humiliating kick up the backside he'd needed. Even now, the main thing he could remember from the night he'd set out to drink himself to death, was that he'd been overly concerned about protecting Fiona's roses.

And now this bastard had trashed them.

"Morning, Mr Stewart," the man said. "Another fine day in paradise."

Duncan had only met the gardener once before, when Donna had introduced them, and he hadn't warmed to him then. And he definitely didn't feel any warmer now. He'd met his type before, he was one of those men who couldn't take orders from a woman, no matter how much smarter and more capable she might be. His blatant disregard for Donna's instructions was another mark against him. Only Duncan got to ignore his housekeeper, everyone else had bloody well better toe her line.

"Tell me something," Duncan asked, his keen artist's eye taking in details about the man. It told him that the gardener was in his fifties and fit for his age. There was an arrogant air about him that rubbed Duncan up the wrong way—probably because the only arrogance he tolerated was his own. "Did my housekeeper tell you to leave the roses alone?"

The man puffed out his chest and scoffed. "Aye, that she did. That lassie doesn't know the first thing about gardening, and I told her so."

Another strike against the man. It wasn't his place to give Donna a hard time—that was Duncan's job. And his alone.

"Well, you can pack up your gear. You're fired. The order to leave the roses alone came directly from me."

Bill's face turned purple, and his hands clenched into fists.

"You can't fire me. I might have only been working at the mansion for a few months, but I've been doing this job for thirty years. I know how to care for roses."

"You were told to leave them alone, but you didn't. So you're fired." As far as Duncan was concerned, this conversation was over. He turned to leave.

A hand curved round his forearm, making him stop. He glared back at the man, watching as the awareness hit him that not only was Duncan at least twenty years younger, he was a good head taller and twice as broad—all of it muscle. The gardener released his hold as though his fingers were on fire, but the outrage in his eyes didn't dim.

"You can't fire me. Your housekeeper does the firing."

"My housekeeper works for me."

Bill licked his lips in an action that reminded Duncan of a cold-blooded lizard. "I want the same severance she gives everybody else you fire. I won't be missing out just because you decided to man up and do the deed yourself for a change."

Duncan stilled. "I don't give severance pay, and I won't be conned into starting now."

"That's a bold-faced lie," Bill snapped. "Everybody knows when you're fired from Kintyre Mansion you leave with a hefty cheque to see you over. I want my cheque. You can't steal from me. I want what I'm owed."

Duncan took a step towards him, looming over the man. "I don't hand out severance pay. Get your gear and get off my land before I physically remove you from it."

Bill's face twisted in rage. "You're trying to steal from me. That money is mine by rights. You're just being tight-fisted because you haven't sold a painting in years. Everybody knows you're a washed-up has-been, but I'll be damned if I'll suffer an unpaid, unfair dismissal because you're tight for money. You haven't heard the end of this. I'll get the money owing to me, one way or another." He turned and strode back around to the front of the house.

What the hell? Severance pay? Duncan watched him go as suspicion bloomed. If Donna had been handing out cheques when she fired staff members, they weren't coming from the house account. Which meant they could only be coming from one place: her pocket. The staff had been taking advantage of her soft heart. And he was damn well going to put a stop to that straight away.

Frustrated, he kicked at the nearest bush, and to his surprise, a book came flying out. Duncan retrieved it and dusted the cover off. It was a copy of *The Hobbit*. One of his staff must have dropped it, or one of the work crew who'd been painting the windows over the past few weeks. He'd give it to Donna and have her track down the owner. For some reason, he flicked through the pages—and stilled.

He lowered himself to sit on the steps leading up to his kitchen door and started slowly leafing through the book. It was full of drawings. Pen and ink doodles in the margins, and full-colour drawings that filled whole pages. He recognised the images as being illustrations from the text. A hobbit on one page, a troll on the next, a large snarling dragon flowing across a double-page spread at the back of the book. His heart raced at the sight of the work. They were some of the best illustrations he'd seen in years. The drawings almost had a life of their own, a style that made them jump from the page. Whoever had done these had serious talent.

He frowned. Why were they working in Arness instead of making a living from their work? Was it possible someone was trying to get close to him, hoping he'd use his connections in the art world to help them get ahead? It wouldn't be the first time it'd happened to him. But if that was the case, why hadn't they approached him already? Or, was this person hiding their talent? A shiver ran down his spine, and he wondered if he'd hit on the truth.

He flicked through the book, stunned again at the quality of the artwork, before turning to the front of the book. No name. No mark of ownership at all. Whoever had done the drawings hadn't claimed them, and Duncan suspected he was right about them hiding their talent. There had been a time, years earlier, when he would have searched the artist out and demanded they fulfil their potential. That was back in the days when he cared enough to mentor the talent that impressed him.

Still, these drawings, they deserved a second look. Maybe later, when he'd finished dealing with his errant housekeeper, he'd track down the artist and return the book to them personally. In the meantime, he tucked it into his back pocket. It was a mystery, and for the first time in years, he'd found something that intrigued him. Something that stirred up his curiosity and made him want answers. Aye, he'd keep hold of the book for now—until he solved the mystery of the unknown artist.

But before that, he had a housekeeper to sort out.

* * *

Donna wasn't proud. She ran from the mansion. And from Duncan. Unfortunately, she ran into town. And it was only when she was cornered by the local branch of the Scottish Women's Institute that she remembered she was also running from them. It was clear she needed a new life strategy. Avoiding people wasn't working for her, they just tracked her down. Like the three old women who had her hemmed against the wall outside the bank.

"Hello, ladies," Donna said. "You all look lovely today." She stumbled over the words when her eyes landed on Joyce

MacDonald. The seventy-eight-year-old was wearing a bubble gum pink jogging suit and had dyed her hair to match. Donna cleared her throat. "Um, I'm sorry I can't stay and chat. I have a lot of errands to run."

She took a step forwards, but Joyce—moving with the speed of a woman half her age—blocked her escape with her walker. She gave Donna an angelic smile, revealing teeth smeared with pink lipstick.

Ann Dunbar, a retired head teacher, gave Donna a look that made her squirm. "You've been avoiding us."

There was nothing she could say to that. It was true. She wasn't even good at hiding it. Ever since they'd approached her months earlier about using the mansion's ballroom, she'd been dodging their calls, hoping they'd give up and find another venue for their fundraiser. She'd completely under-estimated the tenacity of the women. It was like a leg of pork trying to outrun three pitbulls.

"Have you spoken to Duncan about letting us use the ball-room yet?" Flora Reid, Campbeltown's reigning bingo queen, gave her a sympathetic smile. In her perfectly styled grey hair and peach coloured twinset, she looked like everyone's favourite grandmother, but Donna wasn't fooled—she'd seen Flora play bingo. Nothing stood between the woman and a winning line.

"Eh, no." Donna cleared her throat. "But I plan to." She'd scheduled for it the twelfth of never.

"You've been *planning* to talk to him for months now." Ann's frown made Donna feel like she was about to get detention. Something that had never happened when she'd been in school because she'd been too worried about disap-pointing her teachers to do anything unruly.

"Has it been that long?" Donna gave them a wide-eyed look. "Time sure does fly."

Ann was undeterred. "Are you seriously trying to make us

believe that in all these months, you couldn't find five minutes to talk to him about the ball?"

"He's been…um…busy." Her cheeks burned, and she couldn't look them in the eyes.

"Doing what?" Joyce demanded. "Moping?"

Her eyes shot up to glare at the woman, and she felt a flush of fury that she quickly tamped down. "He's mourning. He lost his wife."

Joyce snorted. "That was two and a half years ago. My Graeme died ten months ago and do you see me moping? No, you don't. That's no way to honour the dead."

Donna bit her lip to stop from pointing out that Joyce and Graeme had barely spoken to each other for decades before he'd died, they hadn't exactly been the town's great love story.

"I will talk to him, I promise," Donna said, hoping to appease them enough for her to escape.

"That's good," Flora said. "Because the programme we're raising money for helps cancer patients and their families with ongoing costs. Things like travelling to the hospital to stay with their sick children." She gave Joyce a pointed look.

Joyce's eyes went wide. "Oh, aye," she said. "Some families can't work for months because they're going back and forth with wee ones."

"Wee *sick* ones," Ann clarified.

Flora sniffed and wiped at her eye. "Even babies."

It was the last straw. How could she stand in the way of helping families with sick children? With babies? Her shoulders slumped. "I'll talk to Duncan."

"Today?" Ann pushed.

"Yes, today." Maybe she could do it over the phone? From Spain.

Three smiles of triumph met her words, and a cold dread ran up her spine. Had they been lying to her? Conning her?

She wished one of her sisters were here—they'd be able to tell. The ability to read people had skipped right past her in the Sinclair family tree.

"We knew we could depend on you," Flora said sweetly. "You have a good heart."

In other words, she was a soft touch. She didn't need the ability to read between the lines to know that—her sisters told her often enough. Donna the Doormat was her family nickname, and she couldn't thank her sisters enough for it.

"We knew you wouldn't let us down," Joyce added.

"That's why we sent out the invitations months ago," Ann said.

Donna's stomach jolted in shock and then tried to crawl up her oesophagus to escape. "The invitations have gone out already?"

"Of course," Joyce said. "You can't leave it to the last minute to invite people to an event like this. Not to mention, you have to allow time to organise the thing. We decided we'd best have the groundwork done, in preparation for you getting us permission to use the manor ballroom."

Donna gaped at them. They seemed completely oblivious to her shock. Either that or they didn't care. She suspected it might be the latter.

"We'll have a great turnout this year," Joyce carried on. "Having it at the mansion is a big attraction for folk. Nobody's been able to get in there since Fiona died—well, unless you're one of the contract workers doing the place up. Made me wish I'd trained as an electrician."

Flora elbowed Joyce. "What she means is that we're really excited about raising enough money to help those families."

"And the babies," Ann said. "Don't forget the babies."

Joyce rubbed her side. "Do you sharpen those damn elbows? I have osteoporosis, and I think you just broke one of my ribs."

Flora rolled her eyes. "It was just a wee jab."

"Don't worry," Ann said. "We've still got a couple of weeks 'til the ball, and like Joyce said, we've done most of the prep already."

"A couple of weeks?" Donna said. "As in two?"

They consulted each other with a look.

"Almost three," Joyce said.

She was going to faint. "The ball's in less than three weeks? At the mansion? The one you don't have permission to have a ball in?"

"We aren't worried," Flora said. "We have faith in you to sort it. Don't we girls?" The other two nodded. "After you talk to Duncan, why don't you stop by my house for a nice cup of tea and a slice of cake to celebrate?"

"And don't worry about anything else," Joyce added helpfully. "We've heard Grace Blain is going to be your new cook. We all know Grace, so we're happy to arrange caterers and kitchen access with her. Just leave that to us."

"Nobody will bother Duncan," Ann said.

"Nobody will bother him?" She practically screeched. "You're having a party in his house. How will that not bother him?"

This was getting worse with every word coming out of their mouths. She eyed the travel agent across the street and wondered if Esther could sort her out with a one-way ticket to Spain.

"Well, we mean with the arrangements, of course," Ann said. "We'll keep all of our dealings to you and Grace. He won't even know we're there."

"Aye, we'll liaise with you over the decorations," Flora said. "And the sound system. We've got a great band this year. It's going to be the best ceilidh the Mull of Kintyre has ever seen. I'll email you the details. Or I can message you. Or we can Skip, no wait, it's Skype. Are you on Facebook? I can friend you." She grinned wide, clearly proud of her online abilities.

"Well," Ann said. "I think that about covers it. We'll be in touch."

"Thanks Donna," Flora said.

"Should we leave her like this?" Joyce looked sceptical. "She looks a bit shocked."

Ann waved a dismissive hand. "She'll be fine."

And they headed off down the street, without so much as a backwards glance to see if she'd had a heart attack from the stress and needed them to call an ambulance.

CHAPTER 3

"What do you mean you can't tell me what cheques she writes?" Duncan stood in the middle of his office as he barked down the phone to his bank manager.

"It's private information, Mr Stewart," the weasel whined. "We can't hand out that sort of information to just anyone."

"I'm not *anyone*. I'm your biggest customer. And you aren't the only bloody bank in Campbeltown either."

"It's against bank policy to give out information concerning other clients to anyone who asks."

"I don't give a crap! I want to know if my housekeeper has been paying off the staff I tell her to fire. Technically, this is my business. The cheques were written to people I employed."

"But they were written from a personal account."

He felt like his head was going to explode. His free hand clenched and unclenched as he stalked back and forth across his office. Fiona had decorated the room in traditional Georgian style, and he hadn't had the heart to tell her he hated it. He was a modern décor sort of man: sleek lines and light colours. White. He'd paint everything white if he could, it made a great background for his paintings. Not that he painted anymore, he hadn't been able to do that since Fiona died, but if he did start painting again, he would need white walls not dark green or, heaven forbid, burgundy.

"Just give me the information I need, McLean," he snapped at the bank manager. "I'm not some stranger. You know me, and you know why I'm asking for this. Damn it man, don't make me come down there."

He thought he heard the weasel swallow hard. "If you come down here, I would have to call the police to deal with you. Be reasonable, Mr Stewart, you can't just call up the bank and demand access to someone else's account details."

The man had a point, but Duncan didn't feel reasonable. He felt mad. "I need that information."

"I understand, but you won't get it from me. Perhaps you'll find a record of all the people Ms Sinclair has let go in her housekeeping files, and you could deduce from that how many cheques she's written."

"But it won't tell me how much I owe her."

"I'm sorry, but I can't help you."

"I'll remember this," Duncan growled.

"Please do," the weasel said. "We pride ourselves in protecting our clients' privacy."

Duncan clicked off the phone and barely resisted the urge to throw it across the room.

Instead, he pulled out his desk chair and sat down at his laptop. He had access to the housekeeping files. He'd just never looked in them. There'd never been a need to look. Donna took care of everything while he…well…he focused on getting through the next minute without Fiona at his side. And then he focused on the next minute after that. He'd been focused on minutes for over two years. Although, for the past couple of months, there had been days when those minutes had passed him by and he'd gone an hour or more without remembering he was alone.

The realisation stabbed him in the heart. Was it a betrayal to Fiona's memory that he no longer had to fight every minute to live without her? In a year or two, would he wake up and realise he hadn't thought of her for days, maybe weeks? And would his damaged heart break further over the knowledge that even the memory of her was slipping away from him?

He rubbed his eyes with the heels of his hands. How could a person long for the relief of forgetfulness and hate himself for forgetting at the same time? When he opened his eyes, his gaze rested on the pen and ink drawings on the opposite wall. They were all studies of Fiona. For years, it had hurt to look at them and be reminded of everything he'd lost. Now, he found himself wondering why he hadn't used colour. His wife had been full of life, black-and-white drawings didn't do her justice. If he were to paint her now, he'd use the colours she loved: the ones she'd planted in her rose garden. And then paint the damn wall white to hang the finished work.

He dragged his attention back to the household files. Three hours later, he had a long list of names written out on a sheet of paper beside his laptop. There were check marks beside the people he'd managed to contact. His ex-employees had been happy to tell him how much severance pay Donna had given them. One or two of them had even asked if they could come back and work at the mansion.

Duncan eyed the list with grim resolve. This had to stop. The woman had spent thousands of pounds she didn't have on payoffs he hadn't asked her to make. He would pay back every last penny she'd spent in his name, and then he'd wring her neck. Possibly not in that order, unless he'd managed to calm down by the time she got back. He pulled out his phone, with the screen he'd cracked earlier, and sent a text to his errant housekeeper: *I need to talk to you.*

The reply wasn't as speedy as he would have liked. *I'll be home as soon as I'm finished in town.*

Duncan stared at the message for a moment, the word home jumping out at him. He hadn't really thought about it until earlier that day, but the mansion was as much home to Donna as it was to him. She was the only staff member who lived on-site, and for the past two years, it had only been the two of them rattling around the vast house. He supposed people might have thought it a strange arrangement, but it had never occurred to him. There were days when he felt Donna belonged here more than he did.

Come home now. He typed the order.

Won't be long, came the reply. *I have a family emergency. Will be back right after it's sorted.*

Family emergency? Yeah, right. That was Sinclair sisters' code for 'we're up to something.'

He growled at the phone before dialling her number to talk to her. His call went straight to voicemail. Annoyed, he stabbed out another text, but he knew there wouldn't be a reply. Donna had mastered the art of avoidance. Obviously, it was easier for her than actually telling people no—a trait he'd played off the past couple of years. Something he wasn't proud of, but he'd needed a buffer between him and the world and Donna was it. For some reason, he didn't find her as annoying as he did almost everyone else on the planet.

He flopped back into his desk chair. There was nothing he could do now but wait for her to return. Knowing Donna, if she didn't want to deal with him, she'd sneak in after dark and use the back stairs to avoid him. It wouldn't be the first time. But this time he was on to her, and he planned to be waiting.

Whether or not she liked it, they were going to have a

conversation about the unauthorised severance cheques she'd been writing on his behalf.

* * *

"I'M IN TROUBLE," Donna said as soon as she let herself into her sister's flat, over the only garage in Arness.

Mairi and Agnes had both lived in the flat for years while Donna had lived with her eldest sister, Isobel, and her kids because she was the sister least likely to lose patience with them and lock them all in the closet to get some peace. Now Isobel was married and living in London, and Mairi was back with Keir and had moved into his house in Campbeltown. That meant Agnes had the place to herself. Not that you would know it as Mairi was usually there, sitting at the tiny kitchen table with her laptop. She was setting up an online matchmaking business and had decided she liked working above the garage Keir owned instead of staying home alone. Knowing Mairi, it was best for everyone if she wasn't left by herself too long, so this arrangement worked well all round.

"What did you do this time?" Agnes asked. As second oldest, she considered herself their leader, now that Isobel was at the other end of the country.

"Don't you mean, what has she let someone talk her into this time?" Mairi said, as she tossed her wild, curly red hair over her shoulder.

"I hate you both." Donna flopped into the old sofa, with its springs sticking up and threadbare armrests. "And I need a cup of tea." She batted her eyelashes at them. "Please."

"You are so pathetic." But Agnes got up to put the kettle on. "What did you do? Spit it out." She leaned back against the kitchen counter, folded her arms and did the toe-tapping thing that drove her three sisters mad.

"The Women's Institute are holding their bi-annual fundraising ball in the mansion."

Agnes' eyebrows shot up into her pale blonde hair. All four sisters had different hair colour—Isobel's was chestnut, Agnes' was white blonde, Mairi's was wild red, and Donna's was mousy blonde/brown. Which just about summed up her whole personality. Her sisters call her hair strawberry blonde, but she had a mirror and could see for herself that they were only being nice. All sisters had the same short, curvy stature and green eyes. Although, Donna's were more of a mould green than grass green. She was the only one who'd inherited their mother's nose, which was a dot on her face. If she painted the end red, people would think it was a clown's nose.

Agnes stared at Donna with her emerald eyes, before looking down her lean nose. Now, why couldn't she have inherited *that* nose? "Duncan's letting the women hold a ball in the mansion?"

Mairi snorted. "Don't be daft. He doesn't know anything about it, does he?" As usual, she was enjoying the chaos.

"Not yet," Donna admitted. "Possibly never—if I have my way."

"Those bloody women have been preying on your good nature again," Agnes snapped. "I'm going to kill them."

"No! Don't. I can take care of myself."

Mairi burst out laughing. "Oh, honey, no you can't. We love you, but you fall for every sob story that crosses your path. You're a conman's wet dream."

"Ew!" Donna scrunched up her nose.

Agnes frowned at them. Obviously, they weren't being serious enough for her. "When's this ball supposed to be happening?"

"Flora sent me a text, it's two weeks on Friday." She

ducked her head as she admitted the rest of it. "They've already sent out the invitations."

"I don't know whether to be outraged that they played my sister," Mairi said. "Or impressed by their technique."

Agnes reached over and smacked Mairi on the back of her head. "We're outraged. And you"—she pointed at Donna, in case there was any doubt whom she was ordering around —"need to tell them to cancel. Duncan will lose his mind if a bunch of strangers rock up to his house."

"I was kind of hoping he wouldn't be there to see them." She looked up at Agnes through her lashes.

"Please tell me you aren't planning to go ahead with the ball?"

"I don't think I have a choice. The invitations have gone out, and people have already said they're attending. Plus, it's for a good cause. They're raising money for a programme that helps young cancer patients and their families who are struggling financially." She batted her eyelashes at them. "There are babies in the programme, Aggie. Sick babies."

Mairi grinned. "They used babies? That is so dark. I'm seriously impressed."

Agnes glared at Mairi, who was unrepentant in her admiration of the three witches of the Women's Institute. "You need to stand firm and tell them no."

"Or…I could try something else. I've been thinking about it on the way over." Which was five whole miles from Campbeltown. "My first instinct was to hop a flight to Spain, but Esther in the travel agency couldn't find me one within my budget. So, I've moved on to plan B—hold the ball in secret. If we can get Duncan out of Kintyre for the weekend, then there's no reason he'd know there had been a ball at the mansion in his absence. I mean, who's going to tell him? I'm the only person he talks to, and there's no way I'd say a word."

"You can't be serious. You aren't really thinking about holding the ball behind his back. Do you have any idea how crazy that sounds? He'll kill you. And then he'll bury your body under Fiona's precious roses."

Mairi burst out laughing. "I was thinking exactly the same thing!"

"I'm glad you think this is funny. Because it isn't." Agnes pointed at Donna again. "Our sister is going to die a slow and painful death."

"Drama queen," Mairi muttered, but they all heard her.

"No biscuits for you," Agnes declared.

"*Mean* drama queen," Mairi amended.

They were getting off track. "Aggie, you know Duncan wouldn't hurt me, right? He'd just shout a lot. And maybe fire me. Or lock me in my tower so he could shout at me until he gets it out of his system."

Agnes shook her head slowly. "You have a deeply disturbing relationship with your boss."

"You have no idea. But that's not the issue. The issue is that I can't say no to the Women's Institute, even if it means suffering Duncan's wrath. The ball's raising money for sick babies and children. They're even calling it the Fiona Stewart Memorial Ball. How can I stand in the way of that?"

Her sister rolled her eyes. "Mairi's right, those women played you like they were virtuosos and you were a violin." She scooped the teabag out of the mug, added milk and brought it over to Donna.

"Maybe," Donna conceded. "But it's too late to change things now."

"I'll talk to them for you," Agnes said with a sigh.

"I'll be her muscle," Mairi said cheerfully. "She's going to need it to deal with the three witches."

Great, just what she needed. Her sisters rescuing her—again. She straightened her shoulders. "No. I'll sort it." She was twenty-eight years old, and it was time to stand up for herself. Past time.

Her sisters shared a look before Agnes raised a sceptical eyebrow. "You'll sort it?"

"Yes." She nodded firmly as her stomach lurched.

"How?"

"Give me a minute. I'm still working on that part. First, I need to find a way to get Duncan out of the mansion for the weekend. In fact, out of Kintyre would be even better."

"That isn't sorting it," Agnes snapped. "That's carrying on with your crazy plan to have the ball behind Duncan's back."

"When was the last time he left Kintyre, anyway?" Mairi said. "And where's my tea?"

"You can make your own tea as punishment for admiring the three witches' technique."

Mairi stuck her tongue out at Agnes and headed for the kettle. "That kind of attitude is exactly why I moved out."

"You moved out to get it on with Keir," Agnes said.

"That too." Mairi grinned before turning to Donna. "So, when was the last time Duncan spent a night away from the mansion?"

"I'm thinking." Donna wracked her memory. "It was before I started working there. It might have been for Fiona's funeral in Glasgow."

"Great," Agnes said. "I'm glad that's sorted. All you need to do to get him out of town is wait for someone else to die."

"Aggie! That isn't funny."

"I wasn't trying to be funny. He has no friends, and he doesn't go anywhere. All he does is lurk in the mansion, brooding. Getting him out of there might take a stick of dynamite."

"Have you thought about having the cook lace his food with sleeping pills?" Mairi said. "He'll sleep through the ball and your problems will be solved."

Donna glared at them. "I seriously worry about the moral standards of this family. You especially."

The glare had no effect.

"So, you don't want to drug him." Mairi drummed her fingernails on her chin. "What about propositioning him? You could tell him you want to have a sex-filled weekend away."

Donna almost choked on her tea. "You want me to have sex with my boss to keep him busy?"

"She's not having sex with Duncan," Agnes said.

"Not right now, but she could do it." Mairi was undeterred. "Really, would it be so bad? He's hot, if you can get past the whole mountain-man thing he's got going on. And she obviously has a thing for him."

"I do not!" Donna blustered, but she could feel her face turn red.

"Do too," Mairi said.

"Kids!" Agnes shouted, and her sisters turned their frowns on her. "She can't solve her problem with sex."

"I don't see why not. I solve most of mine with sex. Keir doesn't want me to overspend doing up the house—we have sex—I get to spend what I like. Keir doesn't want to visit Hong Kong on our trip—we have sex—we're going to Hong Kong. You shouldn't mess with something that has a proven track record."

"Your attitude sets women's rights back about a hundred years," Agnes lobbed the packet of milk chocolate Hobnobs at her. "Have a biscuit and stop talking. You aren't helping."

"I'm not sleeping with my boss," Donna said when she could get a word in. "The Women's Institute might be raising money for a good cause, but I'm not willing to offer my body up for it." Especially not when she knew it would be rejected. Apart from the fact Duncan was still in love with his wife, she'd seen photos of Fiona, and there was no way she could compete with that. Fiona had been tall and slender, with long black hair and violet eyes. She was Arwen the elf and Donna was a hobbit.

"I think it would solve your problem," Mairi said.

"And I think you are both deeply disturbed," Donna told them. "Do either of you have any ideas that don't involve something illegal, immoral or just plain pimping out your sister for the cause?"

There was silence.

"Thanks!" She threw up her hands in disgust. "Give me the biscuits. I need chocolate to think. And once I've eaten my way through the packet, I'm calling Isobel to see what she can come up with."

Mairi threw the biscuits at her. "That's not a bad idea. Maybe she can get Callum's business to kidnap Duncan for the weekend. They do stuff like that, right?"

"Wrong." Agnes gave her a look that said she worried about her sanity. "He runs a security company. They hire out bodyguards, run background checks on people, install security systems. They don't kidnap people."

"Oh, well, that's disappointing." Mairi slumped back into her chair.

"Can't you get a gallery to call him up and ask him to show his work that weekend? Wouldn't he leave town for that?" Agnes said.

Donna sat up straight. "Aggie, I think you might be a genius."

"I've been telling you idiots that for years."

Donna ignored her. "A gallery wouldn't work, but his old art school might. The dean of Fine Arts has been hassling him for almost a year to take a turn as a guest lecturer. All I need to do is get her to ask again, then convince him to take her up on it." Okay, that didn't sound so easy when she said it out loud.

"So, you're going to call this art school woman up and say, 'can you invite Duncan to come in two weeks' time and don't take no for an answer'?" Agnes arched an eyebrow that said eloquently what she thought of that plan.

"Or"—Mairi pulled her laptop towards her with a grin —"we could hack the art college system and have someone impersonate this art school dean. That way, she'd say exactly what we want her to say."

Agnes wasn't impressed. "And what happens when Duncan turns up, and the dean had no idea he was coming?"

Mairi shrugged. "We hack the other direction too. Send an email to the art school from Duncan offering to lecture that weekend. Get it? We pretend to be the dean for Duncan and pretend to be Duncan for the dean."

"We don't need to hack Duncan," Donna said. "I have access to his email accounts. We only need to hack the dean."

"He lets you answer his personal email?" Agnes said.

"He doesn't get personal email. The man is an island, and it isn't Ibiza."

Agnes pinched the bridge of her nose. "I see a problem with this plan. None of us knows how to hack anything."

"Ah, but we know someone who does." Mairi reached for her phone. "And he owes me big time."

"Oh," Donna said. "Keir's brother."

"Keir's brother." Mairi nodded as she dialled him. "He hacked my life without being asked, now he can do some hacking for us that we actually want." She held up a finger to tell them he'd answered. "Sean, it's Mairi. I have a job for you. Come over to the flat above the garage. Bring your laptop and don't tell your brother why you're here." There was a pause. "Of course it's legal." She snapped the phone shut and then looked at Agnes. "It is legal, right? Sort of. I mean, we're hacking an art school. It isn't like we're hacking the government."

"Hacking is hacking. It's all illegal. There aren't shades of it."

"Yeah, but nobody's going to send us to jail for hacking an art college. Right?" Mairi looked at her sisters. "I mean it. I can't wear orange. It clashes with my hair."

"No," Donna said with a certainty she didn't quite feel. "We won't go to jail. The worst that will happen is that I'll get fired." Maybe. Or he might keep her around to make her suffer.

"Good." Mairi sounded relieved. "I mean, not good you'll get fired, but good I won't have to wear orange. Okay then, I'm running over to the shop. We need more chocolate if we're going to hack people." She headed for the door.

"That sounds so wrong," Agnes said as she watched her go.

CHAPTER 4

Duncan sat in the kitchen's breakfast nook, in the dark, waiting for his housekeeper to sneak back home. Why he didn't put on the light and leave a politely worded request that she meet him in his office in the morning, he didn't know. Sure he was annoyed, but even he could see this wasn't the way a man treated his employee. But then Donna didn't quite feel like an employee. She felt…more. And he couldn't quite figure out what that meant. Nor did he have the time to spend on it because his prey had just sneaked in the back door and was currently tiptoeing across the kitchen to the fridge, muttering to herself as she did so.

"Stop calling him master," she said. "He isn't my master."

Duncan cocked his head while he watched her. Maybe she wasn't talking to herself after all. Maybe she had an earpiece for her phone. It was hard to tell under that thick mass of hair sitting around her shoulders. And who the hell was this *master*?

She took a carrier bag over to the fridge and opened it. The light surrounded her like a halo, and the contrast of the dark kitchen and the stark light from the refrigerator, made him think of Caravaggio's paintings. He could see this scene on a canvas, only she wouldn't be dressed in slacks and a shirt, she would be wearing a white cotton men's shirt—his shirt—and the light from the fridge would shine through it, showing her curves in shadows through the cloth…What was he thinking? With a shake of his head, he refocused his attention on Donna and the issue he needed to resolve with her.

"I'm not taking advice from you," she said as she put food from the bag onto a plate, then headed for the microwave. "You were given your freedom, and you're still wearing a sack. Why don't you put on some decent clothes?"

Master? Freedom? A sack? This was one weird phone call. It sounded like some sort of master/slave sex game. His stomach clenched. Donna? Sex games? He blinked hard at her. Donna in her buttoned-up clothing and her meek attitude? Meek? He felt like a weight had been dropped on his head. Another word for meek was submissive. This was getting weirder and weirder. Was she talking about having a master? Was she into BDSM?

Donna?

For two years, he hadn't looked at her in any way other than as the woman who smoothed out his life and let him focus on missing Fiona. He definitely hadn't thought of her as a sexual being. But now, hearing this, there were all kinds of sexual images in his head.

He shifted in his seat as his body reacted to the images. A reaction he hadn't had in years, followed by a sharp, but short-lived, pang of guilt over betraying his wife. His long-gone wife. And for once, that thought didn't bring him to his knees. It only produced a dull, throbbing ache in the region where his heart used to be—before it had been taken out of his chest and buried with the woman he loved.

"I don't care what Harry Potter would say," Donna

snapped. "I don't live to please a master. I don't have a master. And I don't need someone to free me with a sock."

Okay, they'd passed weird and entered completely bizarre. He shouldn't be listening in on Donna's freaky phone calls. It was none of his business if his housekeeper was into kinky Harry Potter sex games. Although the thought of her with a man he didn't know disturbed him. Actually, the thought of her with *any* man was disturbing. Who was looking out for her? Who was making sure she was safe? Protected? What if this guy took advantage of her? His eyes narrowed. Just like his ex-employees had taken advantage of her. He needed to remember why he wanted to talk to her and not get distracted by anything else.

As she took the steaming plate from the microwave, Duncan cleared his throat. "Donna, I need a word with you."

She screamed. The plate flew into the air, then landed with a crash on the kitchen floor.

"Duncan?" she whispered as she leaned against the counter with her hand over her heart.

Maybe he should have put the light on after all. "Who else would it be?"

"I nearly had a heart attack. What are you doing sitting there in the dark?"

"Waiting for you. You've been ignoring my messages, and I need to talk to you."

Her brow puckered as she frowned. "I didn't ignore you, I told you I had a family situation to deal with."

"What was it this time? Did Agnes' flat blow up? Did Mairi fall off another cliff?" Donna's sisters didn't have normal emergencies—they had epic ones.

She ignored him, her eyes on the floor. "The chicken pie is all over the place." She sounded so mournful that he almost felt guilty.

"Maybe if you'd come to talk to me like I asked, instead of

avoiding me, you'd be eating your dinner right now instead of staring at it on the floor."

Her eyes flashed luminous green in the low light. "And maybe, if you hadn't scared me half to death, I would have eaten my dinner and then come to find you."

"Aye, right you would." She wasn't fooling anyone. "Did you get me a pie too?"

"It's in the fridge," she said mournfully, her eyes still on the mess covering the floor.

Of course, she got him some food. Donna would never have forgotten him. "Then eat my pie."

"I can't do that. What will you eat?" Her wide eyes stared at him. "It's fine. Once I clean up this mess, I'll make myself a sandwich from the stuff I bought. I cannot wait for the cook to get here." She glanced at the kitchen clock. "Only twelve more hours."

"Heat the other pie. It's massive. We can share it. I'll clean up the mess while you get the food."

"We'll share?" Her voice was a squeak. "You'll clean?"

He wasn't sure what upset her the most—sharing with him or watching him clean. "Aye," was all he said as he flicked on the lights, grabbed the dustpan and brush, and headed for the mess.

Donna looked sceptical, but she didn't argue. She took the remaining pie from the fridge and set about microwaving it, all the while keeping an eye on him in case his head exploded or something. Who knew what women thought?

As he swept up, Donna pulled an empty plate from the cupboard, presumably to divide up their food. For some reason that bothered him. They didn't need another plate. They were perfectly capable of sharing. "Don't dirty dishes needlessly, we can eat from the same plate."

From the look she gave him, you would have thought he'd suggested they lick ice cream off each other's bodies. An image of doing just that flashed in his mind and his jeans became perilously tight. After years of reacting to nothing, his body felt like it was out of control. And it was out of control over his housekeeper. Even he knew that was deeply unprofessional.

And yet, he couldn't stop himself from crossing the line into personal territory, because his mouth opened and a question he shouldn't have asked popped right out.

"Who's this master guy?" he said.

She jerked, and the empty plate slipped from her hand to smash on the floor in front of him.

"What?" Her cheeks were red as she stared down at him.

"Go sit down before you trash all the dishes," he told her. "I'll bring the food over."

"It was only two plates," she muttered. "And you were the reason I broke both of them, with your random questions and your creepy sitting in the dark thing."

She had a point, and he knew he should let the subject drop, but he couldn't. What if she was in danger? What if she was involved in something she shouldn't be? Wouldn't a responsible employer look out for her? Aye. He owed it to her to be responsible.

He cleared his throat. "So, who's this master guy you were talking about? A boyfriend? Is he treating you right?"

When she didn't answer immediately, he looked up to find her staring at him open-mouthed.

"You think I call my boyfriends *master*?"

"You have more than one of them?" He felt his blood pressure rise.

"What? No! I don't have any. Not right now, anyway."

Did that mean she was calling some casual hook-up her master? He didn't like that one bit. Did her sisters know what she was doing? Was anyone looking out for her? Anyone at all? It suddenly occurred to him that he had no idea what she did in her free time. Did she even have any free time? She was always available when he needed her. Except when she was off scheming with her sisters.

"Who were you talking to?" He assured himself it wasn't nosiness that made him pry, it was a concern for her safety.

Anyone else would have told him to get lost, that it was none of his business. Not Donna. Instead, her cheeks burned even redder, and she told him what he wanted to know. "I was talking to Dobby."

"Dobby? What the hell kind of name is that?"

Her eyes hit his for a second, flashing with a fire she quickly snuffed out. "Dobby is the house-elf in Harry Potter. I was…um…imagining a conversation with the character."

"You were imagining a conversation?"

"Yes." She didn't look at him.

"You weren't on the phone?"

"No."

"You were talking to a fictional character?"

"Yes." She studied her knuckles.

"About your master?"

Her head shot up, and her eyes flashed again. "I don't have a master. Dobby was mistaken."

"The *fictional character* you were having an *imaginary* conversation with was mistaken?"

"Yes." She was back to focusing on the table again.

Okay then. "So, who's the master guy you were talking to your imaginary friend about?" And why did it matter? "Is he real?"

"Oh, for goodness' sake," Donna said, sounding slightly exasperated, which was the most he'd ever heard her sounding. "It's you. Dobby calls you the master because you own the house and employ me."

He just stared at her. She was having an imaginary conversation about him? He looked around. Definitely in the kitchen. For a minute he'd thought he was in bed and this was a bizarre dream. His brain went over the conversation she'd had with her imaginary friend, and a slow, wide smile broke out on his face. It felt strange, and he realised it had been a very long time since he'd smiled, and his muscles weren't used to it.

Donna caught sight of the smile, and she seemed as shocked as he felt, which turned the smile into a grin. "This Dobby thinks you should live to please your master then?"

For a fleeting second, her eyes narrowed at him, and then it was gone, replaced by her usual wide-eyed expression. "You aren't my master."

"I don't know." He walked over to the bin with a pan full of broken plates and battered food. "I think your imaginary friend is right. I think you should call me master. It suits me."

"Of course, you think that," she muttered. "You're king of the world in your own head."

"You do know I can hear you, right?"

"Hear what?" she gave him an innocent look that had him fighting another smile. And then she muttered something even quieter. The only thing he could make out was the word Dementor.

Before he could ask her what she was talking about now, the microwave pinged, reminding him that not only did they need to eat, but that they had more important things to talk about than Donna's imaginary friends.

"Don't forget to add the salad," Donna ordered. "It's in the fridge."

"You bought salad?"

"It's healthy."

"Only if you eat it." Any salad either of them had tended to be purely decoration.

He took the plate from the microwave, added the point-less salad, grabbed cutlery and headed for the breakfast nook. Instead of sitting opposite Donna, he slid into the bench seat beside her and handed her a fork.

She pointed at the other side of the booth. "Wouldn't it be more comfortable if we divided this between two plates and you sat over there?"

Probably, but he didn't like the thought of that. He liked things exactly the way they were. And if he didn't understand why that was, there was no way he could explain it to her.

"Just eat." He cut the pie and nudged her half over to her. "I don't see why we have to have salad." He poked at it with his fork. "And why is it full of sprouting seeds? Oh, a nut. I can eat a nut." He popped it in his mouth.

"I don't understand how you can be so fit when all you want to eat is rubbish." Her tone was haughty, but he noticed she too avoided the salad and went straight for the pie.

As soon as the forkful of creamy chicken and crumbling pastry passed her lips, her eyes closed in ecstasy, and Duncan found himself holding his breath as he stared at her mouth. Her top lip was slightly fuller than her bottom one, and the bow made a deep curve. His fingers itched to reach out and trace the outline of her lips, to feel the slight curve beneath his fingertips, to see for himself if they were as satin soft as they looked.

"Perfect," she said, breaking the spell she'd woven. Without another glance in his direction, she concentrated on their meal.

Duncan tried hard to do the same, but his thoughts kept straying to the bow of her lips as though it was the most fascinating sight he'd ever seen.

"What did you want to talk to me about?" Donna said between bites.

Right. Business. He cleared his throat and worked to get his mind on the reason for his ire.

"I spoke to the gardener today."

Her eyebrows shot up. "Oh?"

"Aye. I told him he was fired."

"Okay…well, I'll strike that off my to-do list then." She avoided the salad and stole a forkful of his half of the pie.

"The funny thing was, when I told him he was done at the mansion, he held out his hand for severance pay."

The fork stopped halfway to her mouth, and her cheeks turned pink. "Strange," she said before the fork continued to her mouth.

"That's what I thought too," he said dryly. "You wouldn't know anything about severance pay, would you? Because he seemed to think it was normal practice here at the mansion, and I don't remember authorising you to give anyone cash when you kicked their arses out of here."

She grabbed another bite of his pie and made a big show out of not being able to talk because she was chewing. He twisted in the seat, folded his arms and waited her out. She couldn't run. He had her hemmed in. And at some point, there wouldn't be any food left for her to stall with.

Her thigh touched his as she angled away from him although he noticed she slid the plate closer to herself as she did so. He felt the warmth of her touch through his body, and for a second, he lost track of what they were discussing. All he was aware of was her leg against his.

"You're right," she said, making him fight to focus on the conversation and not the heat of their legs pressed together. "You never okayed any severance pay. He was obviously mistaken."

His eyes narrowed. She was a crap actress, and her attempt at looking innocent fell far short of the mark.

"That's what I thought too," he said. "Until I made a list of all the people we've fired in the past few years and called them to find out if they'd received any severance pay."

"Oh." She looked around, and he wondered if she was

trying to figure out a way to slip under the table and away from him.

"Aye, *oh*. Everybody I spoke to had received a cheque. Some of them hefty."

Wide eyes blinked up at him. "Are you sure they weren't *all* mistaken?"

"You want me to believe everybody I called lied about you writing them a cheque?"

"It could happen."

"Aye, and pigs could fly if they put the effort in." He leaned into her, her vanilla and cinnamon scent filling his nostrils and making his mouth water. Had she always smelled like baked goods? Or was this a new thing? He racked his brain trying to remember, but he honestly didn't recall ever noticing how Donna smelled. "You wrote those cheques. What the hell were you thinking?"

She let out a heavy sigh and pushed the plate away. "Mainly I was thinking that I wanted to get them out of the mansion without any drama."

"And you thought the best way to do that was to give them money?"

"These people have lives, Duncan. They have bills and commitments. You can't just turf them out with nothing and hope they'll survive until they find another job. That's why companies offer severance pay. To help people out."

He pinched the bridge of his nose while he took the time to get his head around her crazy reasoning. "I'm not a company, Donna. I'm a man trying to run a historically significant building that his wife had set her heart on. And you don't give severance pay to people who haven't even worked here much more than a day. Most of the folk you fired hadn't been here long enough to get a normal pay, let alone anything extra."

"To be fair, you were the one firing them. I was only the

messenger. And because I was the one firing them, I was the one who had to watch them cry and worry about how they'd make ends meet until they got another job. I *had* to give them the money. It was the right thing to do, and I didn't want anyone to think you were mean."

It took all his self-control not to roll his eyes. She was unbelievable. A walking magnet for every conman and loser in Scotland. After the calls he'd made to past employees, he knew for a fact that some of them had only taken the job at the mansion because they knew Donna would hand them money when she let them go. They'd abused her soft heart. And he wasn't going to stand for it any longer.

"I'll do the firing from now on." He was firm.

Donna looked like she'd swallowed sea water. "I'm not sure that's the best idea. You tend to scare people."

"Aye." And from the sounds of it, some of them needed a good scaring.

"And it's my job to oversee the staff."

"You can oversee them. I'll step in when the firing needs to be done."

"How about, we change our policy and don't fire any more people? Wouldn't that be a good compromise?" She gave him an angelic smile.

"No. It wouldn't. We aren't keeping incompetent people on at the mansion just because you feel sorry for them. From now on, I'll do the firing. And you won't be writing any more cheques. Am I clear?"

"Unfortunately." The smile disappeared, and he felt like he'd turfed a kitten out into the snow.

He wasn't going to let her sidetrack him. This had to be done. The townsfolk were walking all over her, and him by default. "And another thing, I'll be paying back every penny you spent in my name."

She shook her head, and her cheeks flushed to that fascinating shade of pink that made him itch to reach for his paints. "You don't have to do that. I never asked you for the money."

"Exactly." She had to be the world's most infuriating woman. "That's my point."

She stared at him for a moment, and he found himself getting lost in her sea green eyes. "Are we done now?" she said.

He pinched the bridge of his nose. "Aye. We're done. But no more paying people off. I'm serious. If I find out you've been paying people, I'll skin you alive and bury you under the roses." It was an empty threat because he wasn't sure what he would do if she went against his wishes. He couldn't fire her. The thought of living in the mansion without Donna was unbearable. That left him with very few options. Something he hoped she never figured out.

To his surprise, she burst out laughing. "I knew you'd say that."

Strange woman. His intention had been to lay down the law, but instead, he was reeling from his mystifying reaction to her and wasn't entirely sure if she'd taken anything he'd said seriously.

"Well then," he said as he stood. "I'm glad we got that sorted."

And then he did the only thing he could think of to do. He left her to finish his meal.

CHAPTER 5

Donna awoke to the *Doctor Who* theme tune. She groaned, rolled over in bed and grabbed her phone.

"It's five a.m.," she whined at Mairi when she answered.

"And some of us have been up all night helping you defraud your boss," Mairi snapped back.

"Is it really fraud?" Donna lay on her back and slung an arm over her eyes to shut out the early morning light. "What does Keir think you've been doing all night?"

"Something illegal," Mairi's boyfriend shouted in the background, making Donna realise she was on speakerphone.

"Keir knows?" Donna groaned.

"Sean, the back-stabbing hacker, sold me out to his brother." Mairi's words produced a male groan—Sean, presumably. "The rat fink cracked under pressure. All it took was one teeny phone call from his brother, and he spilled everything."

"You shouldn't be doing this," Keir called out. "It's dumb, and it's going to backfire on all of you."

"Whatever," Mairi said. "I have news. We've cracked the

art school's email. Now you need to draft an email from the Fine Arts dean to Duncan, and one from him to the dean. Then we can send them and get this ball rolling." She practically tripped over her words.

"How much caffeine have you had?"

"Lots. Lots and lots and lots."

Great. Mairi was at her worst when she was hyperactive. "Why do I have to write the emails?"

"Because," her sister said, sounding long suffering. "You know Duncan best. Now, chop-chop, get it done. I want to get this over with fast, so I can have some quality time with Keir before he leaves for work."

"He doesn't start work for another three hours."

"I'm going to need every minute. I have a lot of excess energy I need to get rid of, and I'm not going to the garage to get serviced. Get it? Serviced?" She laughed at her own joke. She was the only one. Everyone else groaned. "The last time we did the deed in the garage I got oil in places that didn't need oiling."

"Well, you are *Rusty*," Keir quipped.

"It's a nickname," Mairi snapped. "Not the condition of my parts."

"That's it," Sean said. "I'm taking my laptop to the car. I'll work there."

Donna couldn't blame him for running. "TMI," she wailed. She was going to be sick.

"You think that's too much information? If you don't get those draft emails to me within the next fifteen minutes, you'll hear all about the time Keir and I did it on the back of his Harley—in detail. Tick-tock."

"Why do you need to be involved in this? I can send the dean's email to Sean. You can go do other stuff."

"I can't. I'm supervising. You lot would be lost without

me." With that, she hung up, leaving Donna with images in her head that she really didn't want to have there.

Donna dropped the phone back onto her nightstand and groaned.

Master won't like this. Donna isn't being respectful.

She lifted her head to find Dobby sitting on the end of her bed. It wasn't the Dobby she'd drawn, no, it was the movie version—damn those movies for messing with her imagination—and he was still wearing that stupid sack.

"Go away. You aren't real."

Donna needs to be nice to Master Duncan, another voice said, and Donna groaned again. She looked around to find Gollum, from *Lord of the Rings*, crouching in the corner of her bedroom. His wide eyes were staring at Donna in disgust. *Gollum loves Master Duncan. Bad Donna will make him sad. Master Duncan is sad enough. Bad Donna! Wicked, tricksy, false Donna!*

Dobby nodded in agreement. *Master will never give you clothes and free you if you're disrespectful. Dobby was very respectful to Harry Potter. That's why he helped Dobby get the sock of freedom.* He held it up and stared at it, a look of rapture on his face.

"I swear, if you go on about that sock one more time, I'll erase you from every book I own." She dragged her pillow over her head and shouted into it, "Everybody, out now!"

When there was silence, she peeked out from behind her pillow. The room was blessedly clear of imaginary characters giving her unwanted advice. She swung her legs over the side of the bed and dragged herself out of its warmth. Spring in Scotland was still chilly, and the central heating hadn't kicked in yet. She reached for the silken robe on the chair beside her bed. It had massive red cabbage flowers over a black background. The red matched the lace two-piece boy short and tank set she wore to sleep in. It was a far cry from the old terry robe she'd worn when she'd first taken the job at the mansion.

She tied the robe tight and padded through her small apartment to the desk in the corner of her living room, nabbing a can of Scotland's other national drink, Irn-Bru, on the way because she was too lazy to make tea, and she needed the caffeine.

The chair felt cold on the backs of her thighs as she sipped her Irn-Bru and waited for her laptop to wake up. As soon as the screen she needed appeared, Donna started typing.

Dear Zoe,

No. Duncan would never write dear. She drummed her fingers on the desktop while she thought. And then she started again.

Zoe,

I'll be in Glasgow the weekend of the 8th. If you still want me to give a guest lecture, let me know and I'll see if I can fit you in, Duncan.

Yep. that sounded like him—terse, to the point.

Now, to sound like Zoe. She flicked through the old emails in Duncan's account, found one the art school dean had written to him months earlier and used it as the basis for hers.

Hi Duncan,

I thought I'd check to see if you're up for a spot of guest lecturing? We have space on the weekend of the 8th and would love to book you in. Maybe you could come up to Glasgow on the Friday night, and we could have dinner together? Catch up on old times? What do you say? Don't let me down this time!

Zoe.

She sat back and considered it. Maybe she shouldn't put in the bit about dinner. She didn't like the idea of Duncan having an intimate meal with a woman she didn't know. She had to look out for him. He was still so vulnerable. Maybe the dinner wasn't a good idea. Unless…She brought up Google and searched for the dean of Fine Arts. It was a relief to discover she was a woman in her early sixties who'd been happily married to an equally famous sculptor for thirty-plus years.

"That's much better than some man-eater," she muttered to herself.

When she'd finished the forgeries, she sent the fake emails to her sister. Her phone rang almost immediately.

"Are they okay?" Donna asked her sister.

"They read fine to me," Mairi said, "but Keir's made a good point. What if this art school woman calls Duncan?"

Donna sat up straighter. "I never thought of that. I'll add a line telling her he only wants to be contacted by email."

"What if he decides to ring her?" Mairi said. "You need to make sure that doesn't happen either."

"How?" It wasn't like she could monitor him twenty-four seven.

"I don't know," Mairi snapped. "I have to go burn some energy. Sean will intercept all emails before they reach their targets. He'll alert you when he has them, and you can substitute your versions for the real thing."

"Targets?" Donna was beginning to regret this plan.

"What else are we supposed to call them? Targets sounds professional."

"Professionally criminal," Keir shouted in the background.

"He's so dramatic," Mairi said. "Anyway, I need to go. Keir is looking particularly fine this morning, and I need some of that. Tatty-bye."

"Now I need to wash my ears out with soap," Donna muttered as she hung up.

Why hadn't she thought about the dean calling Duncan? She amended his message, telling Zoe he only wanted to be contacted by email. Then she made a quick call to Sean, to ensure he didn't send the email from the dean's account until she was ready to deal with her boss. Now all she had to do was stop Duncan from ringing Zoe. Not that she thought he would, but it was better to be safe than sorry.

Her life was getting more complicated by the second.

As she headed for the shower, another character walked out of the pages of *Lord of the Rings* and into her home—Gandalf, the wizard. Today, he was in his Gandalf the White incarnation, meaning he was less playful and more judgemental. He looked down his hooked nose at her, tugged on his waist-length beard and pointed a gnarly finger in her direction.

Oh, what a tangled web we weave, when first we practise to deceive! he said in a voice that would have resonated around a London stage.

"Oh, shut up, Gandalf," Donna said and slammed the bathroom door behind her.

* * *

DUNCAN HAD DREAMED OF PAINTING, and he woke in a cold sweat. It had been years since he'd planned paintings in his sleep. As soon as Fiona had been diagnosed, his nights had been filled with nightmares about losing his wife. Those nightmares had eased somewhat over the past few months, but he'd given up any hope of every dreaming about art again. He'd thought that part of his life had died along with his wife. Now, his mind was full of paintings again and he wasn't entirely sure he liked it. Because each one of the images his subconscious had planned involved his housekeeper in some way.

It had all started with the sight of her in front of the open fridge. He couldn't get the image out of his mind. It had ignited a flame within him. One that had been doused by the loss of his wife. The burning need to paint.

And now, it was alight again. Only this time, the need to work somehow felt like a betrayal of Fiona's memory. He wasn't sure if it was because the paintings in his head involved another woman, or because his art had somehow become entwined with his need for his wife.

He scoffed as he paced the halls of the mansion. It would take a team of professionals working round the clock to sort out his mind. Everything in his life had become a measure of his enduring love for Fiona. From painting to ensuring her dreams for the mansion were carried out to the letter. Hell, he couldn't even leave the building without feeling like he was abandoning her.

He stopped in front of the picture window on the first floor, at the top of the grand staircase, and looked out over the mansion estate. Fiona had loved the symmetry of Georgian architecture, whereas to Duncan, the house had always looked like a huge, grey cube with windows. But he'd put aside his apathy for the place because Fiona wanted to restore the mansion and live in it, and he would never have stood between her and her dream.

He could feel her touch in every colour she'd picked out for the walls and carpets, in the fancy curtains that hung in fussy ruffles, in the antique furniture that seemed to fill the place to bursting. When she'd been alive, her laughter and enthusiasm had filled the building, and he couldn't help but get swept up in her joy for everything Georgian as she restored the house to its former glory. Now, he felt hemmed in by the dark wood, patterned wallpaper and plaster detailing. It was everywhere, and it made him feel like he was trapped in a Jane Austen period drama.

He needed to breathe. He needed somewhere plain, and bare, and white, to rest his mind. He needed his studio. But going back in there without her felt like the worst betrayal of all—which made no sense because he'd been painting for years before he'd met Fiona.

He was stuck. Mired up to his neck in murky clay that hardened around him until he struggled to breathe. There was no solace to be had in his studio, no place to rest in the fussy mansion, and only guilt when he tried to leave. There wasn't even any relief to be found in the rolling hills and manicured gardens that led down to the ocean. He couldn't go on like this, and he knew that, but he didn't know how to change things. He didn't know how to let go of his dead wife and the remnants of the life they'd started building together.

"Good morning, Duncan."

The sound of Donna's voice was a fresh breeze blowing through the mansion. He turned away from the window to see her coming up the stairs from the foyer below. She was dressed in plain black trousers, flat black shoes and a sensible blue blouse. That inner light of hers, which shone so brightly, was in startling contrast to the mausoleum they lived in.

He shook his head to get rid of his maudlin thoughts. "I told you to wear whatever you wanted to work."

"This is what I want to wear."

"I like your Snoopy T-shirt better." It was fern green and matched her eyes.

"Feel free to wear it whenever you like."

He cocked an eyebrow at her to let her know he wasn't impressed by her comeback. Although, to be honest, he was a little. "What's up?"

"Have you checked your email today?"

"Why would I do that?" It was full of people begging him to exhibit or to paint something new for them. He didn't need that kind of pressure. "I put you in charge of my email."

She huffed out a sigh, and he found himself mesmerised by that bow of her top lip again. The curve was sublime. Actually, come to think of it, Donna was full of curves. Knowing women, she probably thought she was fat, but to an artist's eye—purely objectively, of course—he would term her more Rubenesque. Yes, he could see her in a decadent painting by Ruben, all plump flesh and come-hither gaze.

She stepped to the side, and the light from the open window caught her hair, making the many tones within it come alive in a halo of warmth around her face. His breath hitched. Not a Ruben, more like the carefree models in a Renoir. He could imagine her painted in wild, swirling strokes of colour that flowed out from her, carrying sensuality and softness into every corner of the canvas.

He was doing it again.

Planning paintings that revolved around Donna. He could even feel the tingling in his fingertips as they itched to move over canvas, spreading paint in their wake. His hands suddenly felt empty because they didn't hold a brush, and he wanted to feel the texture of charcoal dragging over paper again. He felt the pressure of need building inside him and knew that soon, no matter what crazy objections he might have, he'd have to paint again.

And he wanted to paint Donna when he did.

"Are you listening to me?" she said.

He blinked at her, feeling as though he was coming out of a daze. "No."

"Duncan." She let out a gentle sigh. "Are you okay? Is today a hard day?"

Aye, it was. But probably not in the way she meant, and he hated to see the sympathy in her eyes. He wanted to see them blazing, the way they did when he annoyed her. That was when the soft green came to life and sparkled like emeralds. He'd render those eyes in Winsor Emerald, with a splash of Chrome Green and a touch of Cobalt Green. He shook his head to clear it.

"This damn house is closing in on me," he said gruffly. Surprised that he gave her any explanation at all.

Her reaction was not what he expected. She barked out a laugh and her eyes danced. "This house is over eight thousand square feet. You could run a marathon through the corridors. There's even a room that's made entirely of glass. Not your usual set-up for claustrophobia."

She had a point. He felt the tension in his spine ease somewhat. "What were you saying?"

"There's an email from Glasgow School of Art, they want you to take part in their visiting lecturer programme."

"No."

"You always say no. You sound like a toddler who's only just learned the word. I think you should do it."

Duncan stilled as he studied her. There was nothing in her demeanour to set alarm bells ringing in his head, yet they were blaring. "I don't remember asking your opinion."

"You never ask for it, but that's okay because I'm happy to give it anyway. I think you should go to Glasgow and talk at your old college. Weren't you just saying the walls are closing in on you? This is the perfect opportunity to get out there again."

The bells in his head turned into wailing sirens. "Why are you so keen to get me out of the mansion?"

Her eyes widened further. A sure sign she was up to something. "I don't care either way whether or not you leave the mansion."

Aye, and she probably had a bridge somewhere she wanted to sell him too. "What are you up to?"

"Nothing." A faint flush reddened her cheeks. "You're so suspicious. Is it wrong that I think it would do you good to get away from the mansion for the day?"

"And spend it talking to a bunch of baby artists with stars in their eyes. No thanks."

"What about giving back to the art community and doing your bit to encourage the next generation? What about getting out of the house and giving your staff a break from your angst?"

Her smile was sweet, distracting him enough that it took a second for the last question to register. "If the staff don't like my angst, they can shov—"

"I get it." She held up a hand. "If you don't want to do it, don't. Now, can you sign off on the carriage house renovation, so I can give the builder the go-ahead?"

"Where's the paperwork?"

"Oh, I forgot it." Those captivating eyes of hers got wider. "Never mind. Look it up on your phone. I emailed it to you."

And the alarms in his head grew louder. Donna never emailed anything. She printed it out, shoved it under his nose and put a pen in his hand. Keeping his eye on her, he dug his phone out of his back pocket.

"For goodness' sake, Duncan. You're moving like a snail. Give it to me, and I'll find the email." She snatched the phone from his hand, but it slipped and went flying through the air.

The two of them watched in horror as sailed over the railing and landed with a crash on the marble floor of the foyer below them.

"So," Donna said. "You'll be needing another new phone then."

CHAPTER 6

Donna had run after she'd trashed his phone, using errands in town as an excuse to get out of the mansion. Little coward. She was up to something, he'd bet the mansion on it. She'd also managed to fill his head with yet more paintings while she'd talked to him, which is why he found himself pacing up and down in the corridor outside his studio. He was so focused on the closed door of the room he couldn't quite bring himself to enter, that he almost tripped over a strange woman.

"Who the hell are you?" he snapped.

"I'm the new cook. And you must be the lord of the manor."

She looked him straight in the eye. No fear, but a healthy sense of self-preservation, he respected that. She clasped her hands in front of her as her lips thinned. In a glance, Duncan knew this wasn't a woman who would let his snarling intimidate her. She wore grey polyester trousers with a pressed line down the front of the legs, a pink blouse that had obviously been starched, and had grey hair that was short and neat. She was all about control, and she wasn't about to give any up to her difficult boss.

"The kitchen's that way." Duncan pointed in the general direction. It was big, and full of appliances, it wasn't hard to find.

"Aye, I know. I'm looking for the housekeeper. I need to sort out the shopping and she forgot to leave me the mansion's account details for the local stores. There's nothing in the house except biscuits, white bread and potato scones."

Duncan stopped pacing. "No bacon?"

"No nothing."

"She must be going through another vegetarian phase then," he said. "Make sure you add bacon to the list."

"I don't think so. If you eat too much of that, you'll have a heart attack."

He stopped dead and stared at her. "I like bacon. And meat. And salt and vinegar crisps."

"Well, you should have hired the guy that cooks at the pub instead of me."

His eyes narrowed. "I could still do that."

"Aye, I heard about your itchy trigger finger. If you're planning on firing me, can you wait until the end of next week? I've got an order of fresh vegetables coming from the farmers' market this afternoon, and I don't want them to go to waste. From what her sisters tell me, if I leave them here for you and Donna, they'll either die of old age or get accidentally cremated."

His lips twitched. The woman was funny. "What's your name?"

"Grace Blain, and you're Duncan Stewart."

"I'll give you until the vegetables run out." He felt the need to be honest. "But you damn well better cook the food I like."

"That might be hard. I threw out the fryer an hour ago."

Now she was just pissing him off. "Why did Donna hire you?"

"Because she was desperate?" The woman grinned at him. "Can you even cook?"

"Aye. And I'm good at it too."

"We'll see," he grumbled. And then a thought occurred to him, and he studied her suspiciously. "Why did you take the job? You didn't, by any chance, hear about the severance cheques she hands out when she fires someone? Because I can tell you now, there will be no money when you leave here. I've put an end to that."

She shook her head at him as though disappointed. "I took the job because you needed a good cook. And I'm a good cook. I won't bother you further. I'll send Donna a text message." She paused at the bend in the corridor. "I also took the job because I understand."

As she turned away, Duncan couldn't stop from asking, "Understand what?"

She looked back over her shoulder at him. "I understand what it's like to lose your spouse."

Duncan felt like he'd been punched in the gut. She was there out of pity? He didn't need pity. He wanted to roar after her. To fire her for daring to suggest such a thing, but she was already gone. And he was left pacing a corridor, outside a room he couldn't enter, because he'd lost the courage to do so when he'd lost his wife.

* * *

"Oh crap." Donna read the text message from their new cook. She'd hoped it would be months before Grace met Duncan. Unfortunately, she'd forgotten to tell her not to hunt him down.

She hurriedly texted Grace back. *I promise he won't fire*

you. Yet. *Just order what you need from the store, and I'll sort things out this end. I'm in Campbeltown anyway. And once I get back, I'll make sure you have all the account info you need. Sorry I forgot to give it to you before I left.* Before she'd run out the door to scheme behind her boss's back.

Life was getting far too complicated, and seriously stressful. There was no doubt about it—she was going to crack. It was a certainty. The only thing she couldn't predict was the timing. She wasn't cut out for subterfuge. Mairi and Agnes were experts, but like her oldest sister, Isobel, Donna couldn't lie worth a damn and the guilt from trying made her stomach ache.

Which was why she'd arranged a meeting at a café in town, to tell the Women's Institute the truth.

"You mean he has no idea the ball is happening?" Flora said with a look of pure bewilderment on her face. "None at all? But it's definitely going ahead?"

Donna put her phone down on the table in front of her and looked at the three women. They were in Campbeltown's Nice 'n' Icy café—because she'd needed the sugar and the café was famous for going heavy on the icing.

"I thought it was best to hold the ball without his knowledge," she confirmed before tucking into a massive piece of chocolate cake.

"In other words," Joyce said, "we're running the thing behind his back."

"Exactly," Donna said around a mouthful of icing.

"And you haven't even asked him?" Flora still looked confused.

"No. I don't need to. He'll be out of the house that weekend, so he won't even know the ball is happening." Fingers crossed. So far, she hadn't managed to get him even the slightest bit interested in talking to his old art school.

"I don't agree with this course of action." Ann scowled

down at her plain scone. It was no wonder she was testy. The woman needed more sugar. "It's underhanded, deceitful, and dishonest."

"And brilliant," Joyce added with a grin. "Everybody wins. We get the ballroom. The guests get an exclusive look inside the mansion. Donna gets to keep her job. And Duncan gets to remain antisocial and oblivious to everyone around him." She lifted her cup of tea and toasted Donna. "Well done, lassie."

"No. Don't toast me," she said. "I wanted to tell him, I just…"

"Didn't have the guts?" Ann said.

"Didn't want to upset him?" Flora said.

"Didn't think he'd agree, so you went around him?" Joyce said with a cackle that turned into a hacking cough, making her face so red that people reached for their phones to call an ambulance.

She held up a hand. "I'm fine. I'm fine," she said once she could talk again. "Just a wee cough. You know what they say, it isn't the cough that carries you off, it's the coffin they carry you off in." She cackled again.

"Stop it," Ann snapped.

Joyce sobered. "You're a killjoy, Ann Dunbar. No wonder you're still single."

"I'm single through choice."

"Or lack thereof," Joyce mumbled.

Donna had a horrible feeling she was getting a glimpse of herself and her sisters in the future. It wasn't pleasant. "Can we get back to the point? If we're holding this ball without Duncan's knowledge, then we need to be stealthy about it."

"Stealthy?" Flora said.

"Sneaky," Joyce said.

Flora frowned at Donna. "Then why didn't you say so."

"I need more cake." Donna waved at the woman who owned the café. "Diane, I need more cake. Lots of it."

Diane glanced around the table and nodded. "I can see that. I'll be right over."

The door to the café opened, and Agnes and Mairi walked in.

"You called in your sisters?" Ann said in disgust.

"Who do you think is helping me get Duncan out of the mansion?" Honestly. She was seriously beginning to regret her decision to help these women out.

Agnes and Mairi grabbed chairs from a vacant table and squeezed in on either side of Donna.

"Sorry we're late," Agnes said. "Please tell me you didn't let the three witches talk you into anything in our absence."

"I resent that label," Ann snapped.

"I resented all the detention you gave me in high school," Agnes shot back. "So, suck it up."

Great. She'd asked her sisters to come as backup, not to start a fight. She rubbed her temples and wondered if she should order migraine medication instead of chocolate cake.

"Ladies," she said. "Let's focus on organising this ball. Okay?"

"Wait a minute," Mairi said. "I'm only here as muscle. Not for a job. You know I don't have time to organise anything. I'm trying to set up my business. There are geeks out there who need my services, or they'll spend their lives sad and alone—like Ann."

"I should have had you expelled," Ann said.

Mairi blew her a kiss.

"That's it!" Donna shot to her feet and jammed her hands onto her hips. "If you lot don't stop bickering and help with the planning, I'm calling everything off."

"You can't do that," Flora said. "Think about the babies."

"I don't care about the babies!"

A gasp went up around the café, and Donna pressed a hand to her stomach as it did somersaults. She really did care about the babies.

"Fine," she caved fast, as usual. "I do care about the babies. But I will call every hotel, hall and pub to find you another venue for this ball if you don't behave."

The three women from the institute lowered their eyes and looked sheepish. Agnes looked shocked and Mairi gave her a thumbs up. Meanwhile, Diane came over to the table with a huge slice of chocolate cake. She patted Donna's shoulder.

"I added extra butter-icing. You look like you need it."

"Thanks." She reached for the cake, but her hands were shaking too hard to hold it.

Diane gave her a sympathetic smile and placed it on the table in front of her. With as much dignity as she could muster, Donna sat back down.

"Now, we need to get people in and out of the mansion without Duncan noticing, and we need to make sure he doesn't enter the ballroom." She picked up her dessert fork. "Any ideas?"

Thankfully, the women were able to stop fighting long enough to actually come up with some. As Donna took notes, she ate her way through enough sugar to keep her going indefinitely.

* * *

Duncan couldn't stand it anymore. He had to draw. Although, he couldn't enter his studio. Not yet. But he suspected it was coming. He felt like he'd boarded a runaway train. The need to paint had become almost unbearable, and he hoped to squash it by sketching.

With trembling fingers, he reached for the sketchpad and

charcoal he'd found in a cupboard in his office and took them over to the window seat in his living room. The window overlooked the garden and the rose bushes Fiona had loved. After the gardener's butchering, there wasn't much of them to see, but he hoped that if he sketched the view she'd loved so much, his working again wouldn't feel too much like betraying her memory.

As soon as he made his first mark on the pristine white paper, something inside of him that had been rubbing wrongly slipped into place. Soon, everything that pressed down on him—the emotions he didn't know how to cope with, the conflicted feelings he had about letting Fiona go, the world in general—all faded away. There was nothing but the view in front of him and his drawings.

His hand moved faster with each sketch. Flying across the page, capturing ideas and images before he was even consciously aware of what they were. He felt like he was soaring. Free at last. He felt the way he used to feel—invincible. Untouchable in this own private universe, made up of line and tone and colour.

It was only when the light changed enough to affect the shadows in his work that he realised hours had passed. Torn pages from his sketchbook lay scattered on the floor around him, and his hands were black with charcoal dust. For the first time in years, he felt a sense of accomplishment. Which was followed by the peace of knowing a day filled with work.

Stiff from sitting in the same cramped space for so long, he stood and stretched as he scanned the pages at his feet. Hills. Rose bushes. Tree branches. And then, in the later ones, a person appeared. His breath hitched as he bent to retrieve one of the final drawings. Had Fiona crept into his work when he wasn't looking? She'd often done that. A lone figure in the distance. Someone peeking out of a house. A person walking through the woods. All Fiona. All unintentional additions to work he'd meticulously planned.

But this one didn't show a figure sneaking into his planned compositions. No, this was something else. This was the painting he'd been dreaming about. The figure was front and centre. And it wasn't his wife. It was his housekeeper.

"Damn." Duncan's head fell forwards as he clutched the page. "Damn it to hell," he muttered.

He sank to the floor, his back against the wall as he studied his work with a critical eye. It was black and white—emphasising the drama of the lighting as he'd seen it the night Donna had stood in front of the open fridge. In his head, he saw the scene in colour. He saw the brush strokes dancing over the canvas, the rich hues he'd use in the shadows, and the saturated colours he'd dab into the lighter areas. He saw it all as though he'd already painted it.

And he knew then, from a lifetime of experience, that the image would haunt him every minute of the day until it was realised. Until he saw it on a canvas in front of him.

Until he'd painted Donna.

"Damn," he muttered again. "Damn."

CHAPTER 7

"I hope you know what you're doing," Grace said when Donna staggered in for breakfast a few days later.

All Donna could manage in response was a hysterical laugh. She hadn't had a decent night's sleep since she'd started scheming to get Duncan out of the mansion.

"Here, drink this, it looks like you need it." Grace placed a mug of tea in front of her.

"You are an angel." Donna sipped the tea while she leaned back into the bench in the breakfast nook.

"Well, maybe you should listen to your *guardian angel* and give up on your daft plan. Duncan isn't going to leave the mansion so you can throw a party."

"I'm not the one throwing the party."

"Aye, that's the most important part. Let's focus on that." Shaking her head, she returned to the state-of-the-art stove. Fiona might have wanted to restore a lot of the mansion's Georgian heritage, but she'd drawn the line at wood-burning stoves. Thank goodness.

"Has he taken the bait yet?" Grace said as she cracked eggs into a mixing bowl.

"No." Donna sipped her tea and resisted the urge to groan.

Duncan was nowhere near accepting the request to lecture at the college. The *fake* request, she reminded herself. The one she'd been finessing in an ongoing email exchange with the art college dean where she pretended to be Duncan. Right now, the dean was excited about having Duncan come out of his self-enforced retirement to teach her students. And Donna had no idea how to get him there.

It was a mess. One of her own making. She pressed a hand to her stomach and added 'buy antacids' to her to-do list. By the time the ball came around, she was going to have a hole in her stomach the size of her fist.

"I hate to add to your stress," Grace said, "but the Women's Institute rang, and they're coming over today to check out the location and work out the details for their ball."

"Kill me now." With a groan she rested her forehead on the table. "I told them to wait until I contacted them."

"Aye, apparently you don't have a good track record for following through on those commitments, so they've taken matters into their own hands. They want to see the ballroom, to plan decorations and table layout. And they want to discuss catering with me." She glanced over her shoulder. "Seeing as I'm the catering liaison."

"I'm…sorry?" Yeah, that didn't sound remorseful at all. She turned her head, opened her eyes and silently begged the woman to cut her some slack. "I'll make it up to you, promise."

Grace snorted. "I won't hold my breath. You girls have been making trouble your whole lives." She shook her head sadly. "I wish your mother had half your backbone."

Donna almost choked on her tea. "My backbone?"

Grace's eyes were dancing when she looked over at her.

"Maybe Agnes' backbone. Now, are you vegetarian today or do you want bacon?"

"I thought you were against bacon?"

"I am." She sighed. "Working here is lowering my standards. Now do you want bacon or not?"

"Bacon, please." She thought about it. "Is there any cake?"

The cook frowned at her. "I'll give you bacon with your omelette, but I draw the line at cake for breakfast."

"Don't you think I've suffered enough?"

"Aye, I do. I also think you could cut it in half just by saying no to people when they corner you."

"That is so much easier said than done. Trust me, I've tried. Now, how am I going to get Duncan out of the way while the Women's Institute are here?"

"You'll think of something."

"That doesn't help at all."

"You know what I think about this situation," Grace said. "You need to come clean with Duncan. Sneaking around and lying to him is just going to backfire."

"How exactly? It isn't like he'll fire me. I'm the only person around here he doesn't want to get rid of." And wasn't *that* an honour?

The smell of sizzling bacon made her mouth water. Donna wasn't a very good vegetarian. It turned out she had a hard time saying no to meat as well as people.

Grace came over and placed a perfectly cooked, vegetable-filled omelette in front of Donna, with three strips of crispy bacon on the side. Donna couldn't wait to get at it and nabbed a piece before the plate hit the table. It had the perfect crunch and tasted like a salty piece of heaven.

"Manners," cook reprimanded, but there was a sparkle in her eye.

"Yum," Donna said around a mouthful of food. "I'm so glad you came to work here, Grace. We needed you."

"You wouldn't have starved to death."

"We might have. Neither of us can cook and the mansion's on the no-delivery list for takeaways."

"That boy needs to start behaving himself," Grace said on a sigh.

"I'm no' a boy," Duncan said from the doorway.

Donna gasped at the sight of him and choked on her bacon. Her eyes streamed as the cook clapped her on the back. When she was done coughing up a lung, she reached for the glass of water Grace had placed in front of her.

"You're a boy to me," Grace told him, making him frown.

"Then I'm the *boy* who pays your wages."

Grace just rolled her eyes and went back to the stove. This was another reason Donna had been keen to hire Grace as their cook—she knew the woman wouldn't let their boss intimidate her.

Duncan slid into the bench seat facing her. "Morning," he said with a knowing smile.

He sat there, perfectly relaxed, as though he did this every morning and it was nothing new, when in fact, it was the first morning in her entire time at the mansion that he'd turned up for breakfast.

"What are you doing here?" she said when she could talk again without coughing.

He cocked an eyebrow at her. "I live here."

Great, she had to deal with an early morning smart arse. "You never come into the kitchen for breakfast."

He reached over the table and nabbed one of her strips of bacon. Donna scowled at him as she lifted her fork. "Do that again, and I will maim you."

"All this time and I never knew you weren't a morning person." His eyes sparkled with amusement and Donna almost choked again, this time on nothing. It was the first time she'd seen him amused, and it softened his features, turning his brooding sexuality into an irresistible rugged magnetism.

She tore her eyes from him and looked away, but not before she spotted cook eyeing them with speculation. Her cheeks began to heat, and she had to fight the urge to run.

"Can I have more bacon, Grace?" she said instead.

"I could use some coffee," Duncan added.

Donna frowned at him. "I'm sure Grace wouldn't mind making you up a tray. You can take it upstairs and eat in your office. Like you usually do."

His lips twitched. "I'm fine here."

"I'm not," she muttered.

She prodded at her food, which had lost its appeal, now that she had company. She shifted uncomfortably in her seat before reaching for her tea and trying to hide behind the mug.

Grace placed a coffee mug in front of Duncan. "I'll make you an omelette."

"I'd rather have a full breakfast. Heavy on the meat if you don't mind." He reached for his coffee.

"I do mind," Grace said. "If you want a plate of fried food for breakfast, you'd better head on out to the pub. You're getting an omelette."

Duncan heaved a sigh and turned to Donna. "Remind me why you hired her?"

"She's the best cook in Kintyre, and I was starving to death."

"Is that right?" Duncan sipped his coffee, but his eyes were on Donna, studying her like she was a math problem he needed to solve.

"Why are you here?"

"I'm here to eat."

He seemed mesmerised by her hair. She self-consciously ran a hand through it as she tried to remember if she'd been awake enough to brush it before she came downstairs. When he continued to stare, she decided she'd had enough of his weird behaviour.

She slammed down her fork and glared at him. "Do I have something on my face? Is my hair tangled? Is my shirt buttoned up wrong?"

"Not that I'm aware of."

"Then why are you staring at me like you've never seen me before this morning?"

* * *

DUNCAN HAD COME to realise that there was no getting away from his need to paint Donna. The only way to get rid of the images in his head was to paint them out. And for that, he required her help. He'd intended to work up to his request. To ease into it. To gently and politely ask her for a favour. Instead, the words rushed out of his mouth and landed on the table between them in a tactless heap.

"I want to paint you."

There was silence. Nothing moved. He wasn't even sure the women were still breathing. He may as well have dropped a bomb right into the middle of the kitchen.

"W-what?" Donna whispered.

There was no going back now. He felt his palms become clammy and his heart race. It would be his first painting since Fiona got sick. His first step towards a new life without her. Bile bit at his throat, and a wave of uncertainty hit him. Could he do it?

And then he noticed the stark vulnerability in Donna's eyes. He couldn't back out now. Not for either of their sakes.

He placed his empty coffee mug in front of him. "I want to paint you. I want you to pose for me."

Grace gasped, but Duncan didn't take his eyes from

Donna. She was stunned and confused, trying to work things out, and knowing her, she would come to the wrong conclusion and run. He had to make things clear for both of them.

He leaned forwards, resting his elbows on the table. "I realise this is a weird request when you work for me. I don't want you to feel obligated to say yes." Cook barked out a laugh, and he shot her a look. She didn't need to tell him that Donna had problems saying no, he'd benefited from it more than once. "Is breakfast coming?" he asked Grace.

She cast a worried glance at Donna before turning. "I'll get it sorted."

He focused his attention on his housekeeper. Her hair was down today, and the soft morning light brought out the deep strands of red. Her hair fascinated him. It wasn't wavy, but wasn't straight either, and so thick a man could get lost in it. He could fill a canvas just with her hair alone. A bizarre abstract study. He cocked his head as he considered it. Maybe another time.

First, he wanted to paint her sitting in one of the picture windows, with the early morning light washing softly over her. Oh, aye, he could use the sunbeams to break up the canvas. It would be as though you were looking at her *through* the light. Excitement washed over him. It was like coming home. As though he'd put on a pair of perfect, worn-in jeans that felt like butter to the touch.

Suddenly, his anxieties fled. Fiona had known he was an artist when she married him. She'd understand his need to work even though she was gone, of that he was certain. And that certainty flowed through his body, calming his overactive heart and steadying his nerves. He was an artist. And he wanted to paint. Right now. Without delay. He'd lost interest in eating. All he wanted to do was get to the studio he hadn't set foot in for two long years.

But first, he had to get his model onto the same page. She

was still staring at him as though he'd grown two heads overnight.

"You want to paint…me?" she said, her eyes on his, searching for something, he wasn't sure what.

All he could do was give her the truth. "Yes."

And then she asked the question he'd been dreading. "Why?"

He didn't have an answer. He didn't know why it had to be her, exactly. It was a combination of the colours that made up her skin tone—the peaches and pinks that blended perfectly—and the soft curves that made up her form. The way the light hit her, changing the colours and luminosity of her skin and hair, was fascinating to watch. She was a walking Pre-Raphaelite painting, and he had to capture it for himself, in a way he knew only he could.

"Why, Duncan, why paint me?"

There was no explaining to her how the sum of her drew him to her. That he wanted to get that essence on canvas. It sounded stupid, even to him. There was something elusive about Donna that he wanted—no, needed—to try to capture in paint. But he couldn't say any of that. How could he explain something he couldn't even understand himself? So, he told her the first thing that came to mind.

"Because you're here and Fiona isn't. I need a subject if I'm going to paint again." It was a minuscule part of the whole reason, and as soon as the words were out of his mouth, he knew they were the wrong ones.

For a second, she looked like she'd been slapped, and then her face cleared and a plastic smile appeared. "I'm flattered, but I have a lot to do today." She pushed away her half-eaten food and stood. "But you should definitely get back into painting. A talent like yours shouldn't be wasted. If you need anything for your studio, let me know and I'll order it in for you. The art shop in Glasgow does overnight delivery now." She turned to Grace. "Thanks for breakfast."

With that, she walked from the room.

A plate thudded down on the table in front of him. He looked up into the glaring eyes of his cook.

"You are a bloody idiot," she snapped at him.

"Is that any way to talk to your boss?"

"It is when he's being clueless and cruel."

"What did I do?"

"Men." She shook her head as she untied her apron, then after dumping it on the counter, she followed Donna out of the room.

Leaving him alone in the huge kitchen. He eyed his food. She'd made him an egg white omelette, filled with spinach. He was obviously being punished. He reached over the table and nabbed the last piece of bacon from Donna's plate. While he chewed, he tried to figure out what he'd said that was so bad.

Maybe he should have explained that he'd been thinking about painting more often over the past few weeks and felt it was time to try again, and that she was the perfect subject. But then she would demand to know why she was the perfect subject. Women always wanted to know the *why* of things. And men never had an answer for them. All he knew was he'd spent the past few nights lying in bed, planning paintings in his head.

And each one of them was of Donna.

CHAPTER 8

Because you're here and Fiona isn't. I need a subject if I'm going to paint again.

Donna strode down the corridor towards her office, her head held high and her shoulders back, but his words still rang in her ears.

Because you're here and Fiona isn't.

A sharp pain hit her in the vicinity of her heart. Of course. What more could there be to it? If Fiona were here, he wouldn't want to paint anyone else. She'd been his go-to model. Not that he was a portrait artist, he just liked to use figures in his canvases to tell the stories in his head. And Fiona had been the perfect muse. Anyone else would be a poor substitute.

Because you're here and Fiona isn't.

He didn't want to paint her in particular, he just wanted someone—anyone—to stand in for Fiona while he attempted to see if he could paint without her. It made sense. Perfect sense in fact. And she was pleased for him, thrilled that he was even thinking about painting again. It was wonderful. It was exactly what she'd wanted for him.

She blinked hard, wiped her cheeks and took a deep breath. She needed to focus on her job and not on Duncan's sudden desire to paint again. He'd hired her to take care of the mansion, and that's what she planned to do. The first thing she needed to do was check up on the contractors, to make sure they were on schedule with the carriage house. And there were emails to send. A new batch in her fake conversation with the Fine Arts dean at Glasgow School of Art. They were ironing out the details of Duncan's lecture. The lecture he knew nothing about and she had no idea how to get him there to give it.

She pushed open the door to her office, and her eyes went to the painting Duncan had given her when he'd found her admiring it. It was one he'd done early in his career, and showed a winter scene with an isolated house surrounded by snow-covered hills. A woman walked in front of the house, her head down as though deep in thought. But you only really saw snippets of the scene, because the surface of the canvas was criss-crossed with lines that made you feel like you were glimpsing the scene through a forest. It reminded her of hand-sewn quilts she'd seen during a school trip to the museum. The colours had been pale—washed out almost— but the feeling evoked by the quilts had been magical. Duncan's work was like that. He wasn't only one of the greatest painters of his generation—he was also a storyteller. His images pulled you into the narrative until you felt like you were part of them, and in the midst of all those swirling brush strokes, you felt like you were touching beauty.

Her chest tightened, and it became hard to breathe. He had such an incredible talent. A gift. He'd find a better subject than her.

Because you're here and Fiona isn't.

She blinked several times as she reached for her handbag. Where had she left that copy of *The Hobbit* she'd been drawing in? She wanted to take it with her, just in case she found a minute to lose herself in it. She checked under her desk.

"He didn't mean it, you know," Grace said from the doorway.

Donna forced a bright smile. "Mean what? Isn't it fantastic that he wants to paint again? I honestly thought this day would never come. You should pose for him. It's a great honour."

Grace stepped into the room and suddenly it felt far too small. "He didn't mean what he said. He's just a man. And a daft one at that."

Because you're here and Fiona isn't.

"I don't know what you mean," she lied as she kept the smile on her face. "You haven't seen a copy of *The Hobbit* lying around have you?"

The cook heaved a sigh. "No. No, I haven't. You should think about taking him up on his offer to paint you though. It would be a good way to keep him busy while the Women's Institute is here."

Donna froze. "I forgot all about them."

"Aye," was all Grace said.

A wave of dizziness overcame her, and she had to sit down. "Maybe you could offer to pose instead."

"He doesn't want me."

"He doesn't care what he paints. A person, a bowl of fruit, a tree—it's all the same to him."

Grace pursed her lips. "Seems he isn't the only daft one around here. I need to deal with the institute's caterer. I don't have time to pose for an instant photo never mind a painting."

"Oh. Right."

"I suggest you clear your busy schedule and sit for the idiot unless you can think of another way to keep him occupied while you scheme behind his back." She turned towards the door. "And for goodness' sake, stop listening to what he says and watch what he does. He's a man. He's genetically programmed to put his foot in his mouth every time he opens it."

With a huff, she left Donna alone to try to figure out another way to keep Duncan occupied for the day. *Any* other way. Unfortunately, none came to mind.

* * *

DUNCAN'S STUDIO was on the ground floor at the north-eastern corner of the house, overlooking the garden and the driveway. He wasn't sure what it had originally been used for, most likely as a music room. It was one of the many rooms the original Georgian owners had used for entertaining, and the irony of him owning a building that was designed for socialising wasn't lost on him.

The room had escaped Fiona's restoration. And for this, he was grateful. A studio was an artist's blank canvas, a place to rest his eye and let his imagination reign. Something that couldn't be achieved with burgundy walls or red flocked wallpaper.

No, his studio had white walls, a bare wooden floor, a double sink in the corner, and uncovered windows. And that was it. The rest of the space held an assortment of tables, trolleys, drying racks, easels, and shelves housing paints. The only seating was a high stool he used when he was tired of standing at his easel, and a sofa he sat on to think.

At least, that was what his studio had looked like the last time he'd set foot inside it.

As he reached the end of the corridor and stood in front of the door, his hands began to sweat. This time, he was going inside. He wasn't going to pace the corridor and chicken out. This was it. As he reached for the handle, he remembered the last time he'd been in the room, and he stilled.

"Are you comfortable there? No' too cold?" he asked Fiona as she reclined on the sofa in the corner of the room where the windows met, and the light bathed her in a soft white glow.

"I'm fine." She adjusted the blanket he'd tucked around her. "I have my scrapbook and I plan to keep busy making notes for the renovation slash restoration."

His throat tightened at the sight of her gentle smile. They both knew she wouldn't be around to see the finished mansion.

"Plus," she said, "if I get fed up with this, I can always watch you work." She batted her eyelashes at him. "I would feel so much better if you'd paint without your shirt on. In fact"—her eyes danced, and for a moment, he lost sight of the black circles beneath them—"why don't you paint in the nude? I'm sure that would help a lot."

"You do, do you?" He tossed the rag he'd been using to wipe his brush at her head. "No nude painting. Anyone walking up the drive can see right in here. And I won't be responsible for giving the housekeeper a heart attack."

"Spoil sport."

She rested her head on the arm of the sofa and watched as he applied the finishing touches to a moonlight scene, with a lone figure standing by the water.

"We would have had wonderful children," she said on a sigh.

Duncan cleared his throat before answering. "Aye, we would have."

When he looked over, she was fast asleep, a gentle smile on her face—and Duncan started a portrait of the woman he loved.

That had been his last visit to the studio. Three months later, she'd been taken from him. Now, here he was again, standing in front of the room that used to be his sanctuary, and he shook at the thought of going inside.

This was pathetic.

"Man up!" he barked at himself, and he turned the handle.

He'd expected to find a room knee-deep in dust and strewn with cobwebs. Instead, the air was fresh and flower-scented, and there wasn't a speck of dust anywhere. Stunned, Duncan slowly walked into the centre of the large room, with its high ceilings, and perfect northern light. Someone had kept the place in pristine condition. It looked like he'd only walked out of it an hour earlier.

He trailed a hand over the trolley table used to store the paints he'd been working with on his last painting. Each tube had been wiped clean, and the lids maintained to ensure they didn't crust up and become impossible to open. His brushes were soft and supple, not hard and dried-out as he'd expected to find them.

He scanned the rest of the room. There were dust cloths over the half-finished canvases he'd stacked in the corner. And someone had fitted white UV-filtering blinds to the windows, to protect the colours in the drawings pinned to the walls. Lastly, he turned to the canvas he'd abandoned, the one still sitting on the easel. That too had a dust cover draped over it.

Slowly, he lifted the cover, to reveal the portrait of Fiona sitting in the garden. The blow he'd been expecting didn't come, only a bittersweet sadness at seeing the half-finished work again. As he moved to drop the cloth, he noticed something tucked into the top of the easel, above the painting.

A rose.

A fresh rose picked from Fiona's garden—one of the few left untouched by the gardener.

With trembling fingers, he gently removed the flower from its perch and brought it to his nose. It was the same subtle fragrance that filled the room. And he knew that the scent couldn't have built in the time the flower had been there, there must have been roses present for months—longer, even. It was a quiet and unassuming tribute to the woman he'd lost, and the art he'd abandoned because of her.

The flower, the careful preservation of the past, the working state of the room…it could only have been one person. The woman he'd relied on for two long years but was now beginning to see.

Donna.

He stood there, trying to absorb the magnitude of what he'd found. The depth of thoughtfulness in caring for his studio, in honouring Fiona's memory, almost overwhelmed him. Donna had stepped in to look after the things that were most important to him when he'd been unable to face them. She'd kept his soul alive. Because that was how he'd always seen his art, as the very core of himself, the best part of him —his soul.

And at that moment, he felt the dark, heavy cloak that covered him split wide open. A cool breeze blew through the crack, sweeping away the musty staleness that prevailed. Bright, diffused light from the sheer-covered windows rushed into the darkness and chased it away. He staggered, holding on to his painting table to keep himself steady. As he felt a smile break out, he lifted his face to the light, breathing the cool, fresh air deep into his lungs.

He'd been sleepwalking through life for far too long, but now he felt…alive. A rush of adrenalin demanded he move. There was no time to waste. He wanted to feel his paintbrushes in his hands, needed to lose himself in the colours and shapes and brushstrokes on his canvas. He wanted to live again.

After sweeping the dust cloths off the canvases, he opened the blinds to let the full light of day flood the room. Carefully, he took the half-finished painting of Fiona from the easel. He wouldn't complete it. It was perfect as it was. He leaned it against the wall, where she could watch him work, and then he unpinned all the sketches he'd tacked to the walls. They were old ideas. His head was full of new ones.

After grabbing his sketchpad and pencils, he strode towards the sofa and settled in to work. To think. To begin again. That's when he heard the door creak open, and he turned to find Donna peeking in at him. Those expressive eyes of hers took in the changes to the room and rested for a moment on the rose he'd left on his painting trolley. Her cheeks flushed, as though she was embarrassed at being found out, and then those eyes settled on him.

"I've cleared my schedule," she said tentatively. "If you still want a model, I can pose."

Duncan didn't give her a chance to change her mind. He covered the distance between them in the blink of an eye, took her hand and swept her into the room. Closing the door tight behind her.

CHAPTER 9

What was she doing? This situation was *not* good for her mental health. And yet, here she was, posing for Duncan because she couldn't think of anything else that would keep him occupied while the women from the institute planned a party in his home.

Lies. Lies upon lies upon lies…

That's what her life had come to. She was lying to Duncan to try to get him out of the mansion. Lying to distract him while people used his home. Lying to the art college about Duncan wanting to lecture there. She'd also lied to all the people she'd fired when she'd written them severance cheques and told them it was from Duncan. She was a liar. That was who she was, and she was going straight to hell because of it.

Well, really, said a voice only she could hear, *you only have yourself to blame.* Gandalf the White appeared beside the easel and frowned over at her. *You should tell everyone the truth. It will produce far fewer difficulties in the long run. I find that honesty truly is the best policy. Things seldom go well when you lie.*

Thanks. Donna scowled at the imaginary figure as another appeared in the corner of the room.

Good Hobbitses are kind to their master, Gollum said as he crawled along the studio floor after some invisible prey. *Good Hobbitses don't tell them fibs.*

You're wasting your time. Hermione materialised behind the sofa. *Donna thinks she knows best and refuses to listen to reason.*

Donna glared at all of them. *Why is it none of my drawings ever turn up to support me?*

Ra-Ra. Go, Donna. A massive hand-drawn troll walked through the room carrying a cheerleader's pompom in one hand while picking his nose with the other. Great, *that* was her support? Yay for her.

"Donna?" The only other real person in the room said, pulling her attention away from her imaginary judges. "Are you ok?"

"Yes," she snapped.

"You looked like you zoned out there."

"No. I'm fine." *Can you all just get out of here?* she shouted in her head.

It was hard enough dealing with Duncan without having to put up with advice from imaginary characters.

Well, I never, said Gandalf, and he disappeared.

I know when I'm not wanted. Hermione followed him.

My precious, Gollum shouted and dove out of the room after his ring.

Yum, said the troll as he took his finger from his nose and popped it in his mouth. Then he disappeared too, leaving her blessedly alone to deal with her latest mess.

She forced a smile. "Where do you want me?"

His dark eyes pinned her with an intense look she couldn't quite decipher. And then he blinked, and it was gone.

"Give me a minute," he said and proceeded to tug the sofa in front of the windows that looked out over the driveway. "Okay," he said, once he'd gotten it where he wanted. "Sit in the corner nearest the windows."

He strode past her, lifted the barstool and positioned it facing the sofa, then he retrieved his sketchpad and pencil and sat on the stool—with a clear view of not only the sofa, but of the driveway leading up the mansion.

*Oh no, no, no, no…*This would not do. The whole point of posing was to keep him occupied so he wouldn't see the Women's Institute arrive at the house. From this angle, there was no way he'd miss them coming up behind her.

"Are you sure about this?" she said. "The light will be behind me. Won't that make it hard to see details? Isn't this bad art practice?"

He cocked his head. "I've been doing this for a while. I know how I want to pose my models. The light is perfect."

And so was his view of the driveway.

"I don't like sitting in the sun."

"The windows face north. There is no sun."

"How about I sit on the stool, and you sit on the sofa That way the light will be behind you, and you'll be able to see what you're doing a whole lot better."

He narrowed his eyes at her. "I can see what I'm doing just fine. If you've changed your mind about posing, say it. I've got some sketching I'd like to do in the garden anyway."

And have him wandering around? Outside? Where he could see everyone, or worse, talk to them? No way.

She sat on the couch with a thump before trying to position herself in such a way that she blocked as much of the view behind her as possible. It was pointless. She was small, the window was large, and Duncan was elevated enough to see over her head.

"Can we at least close the blinds?" she tried.

He ran a hand through his hair, in a gesture that screamed frustration. "What's going on?"

"Nothing." It came out a bit too fast, and her cheeks began to heat.

He looked suspicious, so she scrambled for something else to tell him. "I've never posed for an artist before."

The tension went out of his shoulders some. "Well, it's easy. All you do is sit still and shut up." He gave her a slow smile as his eyes sparkled. "I promise I'll make it good for you."

Oh yeah, her cheeks were definitely heated now. She studied him, trying to figure out if the innuendo was intentional. It couldn't have been. It had to be her imagination.

"So, what's it going to be?" he said. "Are you going to pose where I put you, or do I go outside to draw?"

That was no choice at all. "I'll pose."

"Fantastic. In that case, do you think you could relax? You look like a wooden doll."

Of course she looked like a wooden doll. There was enough tension in her body to solidify her muscles and turn her to stone. She stood, shook out her arms, angled her head from side to side, and did a few stretches while she focused on breathing.

Then she perched on the edge of the sofa with her knees together, hands in her lap, and her back straight. She gave him her best plastic smile. "Better?"

"I can honestly say I've never had a model do a warm-up before they posed for me. It's a whole new experience. You sure you don't want to do some yoga to really get in the zone?"

She frowned at him. "Is. This. Pose. Okay?"

"It would be great—if you were the witness in a trial. I need something a wee bit more relaxed."

"This is as relaxed as it's going to get. How about I offer to stare at you for hours on end, and we'll see how relaxed you feel?"

He pinched the bridge of his nose, and she got the distinct impression he regretted asking her to pose. "How about you sit back and read a book?"

That got her attention. "You want me to read?"

"Aye. You've always got a book in that massive bag you cart around, so go get it and you can read while I draw."

"Do I get paid for this or is it considered free time?"

"Donna, you're on a salary. Not an hourly rate."

"I just want to be clear that this isn't time I need to make up later, right?"

"No."

"And all the things that don't get done while I sit here will remain undone if I can't fit them into a normal day?"

"Aye."

"And you won't freak out if one of those things is something you wanted done?"

"Donna, get the damn book."

Well, that changed everything. If she was going to get paid to read, then this posing thing was looking up. "Back in a minute." She ran for the door.

Ten minutes later, she'd returned with a copy of *The Hunger Games*. She'd chosen it because she hadn't gotten around to drawing on the pages yet, which meant less chance of anything from the book popping out of her imagination and into the real world to annoy her. With a glee-filled smile, she settled into the corner to read.

Maybe this posing thing would be okay after all.

* * *

DUNCAN WATCHED Donna make herself comfortable. There

was a look of absolute glee on her face that made him want to smile.

"Is this how you want me?" She'd tucked her feet under her and pulled a cushion over to use as a prop for her book.

Is this how you want me?

Her innocent question made his mouth go dry as images flooded his mind. Donna dressed in nothing but a white men's dress shirt, reclining on the sofa with the soft early morning light bathing her pale skin. The shirt open to reveal a strip of skin down the centre of her body. Her hair loose around her shoulders, flowing over the blue material of the sofa. Her eyes slumberous with sensuality. He'd paint her surrounded by cool blues and purples, contrasting with the warm tones of her skin and the red gold in her hair.

"Duncan?" Donna's voice jarred him back to reality. He blinked at her.

"What?"

"Is this okay?"

He cleared his throat. "Take your hair down for me." Damn. He shouldn't have added those last two words.

With her eyes on him, she reached up and took her hair from her ponytail she'd put in after their breakfast. "Like this?"

She spread it out over her shoulders. It was thick, luscious, and honey coloured, interwoven with several different shades of blonde and brown, that only truly came to life when the sun hit them in the right way. She was a siren, calling to him. He shook his head to clear it. He was a professional, and he'd painted plenty of people throughout his career. This was no different. He was just a little rusty after more than two years away from his work. That's why Donna posing for him was affecting him strangely.

"Exactly like that." The words came out huskier than he'd intended, and he feigned a cough to cover for himself.

"Should I start reading now?"

All he could do was give a terse nod. With a look of uncertainty, she turned back to her book, and Duncan watched her. No, not watched. He *studied* her.

The graceful line from her neck to her shoulder. The voluptuous curve of her waist to her hip. The elegance of her feet tucked beneath her. Long fingers, caressing the book. A hint of a smile, curving lips that were ripe and lush. Skin so smooth and translucent that it glowed in the soft light from the window.

Today, she wore a peach satin blouse, buttoned up to her throat, with soft pleats down the front. It billowed in the sleeve, falling softly around her delicate wrists. She'd teamed it with grey dress trousers that were far too smart for her pose—barefoot on a sofa with a book. Once again, she'd ignored his suggestion that she dress less business-like, but he knew if he challenged her about it, he would get the same answer: she was wearing what she wanted to wear. For some reason, that made him smile.

"What are you reading?" he found himself asking as he reached for the pastels on his drawing table. He'd sketch her in colour and try to capture the way the peach satin brought out the golds in her hair.

"*The Hunger Games.*" Thick, long, black lashes lifted as she looked up at him. Today, her eyes leaned closer to forest green than sea green.

He stared at her while his hand moved over the page in front of him. Sometimes it felt as though his talent worked independently of his consciousness. "I don't know that one."

"It's a teen book." She paused as though waiting for him to comment on her taste in reading matter. He had nothing to say. Who was he to judge what she liked to read? "I'm at the bit where Katniss, she's the heroine, shoots Marvel, one of the other challengers in the game. She gets him in the throat with an arrow and he drowns in his own blood."

That stilled his hand.

He looked up from his sketchpad to stare at her. "Cheery," he said at last.

With a mysterious smile, Donna returned her attention to her book. And he returned his attention to Donna.

* * *

DONNA PRETENDED to read but was all too aware of Duncan's eyes on her. Even though she was fully dressed, she felt naked under his gaze. His dark eyes studied every inch of her as his hand flew over his sketchbook. Now and then, he'd frown before looking back and forth between her and his drawing, as though trying to work out a flaw in the comparison.

"I thought you were going to paint me?"

"Only an idiot approaches a canvas without a plan."

His absolute passion for what he was doing made her sad that he'd spent so long without it. A talent like his, skill like his, needed to be shared with the world. Which reminded her of the scheme to get him out of the way during the ball. "You should take the art college up on its invitation to teach."

His pastel pencil stilled, and his eyes focused on her in a way that made it clear he was now seeing her as a person rather than an object to study. "Where did that come from?"

She shrugged. "You obviously love it. It would be a shame not to share that passion with people starting out. You've taught before, haven't you?"

"That was a long time ago." He flicked the page over to start afresh, making Donna wonder how much planning one painting needed. When she sketched in her books, she didn't think about it at all beforehand, she just grabbed a pencil and got to it. She guessed that was the difference between a professional and someone who dabbled.

"I think you should accept the invitation. It's only one lecture. It's not like you're committing to something long term. Plus, you said yourself, you're going stir crazy here. Maybe a couple of nights in Glasgow is just what you need. Not to mention, you'd get to talk to people who understand you for a change. I imagine that would be nice."

He cocked an eyebrow at her, and she tried to look as innocent and disinterested as possible.

"Will you stop talking and let me work if I promise to think about it?"

Hope rose within her but she played it cool. "You don't need to promise. It's totally up to you whether or not you think about it."

"Then can I get back to work?"

"Yes." She thought about it. "But meeting up with other artists would be nice, wouldn't it?"

"Donna." He was clearly frustrated. "I'll think about it. Okay?"

"Whatever you feel is best."

He growled at her. "Pose. Don't talk."

She grinned and returned to her book. But it was hard to concentrate. Her attention kept being drawn to Duncan. The blue plaid shirt he wore tugged over his shoulders as he moved. Each gesture he made was precise, fluid and intentional. There were no wasted movements.

She imagined other people might find it offensive to be reduced to lines and shape and colours. Donna was fascinated. Somehow, she had become part of his process, and it made her feel a connection to him that she wasn't sure was wise. It was peaceful, sitting in the soft morning light, listening to pastel scrape over paper. She could have stayed there forever.

And that's when she heard the engines. Her heart jumped as she caught movement out of the corner of her eye. There was a convoy of cars coming up the driveway. The Women's Institute were here, and they'd brought an army along with them. So much for the meeting they'd had about being stealthy. There was a van emblazoned with the logo of a catering company, another with *Party Hire* written on the side in pink glittery letters, and one proclaiming it set up the best sound equipment in Scotland.

A lime-green Mini led the procession. In the front seat, clear as day, sat Flora and Joyce. There was nothing subtle about their approach. They'd ignored everything she'd told them. She was going to kill someone. No, she would let Agnes kill someone.

She glanced at Duncan. He had his head down as he studied his work, but he wouldn't stay like that for long. There was no way he could miss the convoy coming down his drive.

"Stop moving, woman," Duncan said as his head came up to look at her.

Her breath caught in her throat as everything unfolded in slow motion. The cavalcade crawled towards the mansion, in plain view of the studio. Their approach caught Duncan's eye. He frowned and set aside his sketchpad.

"What the...?" he muttered as he leaned in for a closer look.

There was nothing between him and the window.

Nothing but her.

Donna shot to her feet, her future flashing before her eyes. Duncan would lose his mind and fire everyone. The Women's Institute wouldn't be able to raise money for their cause. The art college would be pissed and take it out on Duncan. And she would have to listen to his endless rant because there was no way he'd give her a decent reference so she could get another job. She'd be stuck. Forever. And cook wouldn't even be there to feed her.

She had to do something to distract him.

Anything.

And she had to do it fast.

"Donna," Duncan said absently, his eyes on the window. "Sit back down. We're not finished for the day. I just want to see what's going on out there."

There was no time to waste. And she only had one idea to take his mind off the procession. She swallowed hard. This was so dumb.

Don't do it! Hermione shouted from behind Duncan. *Have some self-respect!*

It was too late. Time had run out.

Duncan frowned. "Who are all those people coming up th—"

Whatever he was going to say was lost. Because Donna did the only thing she could think of to get his attention.

She whipped off her top.

CHAPTER 10

One second Duncan was distracted by some work vans coming up the driveway. The next he couldn't see anything but Donna, standing in front of him, wearing a pink flowery bra where her blouse used to be.

"What. . ." He'd intended to ask what she was doing, but the words caught in his throat because she was unzipping her trousers and shimmying out of them.

"It just occurred to me," she said in a breathless, husky voice that went straight to his groin. "Real artists always paint their models naked." Her cheeks had flushed a deep ruby pink now, and there was a madly determined, slightly panicked, glint in her eyes.

These details Duncan picked up in passing because his gaze was firmly stuck on the smooth curves of her body, shown to perfection in her matching lingerie.

"Wha . . ." He tried again. No, Still no sentences. Because, as he started to speak, Donna turned and leaned over to shut the blind.

She rested one hand on the sofa as she tugged at the cord with the other. The action lifted her behind out towards him, like an offering. His mouth went dry. He lost the ability to think, to speak. All he could see was the voluptuous curve of Donna's backside, encased in silky French-cut panties with pink flowers blooming all over them.

His fingers itched to touch as his jeans became far too tight. A roaring need rushed through him. One he hadn't felt since his wife had died. Or maybe, had never felt. His attraction to Fiona had always been a gentle thing. What Donna's curves made him feel was nowhere near gentle. There was a loud roaring in his ears, and his whole body grew tense, alert and primed for action. Every instinct he possessed told him to touch and taste. He shook with the effort to hold himself back.

This was Donna.

His housekeeper.

There were lines. Ones a man didn't cross. And he was looking at one of them.

Damn it to hell!

Guilt slammed through him, wiping the desire away. What was he doing? She was his employee. She wasn't his wife. He'd vowed forever, and that there would never be another. It was like a bucket of ice water, dousing the flames of need.

"That's better isn't it?" Donna said once the sheer blinds were closed. "We wouldn't want the contractors to think you were up to no good with your housekeeper." She gave him a terrified smile as her visibly shaking hands reached behind her back to unfasten her bra. "Guess I should finish getting undressed then."

"No!" He held up a hand to stop her as he staggered back several steps.

Her hands dropped to her sides, and she cast a glance at the windows before a look of relief passed over her face. "Sorry. My mistake. I'll get dressed, and we can finish off the clothed painting—after you're done with your pastel drawings." She grabbed for her blouse and hurriedly covered herself with it.

Her behaviour confused him. But there was no time to reason it out. Not with Fiona's eyes staring at him from the half-finished portrait leaning against the wall. He thrust a hand through his hair before clasping the back of his neck.

"Duncan?" Donna's voice trembled as her wide eyes stared up at him.

It was all too much. He couldn't take anymore.

"I'm done here."

"What about the painting?"

He shook his head. "I'm done. I'll be in the gym. Don't disturb me."

And with that, he tore his eyes from her and stalked from the room. Removing himself from the temptation of his curvy housekeeper.

In other words—he fled.

* * *

"THAT WENT WELL," Donna said to the door as it slammed shut behind Duncan.

She flopped back onto the sofa, and couldn't help but look down at herself, noting the way her stomach creased and her thighs flattened out.

"No wonder he ran." She clutched her discarded clothes in front of her.

Oh, darling. Harry Potter's mother appeared on the couch beside her. Imaginary fingers drawn in soft, coloured pencil lines attempted to brush back Donna's hair. *Why do you bring these things on yourself?*

Donna looked at the image of the gentle, smiling woman that only she could see. "And why couldn't you have been here earlier when everyone was giving me a hard time?" Harry's mum would have sorted out Hermione and gently reprimanded Gandalf.

A soft knock at the door made the drawing disappear and Donna squeal. "Wait a minute!"

There was no time, the door opened, and Grace's head appeared. She took one look at Donna, nodded to herself, then stepped inside and closed the door behind her. "It's true then, Joyce told me you were in here getting naked with Duncan."

"Joyce is four hundred years old and wears glasses that are as thick as jam jar bottoms. Do I look naked to you?" She was still clutching her clothes in front of her, and even though they didn't hide much, anyone could see she still wore underwear.

"You look like you were trying to get naked." Grace sat on the stool Duncan had vacated.

"I was hoping it wouldn't come to that."

"What *were* you doing then?"

"Distracting him." She gave up trying to hide and swept her hands up to tie her hair back before tugging on her shirt. "I spotted the cavalcade coming up the drive, and it was the only thing I could think of to do. I blame Mairi. She made me watch that movie, *Ten Things I Hate About You*. The heroine flashes the coach to get her boyfriend out of detention. It worked for Julia Stiles, so it seemed like a good idea. At the time. But it didn't go quite as I'd planned."

"Aye, I gathered that by the way Duncan ran for the gym like the English were coming for him."

Donna pulled on her trousers and plopped back into the sofa. "Who saw me? Apart from Joyce."

"Everybody. The caterer said to give you his number. And Flora said you waved."

"I figured it was too late to do anything but brazen it out. Have they gone now?"

"No. They're measuring up the ballroom for decorations." She gave Donna a sympathetic look. "I came to check on you."

"I'm fine." She winced at the lie, and her cheeks burned. "As fine as you can be when you flash yourself to your boss and he runs for it." It wouldn't go down in the annals of time as her finest moment.

Grace smiled softly and shook her head. "This can't go on. You know that, right?"

"I know, but if I can get him to go to Glasgow for that lecture, this will be all over."

"I'm not talking about that."

Donna couldn't look Grace in the eye. She didn't want to hear what she was talking about, because she suspected she already knew. She reached for her shoes and slipped them back on, hoping her apparent lack of interest would deter Grace.

But it didn't. "Donna, my girl." Her voice softened, and Donna's heart clenched. "You know I'm very fond of you."

"Don't." Donna held up a hand. "I'm okay. Honestly."

Grace shook her head. "You can't go on like this. You've been mooning over that man for years. It's the talk of Kintyre."

Her back snapped straight. "I haven't been mooning." She pressed a hand to her stomach. "People are talking?"

Grace waved a dismissive hand. "People always talk. But it's clear that you have feelings for Duncan, and it's equally evident—"

"That he doesn't have feelings for me." Nausea rose as she forced the words out.

"That's not what I was going to say. I think he's very fond

of you, but I just don't think he's capable of moving on from his wife yet."

"I know. That's why I don't have feelings for Duncan. The gossips are wrong. I've just been looking out for him, that's all. Anyone would do the same. He's so…broken."

The painting of Fiona caught her eye and she smiled. Each stroke had been painted with such love, and she was glad that Duncan'd had that in his life. By all accounts, Fiona had been a remarkable woman, and they'd been well-suited. No one could ever compete with a bond like that. Not that she wanted to.

"There's no need to worry," she said, more to Fiona than Grace. "I don't have a crush on my boss."

Liar, liar, pants on fire, the troll said as it walked through the room.

"Well, then, that's good," Grace said gently, sounding like she didn't believe Donna.

"Honestly, I've just been looking out for him, for Fiona. That's what she would have wanted."

She'd come into the studio every day to leave a rose for Fiona. She wasn't quite sure why. At first, it was because she was sad that Duncan missed her so much and his studio was languishing because of it, but then she'd begun to feel a kinship with the dead woman, as though looking after Duncan had given them something in common. Sometimes, she'd even felt like she was taking care of him for Fiona.

She blinked several times before looking back at Grace. "He's painting again, and he's thinking about teaching too. I think he's coming out the other end of his grief. He doesn't need me so much anymore. That's good, isn't it?"

"Aye, it is." Grace got up and patted Donna on the cheek. "If you need anything, let me know. I'd best get back and watch those women. Or they'll be pocketing the silver."

As the door closed behind her, Donna let her head rest on the back of the sofa.

And a single tear ran down her cheek.

She wiped it away. There was no time for self-pity. She had a mansion to run...and jobs to apply for. There was nothing keeping her in the mansion any longer. Duncan had moved on and she needed to do that too. With one last glance at Fiona's painting and a whispered apology, Donna left the room.

Duncan was avoiding his housekeeper, which made him feel like he was twelve years old again and didn't know how to talk to girls. He'd hated that awkward age, and he didn't want to relive it. It seemed he had no choice in the matter though. After their posing incident, and a heavy workout in the gym that had nearly killed him, he'd locked himself in his studio and hidden in his work. He was painting up a storm. It was a creative frenzy the likes of which he hadn't experienced since the weeks before his final degree show in college. But it hadn't brought him the peace he'd hoped for.

It seemed that, although he'd managed to dodge Donna in reality, he couldn't get away from her in his art. She was everywhere. In drawings pinned to the wall and on canvases he'd painted well into the night, before falling asleep on the sofa. Only to find upon waking that the first thing he saw was Donna's face smiling out of the paintings around him.

He was a man obsessed. Even when he slept, she invaded his dreams. Sometimes, he saw her in the compositions he painted when he was awake. At other times, he had blazing arguments with dream Donna, ones he would never have with her in real life and couldn't remember when he woke. But it was the third type of dream that bothered him the most: those were blistering hot. Donna naked, lounging on the sofa in his studio, all glorious curves and willing woman. Donna undressing as she sauntered towards him across the kitchen, before pushing him back onto the table and climbing on top of him. Donna beckoning to him from the shower, water trailing over her skin…

He groaned at the thought. The variations were endless, but they all ended up in the same place, with him suffering a hard-on that would not be sated by his own hand. But the worst part of all was the guilt. Every day he walked into his studio, the first thing he saw was the half-finished painting of his dead wife. And it was a punch to his gut every time. He felt like those dreams were betrayals of her memory, of the promises he'd made. He hated that he had no control over his mind and when he slept it was Donna, not Fiona, who returned to haunt him.

It had been over a week since that day in the studio when she'd stripped in front of him. Seven days of suffering, every single minute. His body was desperate for her, while his mind screamed in protest, and his honour was affronted by the whole thing. This couldn't go on. And he feared that the only way to solve it was to either fire the woman who had saved his sanity these past two years or give in to temptation and sate his hunger—assuming Donna would have him.

It was this thought that brought his painting frenzy to a dramatic halt. In all these days of thinking about what she was doing to him—how she was torturing him with her presence, with his need for her—it had never once occurred to him that she might not feel the same way. He sat down on his stool, in his studio, in front of the latest painting of the woman who tormented him. To add insult to injury, she'd practically turned him into a portrait artist.

With a groan he covered his face with his hands. He needed help. And he wasn't sure where to get it. He'd cut off his friends when Fiona got sick, unable to cope with their sympathy and well-meaning advice. His only brother lived in Australia, and Duncan had barely spoken to him over the past few years. Each time Hamish had tried to talk to him, Duncan had been brusque with his replies, and the phone calls had become less frequent. But brothers could be forgiving, couldn't they?

He reached into his pocket for his phone, only to remember Donna had thrown it off the first-floor landing and hadn't replaced it yet. With heavy legs, he walked to the landline in the corner of the room, lifted the receiver and slid down the wall to sit on the floor while he dialled.

"Is everything okay?" Were Hamish's first words, and Duncan couldn't help but smile. It wasn't until he heard his brother's voice that he realised just how much he'd missed him.

"Are you going to answer me? Is my brother okay?" Hamish demanded.

"I'm fine, Hamish," Duncan said.

There was silence for a beat. "Then what the hell are you doing phoning me in the middle of the night, you arsehole? I nearly had a heart attack."

He wasn't sure who was the most surprised when Duncan burst out laughing.

"It's good to hear your voice," he admitted once he'd calmed down.

"It would help if you picked up the phone sometimes."

There was no arguing with that. "How's the family?"

He heard the grin in his brother's voice while he filled Duncan in on all the things he'd missed with his nieces and nephews. Hamish had four kids under ten, and his house sounded like a war zone. Still, there was no denying he was happy, which made Duncan feel a whole lot better about neglecting him.

"You going to tell me why you phoned?" Hamish said when they were all caught up on his kids.

"Does a man need a reason to call his brother?" He was stalling and knew his brother would hear it.

"Aye, you do. Now tell me what's going on," Hamish ordered, proving that a man never grew out of his role as the elder brother.

Duncan let out a sigh. "I'm having some problems."

There was silence, and then, "Are they of a suicidal nature?"

"What? No!"

There was a sigh. "Thank the Lord for that. I'm not equipped for that kind of crap. I was going to wake Shelley and have her deal with you."

"You thought a high school teacher would be better equipped to deal with a suicidal man?"

"Dunc, if that woman can deal with hundreds of hormonal teenagers every day, she can sort out your sorry arse."

He shook his head to clear that weird reasoning from it. "I'm not depressed. Well, not now anyway. I have a problem with…"

How did he explain his dilemma without sounding like a complete arse? He was talking about his housekeeper after all. He was in a position of authority over the woman, and even though he'd been living in his head the past few years, he'd hadn't missed that there was a whole movement going on to put men who abused their power in their rightful place —on their arses with two black eyes.

"Is this a guessing game?" Hamish said. "Tell me when I hit the right one. You have a problem with…alcohol?

Pornography addiction? Opioid abuse? Inappropriate thoughts about nuns?"

"Stop!" He wasn't sure whether he should be insulted or laugh until he cried. "I have a problem with guilt."

"So, it's the nuns then?" Hamish said, but there was laughter in his voice.

Duncan let his head rest on the wall behind him, and he stared up at the pristine white ceiling. At some point in the past couple of years, there must have been a paint crew in here to give it another coat. Donna again. She was everywhere he turned.

"I'm having inappropriate thoughts, but not about nuns, you numpty, about my housekeeper."

"Mrs Granger? Holy shit, man, that's just wrong."

Duncan burst out laughing again. Mrs Granger had been the housekeeper he'd fired before hiring Donna. She'd been old enough to be his mother, had a permanent frown, thought grey was a prime colour, and reminded him of a jar of pickles.

He wiped his eyes as he calmed down. Man, it felt good to laugh again. "Not Granger, I fired her in a drunken fit two years ago. It's her replacement, Donna Sinclair."

"Please tell me Donna is young and gorgeous?"

He looked at the canvases he'd covered with her image. "Aye," was all he could say.

Hamish let out a heavy and clearly relieved sigh. "About time, brother."

"No, not about time. I made promises to Fiona. Vows before God."

"Ah, I see the problem." His brother's voice softened. "You feel like you're betraying your wife. Like you're cheating on her, maybe?"

"Aye."

"I can understand that. The promises we make before

God are serious business. But remember, you also only vowed to keep them until death did you part."

He sucked in a breath, feeling like he'd been punched in the gut. "Damn."

"Aye."

He stared at the paintings of Fiona and Donna, sitting side by side in his studio, while his brother waited patiently for him to talk.

"How do you let go?" he asked, almost to himself.

"I honestly don't know. I've never been in your shoes, and I have no idea how I would cope if ever I was. Only you know how to move on from Fiona. I could give you all the clichéd advice we give people like you—that she wouldn't want you to pine after her, that she wanted you to be happy, that you should live your life and not waste it. There's truth in all of that, but I'm sure it rings bloody hollow when you're the one going through it. I hate to say it, but you need to figure this out for yourself. Just know that I'm only a phone call away if you need me. And if things get desperate, I can hop a plane with the family and come sort you out in person."

Duncan closed his eyes. "What if Donna doesn't want me?"

"I'm going to pretend that you don't sound like one of Shelley's hormonal students and treat that as a serious question. Here's what I think—if she doesn't want you, it will suck to be you, but at least you tried."

His eyes opened as he frowned. "That's it? That's all you've got? *At least I tried?*"

"That's it. That's all I've got. Can we talk about football now?"

"Fat lot of good you are."

"I get that a lot."

"It's been nearly twenty years since I last dated." Even the thought of going through that again made him feel awkward. Maybe it would be best if he stayed a grumpy-arsed widower forever. But at the rate he was going, his obsession with Donna would drive him over the edge—right off the cliffs of Arness and into the sea.

"You're asking the wrong man for dating advice. I've been off the market even longer than you have. But, as far as I can see, the only thing that's changed is you don't have any physical contact until the tenth date. Up until then, it all happens online."

"She lives in the same house as me, we talk in person, not online."

"Well, you could just try the direct approach. Ask her out for dinner, talk to her about something that isn't work-related—if that's even possible for you—and then try to sneak a kiss on the way home. Oh, wait, it's all 'Me Too' now. You can't sneak a kiss. You need to ask permission first, so you don't get slapped."

"And people say *I'm* a caveman," Duncan muttered.

"At least you don't have far to go to get home after you walk her to her door."

His brother was far too amused for Duncan's liking. "Should you really be laughing at my expense?"

"When it's this funny, aye."

A female voice sounded in the background. "Who's on the phone?"

A pang of sadness hit Duncan as he remembered conversations with Fiona in the middle of the night, when the phone had rung and disturbed them. It was the simple, everyday things that always hurt the most. Those memories seemed to blindside him.

"It's Duncan, he fancies a lassie and doesn't know what to do about it," Hamish said.

"That's not true," Duncan bellowed. "Don't tell her that, you arse."

"Duncan"—Shelley's Australian accent sounded down the line—"we've missed you, when are you coming to visit?"

"I don't know," he said with a sigh, "but I'll think about it."

"That's good enough for me. Is the idiot right? Are you interested in someone?"

"Aye." And he felt like he was thirteen again, and word about his crush had spread round the school playground. Hamish had been to blame that time too and had received a black eye for his interference. Lucky for his brother he was half a world away, or he'd be getting a repeat performance.

"That's wonderful," Shelley said. "Fiona wouldn't have wanted you to be alone."

He stifled a groan as Hamish chimed in, "We're not telling him stuff like that because it's clichéd and makes us want to puke."

"Oh, okay." Shelley sounded confused.

His brother must have wrestled the phone from his wife because he came back on the line. "Here's my advice, stop screwing around, grow a pair, and go after the girl. If it all goes balls up, you can cry into your beer."

"Hamish!" Shelley sounded outraged.

"Got to go," Hamish shouted and hung up.

Duncan found himself shaking his head and grinning. His eyes fell on the painting of Fiona, and the smile faded. "What do I do, lass? Will it break your heart if I touch another?"

The silence was answer enough. Fiona no longer had a heart to break. It was long gone, just like the rest of her. He was on his own. And it was up to him whether he stayed that way or not.

CHAPTER 12

Donna hadn't seen Duncan for days. He'd been holed up in his studio, which was good news for all the people sneaking in and out of the mansion. Unfortunately, today was the day the sound crew were due to set up their equipment, and Flora and the others wanted to start decorating the ballroom. That meant Donna had to take extra measures to ensure Duncan stayed ignorant. And for that, she'd called in her sisters.

"I'm only letting the sound team drive up to the mansion," Donna told Agnes and Mairi as they stood side by side in front of the mansion, staring at the windows to Duncan's studio. "And I told them to come in an unmarked van and park round the back. They can use the kitchen entrance. It's closer to the ballroom anyway."

"What will you tell Duncan if he notices the van?" Agnes said.

"That the ballroom floor is being varnished, and he needs to keep out of there for a few days."

Mairi patted her shoulder. "The more you lie, the easier it gets, doesn't it?"

"I'm going to hell." Donna hung her head in shame.

"What about the women with all their decorations?" Agnes said, her eyes still on the building. If anyone could figure out a way for her to deal with this situation, it was Aggie. She was born to be a criminal mastermind. Her sisters had held her back.

"I told them to park outside the west gate and walk up the path." She pointed at the side of the house Duncan's studio didn't overlook. "They said they had a lot of gear to heft up to the house, so I fitted the ride-on lawnmower with a wee trailer. We can load it and go back and forth until everything's been delivered. I was going to borrow a golf cart from the golf course, but I thought that might attract too much attention."

Agnes stared at her. "And you think having the lawnmower mow the same strip of grass over and over won't?"

"Duncan's used to the sound of the lawnmower. It's white noise to him."

"I've had a thought," Mairi announced. "We'll need to do something about the bald grass once this is over. Otherwise, it will make him suspicious." She pointed at Donna's iPad. "Add grass seed to the list."

"Wouldn't it be easier if you went in there and distracted him?" Agnes said.

"I tried that last time. It didn't go so well." Although to be fair, he had been distracted, just not in the way she'd intended.

"What do you mean *not so well?*"

Donna's cheeks heated, but she tried to appear nonchalant. "I panicked when I saw the convoy coming up the drive, so I took off my clothes. Duncan told me to get dressed, and then he ran. I haven't seen him since."

Her sisters gaped at her.

"I'm going to kill him." Aggie's eyes blazed. "Nobody runs away from my naked sister."

"It's fine." She put a restraining hand on her big sister's arm. "I wasn't naked. I was wearing underwear."

Agnes still looked ready to murder her boss.

"What underwear?" Mairi said.

"The pink set with the flowers."

"That's so cute. I love that set. The one with the boy shorts? Right?"

Donna nodded. She'd never be able to wear that set again without feeling like it was rejecting her.

"I see where you went wrong," Mairi said. "It was the boy shorts. Men don't run from G-strings. You should have worn a thong—that would have frozen him to the spot. Although, they aren't comfortable to wear. It feels like you're flossing the wrong end of your body."

Agnes made a gagging sound. "Too much information."

"Did you undress to seduce him?" Mairi said. "Were you taking my advice to distract him with sex?"

"No! I was posing for him. I thought he might like to draw a nude. Well, semi-nude. I wasn't planning on taking off my underwear unless I was desperate."

"Duncan's painting again?" Mairi's eyes widened.

"I know, it's great isn't it?" She was so proud of him. And sad. Because she would never really be involved in that part of his life. As it should be for his housekeeper.

"Can we focus on the problem at hand?" Agnes said. "As far as I can see, everything will be fine if we stick to the west side of the house. What are the chances of Duncan leaving his studio? Can we lock him in if we have to?"

"If we get desperate." The key was in her pocket, just in case. "But the cook usually takes him a tray for his lunch. He only leaves to go to the toilet, and that's in the same corridor." Something caught Donna's eye and she froze. "We have an audience."

The three women looked up at the mansion. Duncan stood in the window, staring at them. His arms were folded, and there was a frown on his face.

"Everybody, smile and wave," Donna said through clenched teeth.

They waved and smiled.

"Do you think he's suspicious?" Mairi said without moving her lips.

"He'd have to be a real idiot if he wasn't." Agnes glanced at Donna, who was in the middle, and she froze. "Don't look now, but Joyce is charging over the lawn with her walker, and she keeps getting stuck."

Donna couldn't help glancing to the side. Joyce was indeed heading their way. Today, she was wearing a luminous orange leisure suit with clashing purple hair and lime-green running shoes, and every time she put her walker down on the water-logged ground, it sank. She'd yank it up, give it a shake, curse a blue streak and charge on. Behind her, Flora appeared out of the bushes, pushing a wheelbarrow laden with boxes. One of them flew open, and a string of paper hearts floated over the grass.

"I'm going to kill them," Agnes said.

"Please do," Donna muttered.

And then she heard a voice, booming out over the estate. "Donna, I need to talk to you."

Her eyes flew to the studio window, which was now wide open. Duncan was leaning out with his hands on the ledge. All he had to do to see the two committee members was turn his head. Her hands flew to the bottom of her shirt. If ever there was a time to get naked, it was now.

Agnes grabbed her shoulders. "Don't even think about it. Get in there and talk to that man. Preferably, when his back is to the windows. I'll deal with the two witches, and Mairi will keep an eye out for the sound people."

"Yes, you're right. Of course you're right. Stripping isn't the answer." But it was hard to unclench her fingers from her shirt.

"Not this time," Mairi said.

"Donna." Duncan was losing patience. "I want to talk to you. Now." There was a pause, and then he said a word she wasn't even sure he knew, "Please."

The three sisters gaped at him.

"Oh crap," Mairi said. "He has a brain tumour."

Agnes groaned. "Don't make me hit you. Distract Duncan while Donna gets into the house." She pushed Donna towards the mansion. "You deal with your boss." And then she waved at Duncan before casually striding towards the women on the lawn.

"Hi, Duncan," Mairi said. "So, I hear you don't like painting nudes. Are animals more your thing?"

Donna heard Agnes muttering something as Mairi smiled brightly up at Duncan, who looked bewildered. Without a word to her sister, he slammed the window shut.

"Job done." Mairi grinned. "I am totally underestimated by everyone around me."

"Joyce," Agnes called. "What are you doing? Get off the grass!"

With a groan, Donna entered the mansion and hurried towards the studio, feeling like she was heading to her doom.

* * *

THE SINCLAIR SISTERS were up to something. It didn't take a genius to see it or to figure out it involved the mansion. If he weren't so nervous about talking to Donna, he'd have investigated. But right now, he had other things on his mind, and whatever the sisters were hatching didn't take precedence.

He wiped his palms on the thighs of his jeans. This was crazy. He'd asked women out on dates before. Hell, he'd been married. So why were nerves making him pace? He was a grown man. Almost forty. He paused in his pacing across the studio floor. Maybe this wasn't nerves? Perhaps it was a mid-life crisis? Was thirty-eight too early to have a crisis? Maybe men had them earlier. He should have asked his brother about this when he'd called him. At thirty-nine, Hamish was much more likely to pierce his ear and buy a motorbike than Duncan was.

So, nerves then. It had to be. He couldn't remember the last time he'd been this nervous. He thought hard and came to the conclusion it was when he was fourteen and had asked Bernadette to see a film with him. Perhaps he shouldn't have thought of that. Bernadette had said no. What if Donna said no too? He stopped in front of the painting of his wife.

"What do I say to her?" he asked Fiona and then groaned. "What am I doing? I can't ask my wife how to chat up a woman."

He turned the painting so Fiona faced the wall. It was better that there were no witnesses to him making a complete fool of himself.

He looked down, catching sight of the paint stains on the front of his shirt, and he stopped. Should he have changed? Worn something more respectable for this conversation? Or at least something clean? Maybe he should have bought her flowers. Or chocolate. Aye, buttering her up first wouldn't have been a bad idea. But it was too late now.

He stood in the middle of the room, his head hanging forwards, one hand on his waist and the other clutching the back of his neck. He closed his eyes and focused on breathing evenly. He wasn't a boy. He could do this.

He let out a shaky breath. Was he even sure he wanted to ask her out? It was a big step. One huge step away from his marriage. From Fiona. But he couldn't deny that all he was thinking about these days was Donna. Ever since his phone call with his brother, he'd been trying to reason things out. He wasn't a coward, but he definitely felt like one. And then there was the guilt. Part of him still felt like he was betraying his wife.

But, as Hamish had said, he'd fulfilled his vows. Fiona was gone. And he still had, hopefully, a very long life to lead. He was sure that if he'd never become aware of Donna in any way other than as his housekeeper, he would have kept on pining after Fiona forever. But he had noticed Donna. And now that he had, he couldn't stop thinking about her. Dreaming about her. Longing to touch her. To taste her. To…

"What is it, Duncan?" The focus of his obsession stepped into the studio.

Duncan's hands fell to his sides, and he took a step towards her before stopping himself. *Don't terrify her. Use your charm.* The problem was, his charm—if he'd ever actually had any—was seriously rusty.

He saw her glance at the sofa, and then her cheeks turned pink. A deep regret filled him. He'd never meant to hurt her when she'd been posing for him. He'd just been shocked to hell.

"I'm sorry about the other day," he said. "You surprised me."

She let out a nervous laugh. "I surprised both of us. Now, what did you want?"

It was now or never. But he couldn't do it like this. Not with her standing beside the open door, ready to bolt. "Have a seat." He pointed at the sofa, realised she might not want to sit there again, and lifted the stool instead, positioning it in front of him. He pointed to it. "There."

He mentally groaned. Great. That wasn't weird at all.

Slowly, keeping her eyes on him, she crossed the room to sit on the stool. "Okay, I'm here now. Do you want to tell me what this is about?" She paled slightly. "You don't have a brain tumour, do you?"

"What? No! Why would you think that?"

"You said please."

"And that's evidence of a brain tumour?"

"It's the first time I've heard you use the word."

He stared at her as his mind chewed on that little snippet. "I've never said please?"

"Not once since I've been here."

They were getting off track. Duncan put his atrocious manners aside for the moment as he paced again. "I'm fit and healthy. That's not why I called you in here."

"Are you going to fire me?"

He stopped. "No!"

"Because after the other day and the inappropriate stripping, you would be totally justified in firing me."

"I don't want to fire you."

"Okay, thanks for being so nice about it. But I realise I was out of line, and I'm going to start applying for other jobs. I'll let you know as soon as I get one I like. I won't leave you in the lurch."

All thoughts of asking her out fled from his mind. "You're leaving me?" He shook his head. "I mean, you're leaving the mansion? No. Just no. The stripping didn't bother me. I mean, it was fine. You looked fine. It was lovely. Damn it, woman, don't apply for other jobs."

"That isn't your decision."

He took a step closer to her. "Is it money? Do you need more? Does one of your sisters need money? I can give you what you want. You don't need to go looking for another job. Hell, with the money I've made from my paintings, I have plenty to dish out." He glared at her. "But not for people we fire. They don't get any."

"No, I don't need more money." She paused and looked away. "I just think that it might be time to move on. When I start doing crazy things like stripping for my boss, then I need to reassess my life. We live together and work together —lines get blurred. It isn't professional."

Lines get blurred? What lines? And why was she so focused on the stripping? It was perfectly normal to take your clothes off in a studio. She'd just surprised him. And then lust had blindsided him and he'd run like a coward. That wasn't her fault. That was him. He didn't understand her reasoning at all.

"Is someone bothering you? Is that what it is? Do I need to fire some staff and hire nicer ones?"

"It's not the staff." She let out a sigh. "I've been here two years, and I never even intended to take this job. You don't need me anymore. You can run the estate by yourself. Maybe it's time for a change."

"I don't need you? Where the hell did you get that idea?"

She waved a hand around his studio. "You're painting again, Duncan." Her eyes followed her hand, and she seemed to notice for the first time that the paintings were of her. She gasped, and her hand flew to her chest.

Duncan barely noticed. He was still stuck on the logic that said if he was painting, he didn't need a housekeeper. Surely, if he was busy, he would need a housekeeper more, not less? Women. If he lived to be a hundred, he still wouldn't understand them.

"You can get those daft notions out of your head right now. I am painting again, and it means I'm too busy to run the estate. That's your job, and you aren't leaving it." Was it possible to legally block someone from quitting a job? As soon as this crazy conversation was over, he was calling his lawyer. If there was a way to do it, he wanted it done fast.

"These paintings are of me," Donna said in a small, shaky voice.

His attention zoomed in on her. She seemed shocked, stunned, emotional. He cocked his head and studied her, but he still couldn't figure out what the reaction meant. Didn't she like the paintings? He could reassure her on that front. "They aren't finished yet. They'll look better when they're done."

"They're all of me," she whispered.

"You're the one who posed, of course they're of you." She wasn't making any sense.

Her shoulders slumped, and her face closed up the way it had that day in the kitchen when he'd first asked her to pose. "Of course," she said evenly.

His heart raced. Something had gone wrong again, and he wasn't sure what, but this time he wasn't letting it go. "What does that mean? That 'of course' comment."

She shrugged. "Just that it makes sense. I'm the only one here to pose for you."

The penny dropped, and it hit him hard, making him think it had been launched from afar. He took a step towards her, closing the distance between them until he could almost touch her.

"I didn't ask you to pose because you were the only person here. If I wanted to, I could pick up the phone and have my choice of models here in a day or two. I asked you to pose because I wanted, no—I needed—to paint *you*."

A flicker of something that looked like hope sprang into those wide green eyes of hers before it disappeared again. "That's really sweet of you, Duncan."

It was clear she didn't believe him. His mind raced over the conversation they'd had that day in the kitchen. His words came back to him in a rush: *Because you're here and Fiona isn't. I need a subject if I'm going to paint again.*

He was an idiot.

"Donna," he said softly, "listen to what I'm trying to tell you. I don't paint just anyone. I never have. The model has to call to me. A unique call, one that's all them and no one else. And when I want to paint that person, no other will do. My models aren't interchangeable. They never have been. What I said in the kitchen that day was stupid and untrue. I didn't ask you to pose because I needed a model and anyone would do. I asked because I'd been lying awake nights imagining what you would look like on my canvas."

She sucked in a breath. Her eyes became pools of sea green water that would drown a man, and her cheeks coloured with the softest pink. He dreamed about that colour.

"Beautiful," he whispered.

It felt like the surrounding air had become charged. The hairs on his skin stood to attention, and he felt the ache of awareness. Her cheeks were darker now, perfectly matching the colour of her lips.

"Duncan?" she whispered, her eyes searching his.

He was vaguely aware that his nerves from earlier had disappeared. Everything had disappeared. The world had reduced to the woman in front of him. The soft, delicate woman who was looking up at him with such vulnerability in her eyes.

"I have something I wanted to ask you," he said.

"Yes?"

Man, she was beautiful. Inside and out. He felt like he was falling into those pale green eyes of hers. A strange feeling of peace, of floating, surrounded him, and the anxiety and guilt that had wracked him disappeared. There was only Donna, nothing else, and the question he'd been practising and worrying over, dissolved in his mind. To be replaced by one that was much more important. It slipped out of his mouth before he could censor it—not that he wanted to.

"Can I kiss you, Donna?" he whispered. "I hear tell a man must ask first these days, and I would dearly like to taste you."

"Oh." The word was barely a breath, but it wasn't the one he wanted to hear.

"Tell me I can kiss you," he said as he lowered his head towards her, his eyes holding fast to hers. "Let me hear the word."

For an endless moment, it felt like the world stood still and waited for her answer.

When it came, it almost took him to his knees.

"Yes," she whispered. "Yes."

CHAPTER 13

Duncan's hands were steady as he cupped her face, never taking his gaze from hers. Her emotions flitted across her face—trepidation, caring, desire, anxiety. It was all there, laid out for him to see. That she wanted his touch as much as he wanted hers was reassuring, her nervousness wasn't.

With a barely there touch, he stroked the pad of his thumb across her bottom lip, feeling the warmth of her breath on his skin.

"Alizarin Crimson," he whispered. "With highlights of Rose Madder, Jaune Brilliant and white."

She swallowed. Her eyes darkening until the iris turned a Phthalo green. "How do you know the colours? You've barely glanced at my lips."

If he hadn't been standing a hairsbreadth from her, he wouldn't have heard the question or seen the yearning vulnerability in her eyes.

It was the vulnerability that made him give her the truth. "I have your lips memorised. I could paint them with my eyes closed." He inclined his head towards her, closing the scant distance until his words brushed over her mouth. "I paint them in my sleep and wake wondering if the colour will taste as fresh as it looks. Will they taste of peaches? Like the highlights. Or will they taste like ripe raspberries? Like the darker hues. What do you think, Donna?"

She didn't answer, but he felt the pulse under his fingertips speed up.

"Let's find out." His lips brushed hers with each word as he held her eyes captive with his.

Soft. Her lips were softer than rose petals but plump and full like a ripe plum. He pressed a gentle, chaste kiss against them and heard her breath hitch.

"More?" he whispered.

She nodded as her fingers curled into his shirt.

"Aye. More." He angled her head to tease her lips with his, tugging at that full bottom lip until she opened her mouth for him.

With a needy groan, he stepped closer until he was standing between her knees, and he could feel the heat of her body against his. Her eyes lost focus, and her eyelids closed slowly as though they'd become weighted. Dark, black lashes formed a crescent across her pale skin as a rose stain bloomed on the apple of her cheek.

His tongue licked out across her bottom lips. Peaches. Damn. He loved peaches. Slowly, with care and longing, he traced the shape of her lips with his tongue. Perfect. He needed more. So much more.

His hands moved, one to clasp the back of her head, his fingers threading through that thick, luscious hair of hers, the other to span the small of her back. He pulled her up and into him as he deepened the kiss.

Their tongues tangled as he chased her taste. That sweet, elusive peach flavour that he knew he was already addicted to. Tentatively, her tongue chased his into his mouth, and Duncan caught it, sucking on it hard. A desperate moan escaped Donna, and her arms wrapped around him, holding him tight.

A heady feeling of power, lust and need rushed through him as he realised what her hold meant. She wanted him to fly away with her. She was clinging on for the ride, expecting him to keep her safe while he made her soar.

And he wanted to.

But he couldn't.

Not yet.

* * *

SLOWLY, softly, their lips separated. Donna's eyelids felt heavy, and her brain full of fluff. Her only thought was that she needed more. She leaned into Duncan, but his warmth was suddenly gone. She swayed on the stool and forced her eyes open, to see him pacing. His lips were kiss-swollen, his eyes were dark, and his hair was standing on end. He looked like a wild man.

"Crap," he snapped. "This is all wrong."

It was a cold bucket of water right over her head. The shock almost threw her heart into arrest. It was wrong? Kissing her was wrong? She blinked hard. Her mind stunned. Her emotions frozen. She was still dazed from a kiss that had rocked her world, and he was saying it was wrong?

He spun to face her. "Don't worry. I'm going to sort this. I've been reading up on it, and I know what I'm doing. I got carried away in the moment, but I'll fix it."

"What?" She managed to force the word out as her brain reeled. He wasn't making any sense, but she dreaded that he regretted kissing her because he was still in love with his wife.

Her eyes sought out the half-finished painting of Fiona, but she couldn't see it, which confused her further. It was always here. She'd come to think of it as Duncan's anchor to the past.

When hands landed on her shoulders, she jumped, and her eyes flew to his.

He saw her startle and removed his touch. "Damn it. I'm screwing up again."

"You aren't making any sense."

It almost seemed like he didn't know what to do with his hands. Eventually, he settled on thrusting them into the pockets of his jeans. His gaze was intense.

"I've been reading up on the 'me too' movement," he said at last.

"Okaaay." Donna was still lost, but now there was a flicker of hope that him freaking out wasn't about his love for Fiona or any deep regret over touching her.

"There's a power difference." He brought out a hand and gestured from her to him. "Between us. I'm your boss, and I own your home. And you're Donna." He ran his hand through his hair.

At last, the daze began to clear. "I swear, if you don't get to the point soon, I'm going to stab you in the ear with a paintbrush."

His eyes widened. "That's very graphic." A smile tugged at his lips. "I kind of like it." He shook his head and became serious again. "I'm your boss."

He said it like it was a revelation. "You have been for the past two years."

"And you're Donna."

"I have been for the past twenty-eight years. Honestly, Duncan, did you fall and hit your head? Do I need to call a doctor?"

"What? No! I'm just better at painting than I am at talking about personal stuff. The thing is. You aren't good at saying no to people." He raised an eyebrow in challenge, as though she was going to deny what the whole of Scotland already knew. He nodded when she didn't reply. "Well then, what are the chances you would have said no to me kissing you if you didn't want to?"

"Oh."

"Exactly," he said when she didn't say anything more. "I called you in here to ask you out to dinner, but you wouldn't say no to that either, would you?"

His words shocked her so much that she almost fell off the stool. "You were going to ask me out to dinner, and you wanted me to say no?"

He looked at her like she was the slow one, when he was practically talking another language. "No, I don't want you to say no. I want you to say yes. But I want you to do it because you want to, not because I'm your boss and you feel you have to. I didn't think this through properly. I don't want you feeling obligated. Or threatened." He eyed her carefully. "Do you feel threatened?"

"Mainly I feel confused."

"Good." He patted her cheek and then pulled his hand back as though the touch had burned him. "Don't worry. I'll figure this out. I need to call my lawyer."

He turned and strode to the door. When he threw it open, he found her sisters standing on the other side of it. They jumped back, and it was clear they'd been listening in. The finks.

"Don't go near the ballroom," Agnes said. "The guy who's varnishing the floor is here. In fact, it would be best if you avoided that side of the house altogether. I hear the fumes are deadly."

Mairi looked behind him and grinned wickedly at Donna before giving Duncan an innocent smile that meant she was up to no good. "Did you kiss my sister? Is that a new part of her job description? Making out with the boss?"

"See?" Duncan shouted at Donna while he pointed at Mairi. "That's what I'm talking about. I need to sort this out." And he stormed past the women. "I'll be in my office," he called over his shoulder.

Donna was left staring after him, and then she caught sight of her sisters. Mairi was grinning wickedly, and Agnes had a look of disapproval on her face.

"Don't ask me what just happened." Donna held up her hands. "I have no idea."

"Oh, by the looks of it, and from the stuff we heard through the door," Mairi said as she came into the room, "kissing happened."

"What were you thinking, kissing your boss?" Agnes demanded.

There was no reply Donna could give that justified her actions. When he'd asked if he could kiss her, she'd wanted nothing more than to feel his lips against hers. She'd wanted, if only for one minute, to feel a little of the devotion he'd felt for Fiona—so she'd stolen a crumb of it, with a kiss. That's how pathetic she was, she'd stolen a kiss meant for a dead woman.

From her boss.

She groaned. "I wasn't thinking. I should have been thinking." But once the kissing had started, her ability to think had fled altogether.

"Holy macaroni, look at her face," Mairi said. "It was *that* good? Who would have thought Duncan knew how to put a look like that on a woman's face? I, for one, am stunned."

"Will you behave?" Agnes tapped her toe in a sure sign she was losing her patience. "She can't kiss her boss. That path leads nowhere good." She glared at Donna. "Don't. Do. It. Again."

"I'm not stupid. If Duncan has anything to give, it will only ever be physical. His heart belongs to Fiona." And she was okay with that. Honestly. She'd known it was the case from the moment she'd stepped into the mansion. A love like Duncan's for Fiona could never be replaced. There was no room inside him for anyone else. That's why she'd been brutal with herself where he was concerned. She refused to feel anything for him, other than pity, and maybe a dash of caring. That was it. Nothing more. "He just asked so nicely."

"And that's all it took?"

For a second, Donna was worried Aggie was going to have a heart attack. She climbed off her stool. "Maybe you should sit down for a minute."

"Just don't tell her to calm down," Mairi said. "She doesn't take that well."

"Look," Donna faced her sisters. "It was only a kiss. It's over now. You heard Duncan. He's my boss, and this complicates things. He just kissed me because I was the only woman here." She swallowed hard but wouldn't let them see how much that hurt. She'd gone into that kiss with her eyes wide open. "Of course he'd turn to me when he started to feel...*needs* again. I'm the one he's used to. It will pass." And then she would have to watch him kiss another woman like he'd kissed her. Maybe it was time to look for another job.

"I don't have a problem with you kissing Duncan," Mairi said. "He's sexy, in a lives-alone-in-the-wilderness-building-bombs-and-planning-conspiracy-theories kind of way, but that isn't enough to sustain a relationship. You'd be much better off with a nice geeky boy. I have a few I'm still trying to match up. You can join my dating agency, and I'll let you have your pick." She smiled hopefully.

Agnes shook her head. "You just want to get another name off your list. This isn't about Donna. It's about you making another match."

"It's totally for Donna's benefit too," Mairi argued.

This was getting out of hand. "I don't want one of your

lonely-heart geeks, and I don't want Duncan either. I'm perfectly fine on my own. Mr Right will turn up eventually, but at the moment, I don't have time for a man in my life. I have enough problems to deal with."

A hand-drawn troll appeared behind her sisters. *Liar, liar, pants on fire,* it said.

Donna ignored it. "This…" She waved a hand to encompass pretty much her whole life up until that moment. "This is just a phase. Everything will go back to normal soon."

There is no normal, Gandalf said from beside the easel. *Really, you should know that by now.*

Katniss Everdeen, her latest sketch in the pages of *The Hunger Games*, appeared beside Gandalf and looked up at Tolkien's wizard. *Do you need me to take him out? I will if it's for the good of the people.*

"That's great," Aggie said, "but what else are you going to give the guy if he *asks nicely?*"

That was it. She was done with unwanted advice and sarcasm, from real and imaginary people alike. "Out. Everybody out." She pointed at her drawings too. "All of you leave now."

"Donna," Agnes said as she looked around. "Who are you talking to? Have you snapped? It's the pressure of this ball, isn't it? I knew it would be too much for you."

"Oh," Mairi said as she pointed at a painting. "That's your underwear set."

As one, they turned to stare. And there she was, splashed across a massive canvas. It showed her standing in front of the studio windows. The beams of light hit her skin in a pattern that made it glow. She looked beautiful, otherworldly, ethereal.

For a long time, they all stood staring at it.

Agnes wrapped an arm around Donna's waist and pulled

her into a hug. "I understand," she said softly. "If someone saw me like that, I'd kiss him too."

"It's just a painting." But Donna's voice shook.

"That isn't *just* a painting." Agnes stroked Donna's hair.

Mairi looked around Agnes to snag her attention. "What the hell. Just go for it. Have some fun, Donnie, we'll be there to pick up the pieces afterwards. You can count on us."

"I know, but this isn't fun." No, it had the potential to break her heart. If she let it. "It was just a kiss," she muttered.

And her sisters enfolded her in a group hug.

* * *

DUNCAN WAS IN PURGATORY. Suspended between the heaven of kissing Donna and the hell of betraying his dead wife's memory. Only, it hadn't felt like a betrayal. It had felt like… home. A home he couldn't return to if he didn't get things sorted out.

He barrelled through the door to his office, picked up the phone on his desk and dialled his lawyer.

"What now?" Janine Myer said when she answered the call.

"Is that the way you answer the phone to all of your clients?" he barked at her.

She wasn't intimidated. It was one of the reasons he was happy to pay her exorbitant fees. "Only the ones who're difficult and time-consuming to deal with."

He fought a smile. There was no time for amusement. He was a man on a mission. "I need you to rewrite Donna's contract."

"Okay, hit me with it. What changes do you want, and why?"

"First, I want a clause in there that says she can't quit."

There was silence.

"Janine?" He paced his office, scowling at the dark walls as he passed them.

"That's illegal. You can't force a person to continue working for you. There's a word for it. It's slavery."

"Is there anything we can do to stop her wanting to leave?"

"Try being nicer to her," came the droll reply.

"I'm trying. Why the hell do you think I'm calling?"

"I wish I knew." She sighed. "The answer to your first demand is no, we can't amend your housekeeper's contract to stop her quitting the job. What's your second point?"

"I've been reading up about the 'me too' movement," Duncan started.

"Wait a minute," Janine interrupted, then shouted to her assistant. "Brian, cancel my next appointment. This is going to take a while."

"Funny, very funny."

"I wasn't being funny," Janine said. "Carry on. This, I've got to hear."

He pinched the bridge of his nose and wondered if every woman in his life set out to be difficult, or if he just attracted a type. "This whole 'me too' movement is about consent first, right?"

"Basically, it's about asking men to resist the temptation to be arseholes."

"Right." He nodded as he walked over to his window. "And part of that is making sure you don't abuse your position of power."

"Yes…"

"And I'm in a position of power over Donna. I control her job, income, home, transport, that sort of thing."

"Is there a point in here?"

"I need you to amend the contract so that Donna won't

feel as though she has to say yes to any personal requests I make of her."

There was a choking noise on the other end of the line. "You want me to add a clause to her contract stating that if her boss asks for sex and she says no, it won't jeopardize her job? Do you have even an inkling of how wrong that is?"

"Did I say anything about sex? I just want to ask her out for dinner. And you know Donna, she can't say no to people at the best of times. I want to give her the power to say no. As far as I can see, that puts me in the right."

There was hysterical laughter, and Duncan could do nothing other than wait it out. He stared out of the window, and to his surprise, he saw an old woman dressed in a twinset and pearls, pushing a wheelbarrow full of what looked like glitter across his lawn. He rubbed his eyes. No. She was still there. And she was making decent progress too.

"Okay," Janine said when she'd finally calmed down. "You want to date your housekeeper, but there's a conflict of interest, and from your earlier request, I'm guessing you don't want to remove that conflict of interest by firing her."

"No." On that he was firm. Donna needed to stay at the mansion. And he needed Donna. "Just make it so she will feel secure enough to say no to me."

"Have you really thought about this? Are you sure you want to change the dynamic between you and the only member of your staff you haven't managed to get rid of yet?"

"I don't want her to leave, and I don't want her to feel powerless." He wasn't sure about anything else.

"Okay." Janine's tone grew serious. "I can't stop her from leaving, but I can even out the power dynamic some. If you're sure."

"I'm sure."

"All right then. Let's hash out some ideas."

CHAPTER 14

Donna spent the night worrying about her situation with Duncan. Did he regret the kiss? Would he ask her to leave? Or worse, would he give her the speech about how it was all a mistake? How he'd slipped and plastered his lips to hers by accident. She could take rejection, she even expected it, but she couldn't handle Duncan telling her it was a mistake and he regretted it. After a night spent tossing and turning, she decided that her best course of action was to avoid Duncan as much as possible.

Unfortunately, Duncan wasn't on the same page, and he called her into his office straight after breakfast. As soon as she set foot inside, she noticed things had changed. All of the framed drawings, mostly of Fiona, were piled on the floor.

"Oh, good, you're here." Duncan took the last picture from the wall. "Do we have any white paint kicking around? I can't look at the colour of these damn walls a minute longer."

He didn't want to talk about the kiss? This was about paint? Did that mean the kiss meant so little to him that it hadn't even registered? He was carrying on as usual, and she'd been up all night thinking about it. Worrying about what to do. How pathetic was that?

"Donna, do we have any white paint?"

She straightened her shoulders. If he was going to ignore it, then she could too. She was a professional. She could do her job—even if she couldn't look him in the eye while she did it. "You want to paint the walls?"

"Aye."

"By yourself?"

"You have a problem with that?"

She held up her hands. "No. It's just that we normally contract that kind of job out."

"I'm a painter. If I can prepare a canvas with white paint, I can prepare these walls."

"As a canvas?" Maybe it was her, but it seemed Duncan was a whole lot harder to understand these days.

"I just want to paint the damn walls white."

And less patient. Which was saying something.

"Fine. I'll get the paint. Did you have anything else you wanted to talk about, or can I get back to work?" Did that sound snippy? Oh, she hoped not.

His eyes darkened, and she felt his gaze shoot straight to the bits of her she was trying to convince to forget him. She'd had her taste of him. Common sense said it was more than enough. Unfortunately, her horny bits didn't run on common sense, they ran on desperation.

He picked up a pile of papers and handed them to her. "I need you to sign your new contract. As you can see, I've upped your salary, so there's no need to go looking for work elsewhere."

She took the document and stared at him. "I don't need more money." Although, she wasn't an idiot. "But it would be nice, thank you."

He ran a hand through his hair and perched on the edge

of the massive wooden desk. The desk that was big enough to fit two bodies tangled together. The kind of desk that a woman could bend over and press her front to, feeling the cool wood on her skin as a man came up behind her and…

"Are you listening to me?"

The temperature in the room seemed to have shot up a few degrees. "Is it hot in here? It feels like it's hot. I'm just going to open a window." She hurried over to the sash window and proceeded to do just that.

"I was saying," he said. "Janine said it's illegal to make you sign something saying you won't resign. But I don't want you to leave, so I took some other measures."

"Other measures?" She turned to look at him and tripped over a pile of books. When she bent to right them, she stilled. The book on top looked to be her missing copy of *The Hobbit*. Had he looked in it? Had he seen her drawings? She couldn't ask him without giving herself away, and she did not want Duncan to know they were hers. Very carefully, she piled the book with the others. "I didn't know you liked Tolkien," she said as casually as she was able.

He seemed confused for a second until she pointed to the book. "Oh, that. I found it outside. Someone must have dropped it."

"Do you want me to take it to my office and find the owner?" Please, please, please…

"I'll look for them myself. There are some drawings in there I want to talk to them about."

Pure, unadulterated panic swept through her and she had to fight the urge to run. "Are you sure? It's no trouble."

"Forget about the book. I want to talk about the contract."

It was hard to forget about the book. But she reminded herself that she had the keys to every room in the building, and she could sneak in and remove it when he wasn't around.

"As you'd see, if you actually looked at the contract, I'm changing the nature of our relationship. In academic terms, you now have tenure. No matter what you do—unless it breaks the law—I can't fire you. Your job is one hundred percent protected."

"What?" Her legs found the chair behind her, and she sat down with a thump.

"I couldn't gift you your apartment on the third floor, because it's part of the mansion, but I have stipulated that if you felt you had to leave for any reason—which you won't—then the trust would pay for accommodation of your choosing for the rest of your life."

Okay, so now it was hard to breathe. The papers shook in her hands, and she tried to still them, which just made things worse.

"As for the car," he said, staring at her intently. "I've given it to you. The ownership papers are in there." His voice deepened. "And if for any reason you felt forced out or had to leave without a job to go to, I'll pay your salary at the time of your departure for the following five years."

It felt like the room was spinning, and Donna had to bend over to stop herself from passing out.

"Damn it, this was not the way it should have gone," Duncan muttered as he strode from the room.

Donna focused on breathing steadily while the blood rushed back to her head. She only realised he'd returned when she felt a cold cloth on the back of her neck and a glass of water was thrust under her nose.

"Take a drink," he ordered.

She could do nothing other than obey. Her hand shook as she drank, and she looked up to find herself staring into dark eyes as Duncan crouched in front of her.

"What have you done?" she asked him. "This is completely over the top. People don't do things like this."

He shrugged, his broad shoulders rippling under yet another tartan shirt. "I'm trying to be a modern man. I know I'm a throwback, and I'm trying to even out the power discrepancy between us." He ran his hand through his hair again. "I want to give you the tools to say no to me if you want to. Without feeling as though you'd lose something if you did."

The silly, sweet, completely irrational man. "I can't sign this. It would tie you to me forever. You would be paying for me for the rest of your life. That isn't right. You'll only regret it."

His gaze captured hers and took away her ability to breathe. "Don't you know that without you I wouldn't have the rest of my life to regret anything? Before you knocked on my door, I was heading for destruction and I didn't care. You've kept me here these past few years. I don't understand the how or the why of it, but I know that I owe you far more than you could ever take from me. Don't think I don't remember the night you picked me up off the driveway and cleaned out my rooms. You saved my life—even though I resented the hell out of you for months for doing it. Just sign the papers, Donna, so that I can ask you out to dinner."

"And what if I say no?"

"Then we'll carry on as usual."

Bless his crazy, over-complicated heart. "Has it occurred to you that the generosity of this contract might make me feel obligated to go out with you?"

His jaw dropped. "No. That hadn't occurred to me. Thanks for that." He stood and paced. "How the hell do people date these days? It's only been eighteen years since I last did it, and it's like I'm on a different planet."

"Is that what you're trying to do? Date me?" The idea seemed unbelievable.

"Aye. And it isn't going well."

He looked so affronted that she burst out laughing.

"Now, that's good for my ego," he said wryly.

Donna put the papers on his desk. "I appreciate the gesture, and the effort you must have gone to in getting this written up. I know it must have entertained Janine no end. But I'm not signing the contract."

"No!" He picked them up and thrust them at her. "You have to, so we can go out for dinner."

Honestly, it was painful to watch Duncan trying to claw his way into the twenty-first century. "I'm not sure it's a good idea for us to date, and I'm not sure there's room in your life for anyone other than Fiona." There. She'd put the crux of the matter out there. The elephant in the room—his past.

He winced, but his eyes held hers. "Does this have to be more than a few dates? Can't we enjoy each other's company and see where this goes?"

She felt as though someone had clenched her heart and was squeezing it firmly, but she kept the smile on her face. This was going nowhere, and the fact he couldn't see it meant he was just deluding himself. She'd been right when she'd explained things to her sisters—Duncan's libido had woken, and this was him dipping his toe back in the dating pool, with someone safe.

"Donna?" He looked so vulnerable that it was hard to look at him.

She brushed imaginary fluff from her blouse, keeping the smile on her face. She'd taken care of him for two years, and she would give him this too, because it was what he needed. And she always gave Duncan what he needed.

Decision made, she looked back up at him. "I'm going to take all of the worry out of this for you. If the problem is you taking away my control because of your position, then I'll take the control back." She took a shaky breath. "Duncan, would you like to go out for dinner with me?"

His eyes swirled with warmth. "Aye, Donna, I would like that very much."

It felt like a set of jumping beans had taken up residence in her stomach. "Okay, then. I'll make a reservation at that nice Italian place in town." If they went out that evening, it would have the added benefit of getting him out of the mansion while the women were setting up. "How does tonight suit?"

"Tonight would be perfect. Seven-thirty?"

She nodded and turned towards the door, frowning in consternation when her legs felt weak. This was the right thing to do. She would get Duncan out of the mansion and away from the set-up, and she'd help him take the next step in getting over his wife. It didn't have to mean anything. She could keep her distance. After all, she'd been doing it for the past two years.

"One more thing before you go." Duncan's deep voice made her stop at the door.

She pressed a hand to her stomach as she looked back at him. "Yes?"

"I want to be clear. This dinner is a date, right?"

"Yes, this is a date." Wasn't that what this whole weird conversation was about?

The look of triumph that flashed in his dark eyes made wariness creep up her spine. It was the same look he got when he talked her into firing someone.

"Good." He nodded. "Then, during this dinner, this *date*, do I have your permission to touch you? I'd like to get it all out in the open before we go out, so we're not stopping every five minutes for me to get consent. Just to be clear, you understand."

She licked her lips as she looked up at Duncan. "You have my permission to touch, but I think we should set limits, don't you?"

His eyes were molten. "Aye, that sound like a right modern idea. We wouldn't want to colour outside the lines. Would holding hands be permitted?"

"Yes." It came out far breathier than she'd intended.

"And kissing?" His voice lowered, and the sound resonated throughout her body, waking up nerve endings and making cells vibrate.

"Yes." She cleared her throat.

Dark eyes held her captive. "A hand pressed to the small of your back? Perhaps some nuzzling of your neck?"

The image hit her hard, and her mouth went dry. She licked her lips, and Duncan's eyes snapped to the gesture, watching it with dark intent, making her remember the kiss they'd shared.

"And, of course, a man would like to hold his date. To wrap her in his arms while he kissed her and feel her soft curves against him. Would that be okay with you?"

The only sound that came out of her mouth was a needy whimper that embarrassed her, but she could no longer tell if her cheeks were burning from humiliation or desire. She now understood what the phrase 'putty in his hands' meant.

"What's your answer, Donna?" His voice was a seduction. "It would be best if these things were crystal clear between us."

She shivered at his tone even though it made her feel hotter. "Yes, that would be fine."

She turned on shaky legs and almost staggered from the room.

As she left, Duncan said, "Oh, I think it will be more than fine."

Closing the door softly behind her, Donna leaned back against it and wondered how she'd survive their date, when even the negotiations had turned her knees to jelly. So much for keeping her distance.

CHAPTER 15

Duncan didn't even bother saying hello when his brother answered the phone. "What do I wear on a date? Has it changed? Do I wear a suit? Jeans? What are the rules now?"

"And to think I missed your phone calls," Hamish said. "Isn't there a lassie you can ask about this crap?"

"My first instinct was to ask Fiona, but that didn't seem right."

There was a silence for a beat. "And it would scare the crap out of you if she answered."

"Aye, that an' all."

There was a sigh. "Where's this date then?"

Duncan was grateful his brother didn't say anything about him getting his head out of his arse long enough to ask Donna out. The process had been agonising enough without dissecting it. Thank the Lord they were men. If he'd had a sister, he would have been talking about feelings by now, and he'd rather have all of his teeth pulled—without anaesthetic.

"The Italian place in town," he said as he looked at his ties. Did men still wear them for anything other than a funeral or a job interview? "It's a nice restaurant, but it isn't expensive."

"Jeans and a nice shirt," Hamish said decisively. "And have a shower."

"I've had a shower. I can do the rest." He tossed the tie he'd been holding back into his closet. "Thanks." He hung up.

A second later his phone rang. He answered by growling his name.

"How are you, Hamish?" his brother said, his tone sarcastic. "How are the kids? What time is it over there? Is it the middle of the night? Did I disturb you doing anything? Well, now, funny you should ask, Duncan. It's five in the morning here, and I was sound asleep. You selfish bastard." The line went dead.

Duncan burst out laughing as he pulled a fresh pair of jeans from the shelf. Turning to toss them onto his bed, he caught sight of the drawing he'd done of Fiona during their honeymoon. It was a simple pencil sketch of her with her face turned up to the sun. His humour disappeared, and he sank down to sit on the edge of the bed. He leaned forwards, elbows on knees, and put his head in his hands.

"What am I doing?" he asked the silence.

He wasn't ready to spend an evening with another woman. No matter that she knew him inside and out and kissed like an angel with fire in her blood. He remembered Fiona's kisses. Her lips had been thinner than Donna's and her touch more confident. Fiona had thought nothing of climbing into his lap and demanding they make love. He'd had to wrestle for control with his wife during their love-making. It was a challenge he'd more than enjoyed. Donna would never tell him what she wanted. She would wait for him to initiate anything between them. If he was ever able to take that step. Right now, he was struggling to get dressed for a meal in a restaurant.

He glanced at the clock and forced himself to his feet. The question he'd asked his brother rang in his head: *How do you let go?* How did you move on when you'd had everything you'd ever wanted? And how did you stop loving someone just because they weren't there to touch?

He reached into his closet and tugged one of his blue tartan shirts off the hanger before stilling. Hamish wouldn't consider it a nice shirt. He tossed it aside and reached for the white long-sleeved T-shirt hanging beside his many tartan shirts. He'd never worn it, but Donna had kept it ironed and fresh, ready to wear. The least he could do was show her the effort had been worth it.

After tugging on his shirt and jeans, he reached for a pair of brown dress shoes and then grabbed the navy blazer he'd worn years earlier for a gallery opening. His jaw was smooth, his hair—well, his hair was as good as it got, and he was dressed in something that wasn't covered in paint. He was good to go.

As he reached for the door handle, a gleam of light caught his attention, and he stared at the wedding ring on his left hand. It was like a shot to the heart. He leaned against the wall and slowly slid to the floor. As he draped his arms over his knees, his eyes were still on that ring, and he knew he wasn't going anywhere.

* * *

Donna smoothed down the skirt of her mint green sundress as she looked at herself in the full-length mirror on her wardrobe door. Behind her, on the bed, was a pile of clothes. She'd spent the past two hours trying on everything she owned, which wasn't much, so she'd tried them all twice. She slipped on a pair of white sandals and grabbed the yellow knitted handbag she'd bought at the summer fair.

You look lovely, Ron Weasley's mother said from beside her.

"That would mean a whole lot more if you were real," Donna muttered.

I remember Ginny being this nervous when she first went out with Harry and look how well that turned out.

Donna didn't want to break Molly Weasley's imaginary heart by telling her Harry should have ended up with Hermione.

You'll have a lovely time, Molly said.

"Yeah. Right." She was crossing so many lines. Blurring boundaries between her and her boss. And risking her heart. Her fingers brushed her lips as she remembered Duncan's kiss. He'd swept her away from herself, from everything. There had only been him. Her body had been on fire with the need to get closer to him. To touch him. To know him. To claim him. But he wasn't hers to claim. He belonged to his long-gone wife. He would *always* belong to Fiona.

She straightened her shoulders and patted her hair. As long as she remembered that, she would be fine. This was just dinner. Nothing more. She could do dinner. She'd eaten with Duncan before now, and this evening was no different.

Then why did it feel like there was a kaleidoscope of butterflies trying to fight their way out of her stomach? She pressed a hand against it. She was fine. Everything was fine. She was overreacting. Her heart wasn't involved, and that was all that mattered.

Are you completely deluded? Hermione appeared beside Ron's mother. *This is a date, and you plan to kiss Duncan. You can pretend your heart isn't involved all you like, but we know the truth.*

"You don't count because you aren't real." Hermione was wrong. Donna wasn't deluded. She was a realist. She wasn't going to risk her heart with a man who didn't have one to give in return. "I'm just distracting him so that the women can prepare for the ball."

Can you even hear yourself? This is a very bad idea. You need to call Duncan and back out. Before you regret this. Hermione turned to Molly, who nodded her agreement.

Donna frowned at Molly. "You were just telling me this was great."

She shrugged, wiped her hands on her apron, and ran off to get something out of the oven.

Donna glanced at the clock. Six forty. It was time to meet Duncan in the foyer. She patted her hair, wondering if she should tie it back. No, there wasn't time to struggle with her hair. With one last glance at the mirror, she hurried out of her bedroom and through her living room to her front door.

Only she didn't make it.

Her feet stopped moving halfway across the room, and she felt as though they'd become encased in fast-setting concrete. She couldn't do this. She and Duncan could forget one kiss. They could chalk it up to confusion and write it off as a mistake. But a date? There was no getting past that. If she went out with him, their relationship could never go back to what it was. She would lose him. Wait. What was she thinking? She was flustered—she'd meant that she would lose her *job*. That was the problem. She was risking her job, her home, everything. And for what? Another kiss with a man who was still hung up over his dead wife?

Hermione was right—she had to call this off.

Donna tossed her bag onto the settee, kicked off her shoes and walked to the intercom on the wall beside her door. She pressed the button for the foyer, but no one answered. With a frown, she tried Duncan's office. Still no answer. In frustration, she pressed the button that was used to page people through all the intercoms in the house.

"Duncan? Are you there? I need to talk to you."

And then she waited for him to answer.

* * *

Duncan knew he had to cancel their date. He glanced at the clock. Almost ten to seven. Donna would be making her way downstairs to meet him. He groaned and pinched the bridge of his nose. How had his life gotten this screwed up? Once he'd been the toast of the art world and the envy of every man he knew because Fiona was at his side. Now, he was too scared to go out for a meal with a woman who intrigued him, and the art world had forgotten about him.

"Duncan? Are you there? I need to talk to you." The intercom blared above his head, and he swore loudly.

Donna must be standing by the front door, wondering where he was. Feeling like his bones weighed a tonne, he got to his feet.

"Man up," he muttered to himself before he pressed the answer button. "Donna, I'm sorry, but..." But what? He'd had a meltdown?

"Duncan, this date is a really bad idea. I think we should, maybe, you know, leave it for a while," she said in a rush. "Until we're sure it's a good idea."

There was silence. Duncan cocked his head to the side and stared at the intercom as her words sank in. She was dumping him? Before they'd gone out? Was that even possible?

"Duncan?" She sounded worried.

He frowned as he jabbed at the button. "Are you cancelling our date?" he snapped.

It didn't matter that he'd been seconds from doing the same thing, now that Donna was pulling out of it, he was mad. A little voice in the back of his head told him he was being unreasonable. He told that voice to go to hell.

"Duncan, we're boss and employee. This isn't smart."

"I thought we'd been over this. I had a new contract

drawn up to ensure you wouldn't feel pressured into something you didn't want to do. You can still sign it. I'm okay with that."

"I don't need to sign it. And I thought you had it drawn up so that I would feel okay saying no to you," she reminded him.

She was right, but he didn't have to like it. "Are you saying no to me?" His palms began to sweat as he waited for her answer.

There was silence. He could see her in his mind's eye, gnawing on that bottom lip of hers, trying to figure out the least offensive thing to say.

"I'm saying that this is a bad idea. Lines will be blurred."

"I need to hear the word, Donna. Yes or no. Do you still want to go out with me tonight?" He held his breath.

It took a decade for her to answer. "If we go out, it's going to change everything."

He sure as hell hoped so! But the most important thing was that she hadn't said no. A surge of adrenalin rushed through his veins, washing away his earlier doubts. Donna might be having second thoughts, just as he had, but she still wanted to spend the evening with him. This could be salvaged. If he got over himself long enough to make it happen.

"We can forget one kiss," she said in a rush. "If we go out tonight, that will be harder to excuse."

What? He'd obviously tuned out and missed something important. "Forget the kiss? Why the hell would we do that? That kiss was mind-blowing."

He heard her suck in a breath. "Going out with you is confusing things."

"Donna." He lowered his voice, aware from their time in his office earlier that it had an effect on her, and he wasn't above using everything in his arsenal to get what he wanted.

What they *both* wanted. "Why is this confusing? We're two people who know each other well, who live in the same house, and we're going out for a pleasant evening together. We'll eat some food. Talk." He let that sink in, and then he went in for the kill. "Maybe we'll hold hands, touch, kiss. I liked our kiss, Donna. Didn't you?"

The answer was a frustrated groan that had him smiling.

"Have you dressed for our date already?" He poured seduction into his voice. "What are you wearing?" He leaned into the intercom.

She cleared her throat. "My mint green sundress."

He knew the one she meant. It matched her eyes perfectly. "I've often wondered if that dress was as soft as it looked."

She groaned. "You are driving me nuts. You're deliberately trying to talk me around."

"Is it working?"

"Yes. Damn you."

"I'm coming up to your rooms. I'll walk you downstairs. If you still want to call this off, tell me to my face." He hit the Off button.

With a grin, he grabbed his car keys and wallet and jogged out of his room to get Donna.

CHAPTER 16

The date wasn't going well. Donna was too nervous to relax, and Duncan seemed uncomfortable in the restaurant, probably because the other diners were all staring at him as though they'd spotted a Yeti.

"Is everything okay?" Marcus, the owner, asked them for the third time. From the smile he was trying to hide, he wasn't interested in their comfort, but in the *dis*comfort Duncan was experiencing. "Can I get you anything else?"

"Some privacy?" Duncan snapped.

Marcus was third-generation Italian-Scottish and had grown up in Glasgow. He was used to dealing with rude people.

"If you showed your face around town a bit more, people wouldn't stare. A smile would help as well, and you could try calling a halt to firing everyone who works for you over the least wee thing." Marcus shook his head at Duncan. "I can't do anything about the audience, but I can get Rob to up the garlic in your fettuccine, the smell might deter them."

Donna leaned forwards to place a restraining hand on

Duncan's arm before he could get up and punch Marcus. There were a limited number of places in Campbeltown where she enjoyed eating, and she wasn't going to let him get her banned from one of them.

"Marcus," she said. "Is there anything you could do for us? Please."

The gleeful gleam in his eye from prodding Duncan faded as he smiled softly at her. "For you, *bella*, I'll see what I can do." With that, he swaggered off to the kitchen.

She turned back to Duncan, to find him frowning at her. "What?" she said as she reached for a breadstick.

"Is there something going on with you and the owner?"

She almost choked on the bite she'd taken. Although, the comment was kind of flattering. Marcus was in his early thirties, muscled from MMA fighting in his free time, and his gorgeous smile was famous in Kintyre. Women queued up for a date with the man. That Duncan thought he'd choose her over the smorgasbord he had on offer was a boost to her ego.

Although tempted to make up a sordid past between her and the restaurant owner, she thought it wiser to stick to the truth. "I'm a family friend. I went to school with his sister."

His eyes narrowed. "And that's it?"

She felt her cheeks heat. "Are you jealous, Duncan?"

Shock flashed over his face and Donna wanted to kick herself. Of course this wasn't jealousy. She was under no illusions that she was the sort of woman men fought over, or even lusted over. She definitely didn't inspire jealousy. Maybe if she'd had her sisters' looks, and hair, things would have been different, but she was the plain sister, and she was fine with that. There was nothing she could do about it anyway, and she loved her sisters too much to envy them. Well, not *all* the time anyway.

Before Duncan could say something that would mortify her further, Marcus reappeared.

"If you don't care about ambience, I've set up a table for you in my office." He gave her a pitying smile.

"We don't care." Duncan was on his feet before Donna could answer. He threw down his napkin, grabbed her hand and stalked towards the back of the restaurant, glowering at the other diners as he dragged her along behind him.

"Are you sure you wouldn't rather date some guy who can take you out in public? Like me?" Marcus asked from behind her, his voice low and sensual.

Donna smiled at him. He was always joking about her going out with him. She'd often wondered what he would do if she said yes.

"Seriously, bella, I can get rid of him for you, if you want. No trouble. You know I owe you."

She looked over her shoulder at him. "You don't owe me anything."

"Bella." He shook his head. "We all do. We owe you Julianna's life. I've told you this before—all of us have—if you ever want anything, any time, you just call. And stop trying to pay when you eat here. It's driving the family crazy."

And that was the reason she rarely ate at the Italian Garden. "I can pay for my meals," she reminded him.

"Aye, you can, but we won't take your money." When Duncan glared back at them, he pointed at a door at the end of the corridor, past the restrooms.

"You sure you don't want him gone?" Marcus' eyes were on Duncan's back, and for a minute, Donna wasn't sure if he meant from the date, or from her life permanently.

"He isn't as bad as he seems," she said weakly. "But thanks for the offer."

His lips thinned. "Expect a call from my sister."

"Great," Donna muttered as she followed Duncan into the office.

Two waitstaff squeezed out to let them in. They smiled at Donna but ignored Duncan. As she stepped over the threshold, she realised why they'd been in the room. The desk had been pushed back against the wall and was covered with a white linen tablecloth. In the space where it had sat was a small round dining table, set up exactly like the ones in the restaurant, with candles burning in the centre and fresh breadstick in a basket. Behind the table, the office window gave them a view of the harbour lights reflecting on the water. It was perfect.

"Thank you, Marcus." Donna rested a hand on his shoulder, went on tiptoe and pressed a kiss to his cheek.

A loud growl sounded from behind her, and she looked back to find Duncan standing with his hands curled into fists at his side, glaring at them.

"You sure?" Marcus asked her again as he flicked an irritated look at Duncan.

"Yeah," she said on a sigh. "Unfortunately."

She moved to sit, rolling her eyes when Duncan elbowed the owner out of the way, so he could pull the chair out for her.

"I'll send in your waiter with your food," Marcus snapped before leaving.

Duncan helped her push in her chair, and as Donna reached for her napkin, she realised he hadn't moved from behind her. She stilled as his hands rested gently on her shoulders, and then she felt him lean down to her. His breath drifted over her cheek as he leaned into her ear.

"It turns out I *am* jealous, and I would be verra pleased if you kept your hands off that dickhead."

"Duncan!" She turned to glare up at him, but it was clear he was unrepentant.

He also wasn't in the mood to miss an opportunity. He clasped her cheeks and pressed his lips to hers. The kiss was fast and ferocious, leaving her breathless and light-headed.

"So," a voice said from behind them. "That's how it is."

"Aye." Duncan stroked her hair before taking his seat. "That's how it is."

As Duncan and Marcus started a staring contest, Donna slowly floated back to reality. "Would it be faster if someone just peed on me to mark their territory?"

Marcus made gagging noises while Duncan shot her a look of bewildered disgust. She shrugged and reached for a breadstick.

"Don't hurt her," Marcus pointed at Duncan, who nodded once.

As Marcus turned to leave, Donna called after him. "I'm going to need cake. Send in the dessert menu."

There was no way she'd get through this evening without it. Hermione was right. This date was a bad idea—on so many levels.

* * *

IT TOOK ALL of Duncan's meagre self-control not to follow Marcus and teach him not to poach from another man. If the kiss didn't make him back off, then Duncan planned on coming into town in the morning and having a wee word with the man—using his fists.

"Will you stop glaring at the door?" Donna said, bringing his attention back to her.

Man, but he loved the colour of her lips after he'd kissed her. He needed to get that look into a painting. The thought of painting Donna after an afternoon in bed together left him feeling light-headed. He grabbed his water, took too large a gulp and ended up choking.

"Are you okay?" She got up to rub his back. "We can go home if this is stressing you out. I don't mind." The concern in her eyes told him she was telling the truth. This wasn't just another attempt to get out of their dinner.

"I'm fine. I swallowed the wrong way. Sit back down and tell me what you do in your free time."

She froze while bending to sit. "You want to know what I do in my free time?"

"Aye." Was asking that something else he shouldn't be doing? He needed a bloody dating manual.

She sat down, smoothed the skirt of her dress and then sipped at her water. All the while keeping her eyes on him, with a look that made him wonder if he was growing another head.

"It's no' a hard question," he grumbled. "I only want to talk about something that isn't to do with the mansion."

"Ooookaaay." She put the glass down. "I hang out with my sisters. And I used to babysit for Isobel, but she's in London now."

He looked around for something else to say. This was brutally painful, but outside of the mansion, he had no idea what to talk to her about. He didn't have the patience to watch TV, and he'd lost interest in reading when Fiona died. All he did with his time was pace the confines of his home like a caged tiger, work out in the gym, and harass Donna. Well, what did you know? He did have a hobby after all—annoying his housekeeper.

He cleared his throat. "Did you always want to be a housekeeper?" As soon as the question was out of his mouth, he remembered he'd forced her into taking the job in the first place. "Forget that. How are your sisters and the kids?" At last, a safe topic. He hoped.

"Fine. Mairi's starting a matchmaking business. Agnes sits her final exams for her hotel management degree soon.

Isobel's working as a receptionist at her husband's security company. Jack loves school, and Sophie has a London accent now." She sounded wistful, and he imagined she must miss her niece and nephew.

"How old are they?"

"The kids?"

He nodded.

"Jack's seventeen now, and Sophie just turned four."

"Difficult ages for both of them," he said, because he didn't know what else to say and that sounded like something someone normal would say.

"Aren't all ages hard?"

"Aye."

They lapsed into another heavy silence, and Donna nervously spilled pepper while fidgeting with the bottle, then spent the rest of her time making patterns with it on the white tablecloth. Every minute stretched until it was unbearable in its awkwardness. Which made him unreasonably thankful when the waiter came in with their meals.

Duncan was grateful they hadn't ordered starters because it looked like the time it would take to get through their main course would be painful enough. He tried to remember if he'd always had this problem talking to women, but he couldn't. It had been so long since he'd tried, and when he'd been in art school, he'd talked art—or politics. The people around him had plenty of opinions on both.

Halfway through her meal, Donna took her napkin from her lap, dabbed at her mouth, then placed it on the table. She reached over and put her hand on top of his as it curled around his fork.

"This was a bad idea," she said gently. "Let's go home."

The word 'disaster' hung in the air between them, but neither of them uttered it. His shoulders slumped, and he put down his cutlery before pushing back his chair. "Give me a minute to settle the bill. Wait here." He pointed at the table to be clear, noticing the drawing she'd made with the pepper. It looked like an eye, and it was strangely familiar.

She saw where he was looking and blushed as she dusted the pepper away. "Go pay then and make sure you don't give in to temptation and hit Marcus. Especially on the face. His smile brings in business."

"I'm not going to hit him." Although the bastard deserved it. "I'm just going to pay the bill."

She cocked an eyebrow at him and reached for her wine. "Yeah, right."

Duncan left her to it as he headed for the bar. It was tempting to blow off the date, the bill, everything, and ask the bartender to hand him a bottle of top-shelf whisky. But he couldn't do that to Donna. He'd already messed up enough for one evening. She was right. This had been a bad idea. He'd been feral so long he had no idea how to be civilised. If Fiona had been there, she would have been disgusted with him. Thank the Lord she wasn't.

He froze.

Thank the Lord she wasn't.

The bartender asked him something, but Duncan didn't hear it. He was too busy waiting for the guilt and recriminations to slam into him after thinking something so abominable about his wife.

But…they didn't.

Instead, he felt a lightness inside as he realised that he wasn't the man he'd once been. He wasn't the man who'd sweet-talked Fiona into sleeping with him a few days after he'd met her, and he wasn't the man who could entertain a bar full of friends with stories, or debate for hours. That man had died along with his wife. But he no longer mourned who he'd once been either. Instead, he wondered who he'd become and whether Donna liked the man he was now.

"You going to pay or what?" Marcus shoved the bartender aside to glare at Duncan over the bar.

"I am. And you can add two tiramisus to the bill as well. Bag them to go."

Marcus nodded to the hovering waitress, who scurried off, and then he reached for Duncan's credit card. "You're an arse. You know that, right?"

"Aye." He glared at the man. "But I'm the arse who's on a date with Donna. How many times has she turned you down?" He knew he'd guessed true when the man winced.

"She didn't think I was serious." Marcus handed the card back to Duncan as the waitress came back with a paper bag holding his desserts.

"Well, she'd better not start thinking it now."

"Or what?" Marcus folded his arms and glared at Duncan. It was no secret in town that he was a champion fighter. It *was* a secret that Duncan had held his own in the ring right through his twenties.

Without signalling his punch, Duncan shot out his fist and felt the satisfying crunch of Marcus' nose. He didn't feel the need to say anything more. He was fairly certain he'd made his point—and he'd managed to leave the man's business-related smile intact.

As he strode back through the dining room, he noticed that people were no longer staring at him and he found himself grinning. Now, that's what he called a successful evening out. All he had to do now was salvage his date. The old Duncan would have taken Fiona out for dinner and gently seduced her with intelligent conversation and sophisticated moves. The new Duncan had to find his own way, and he had to do it with a woman who was nothing like his wife. Something that gave him hope. Fiona wouldn't like the man he'd become, but Donna sure as hell didn't seem to mind him.

For the first time in years, the thought of his wife didn't bring him to his knees, all it did was make him pause and feel sadness that he was doing something he'd never thought he would—he was moving on.

CHAPTER 17

As Duncan drove them back to the mansion, Donna watched the glittering lights over the water off Campbeltown.

"Why does Marcus and his family owe you?"

She stiffened at the question. "I didn't think you'd heard him."

"Oh, I heard him all right." His knuckles tightened on the wheel, and she guessed that meant he'd heard everything. "Why do they think you saved his sister?"

She stared out over the water and hoped he'd let the subject drop. But she'd forgotten just how stubborn he could be.

"Well then?" he pressed.

She let out a sigh. "His sister was sick, and I helped out. That was it."

He looked at her out of the corner of his eye. "That was all?"

"Yes."

"How sick was she?"

"Pretty sick."

They drove on in silence for a few minutes, and she began to think he'd dropped the subject.

He hadn't. "The scars on your stomach. The ones I saw that day you stripped in the studio. They're small and faint. Could have been from keyhole surgery." He sucked in a breath before looking over at her. "You donated a kidney."

It wasn't a question. The man certainly had an artist's eye for detail. Most people didn't even notice the scars.

She shrugged it off. "It was no big deal. I had two."

"What if something goes wrong with yours? What then?" His knuckles had gone scarily white.

"Between my sisters and me, we have seven kidneys. We figured we could pass them around between us as needed."

For a second, she could have sworn his eye was twitching. As they drove up the dark, empty road away from town and towards home, Duncan reached out and took her hand. He wove their fingers together and rested their hands on his thigh.

"That is the most selfless thing I've ever heard." He gave her a strange look. "I don't really know you at all, did I?"

She flushed and looked away, watching as the softly lit exterior of the mansion came into view.

"I plan to fix that," Duncan whispered as they drove through the gates.

They sat in silence as he parked outside the front door. As soon as they were inside, Donna gave him a polite smile.

"Goodnight, Duncan. See you in the morning." She turned towards the stairs.

"Wait a minute." His hand swamped hers when he took it, reminding her again that he was so much bigger than she was. "It's barely nine. This date isn't over yet."

"I want to go to bed. I'm exhausted." Their date had worn her out.

"Later." His eyes held a dark promise that made her

stomach clench. "First, we have dessert." He held up the take-away bag.

Donna didn't see the point in prolonging the agony. They had no idea what to say to each other, and Duncan aggravated everyone within range. She also had suspicions that he'd hit Marcus. When they'd left the restaurant, the owner was nowhere in sight, and the other diners wouldn't even glance in Duncan's direction. That was *not* her idea of a perfect date. She'd rather have been home talking to invisible people. And didn't that say a whole lot about the state of her life? "Why can't we just give up and go to our rooms?"

He stopped in front of her, making her collide with his back. When he turned, he steadied her. "Because, Angel, that dinner was the worse date in history. It might have been eighteen years since I last did this, but even I could tell how painful it was. If we don't salvage some of this evening, we'll never be able to look each other in the eye again."

He had a point. "One hour. That's all I'm giving you to redeem yourself."

"I'll take it." Without hesitation, he took her hand and led her towards the orangery.

* * *

IF ONE HOUR was all he had, Duncan wanted to make every second count. He would salvage their evening if it killed him.

"Dragging me behind you while you move at the speed of light isn't a good start," Donna complained.

He instantly shortened his stride and slowed as he felt his cheeks heat. It was humiliating. Grown men didn't blush. "I'm sorry. I keep forgetting. Fiona's legs were longer, and I'm used to that. Notice, I said longer, not prettier. I'll take better care."

He moved to keep walking but was pulled back when

Donna didn't follow. He turned to see what the problem might be and found her staring at him with tears in her eyes.

His heart sank. He'd screwed up. Again. "I shouldn't have said anything about your short legs, should I?"

She sniffed. "It's not that."

"What is it then?" He reached out and gently brushed away the tear that had escaped to run down her cheek. "You're breaking my heart, Angel. Tell me what I did wrong, and I'll fix it. I promise you, I will get better at this dating stuff."

Her smile was tremulous. "It was the first time you've spoken about Fiona like it was normal, like you weren't in pain."

Duncan jerked back and went over his words. He hadn't even noticed what he'd said. He'd been more concerned about Donna's comfort than the fact Fiona was gone. At first, he didn't know what to say, and then he just went for brutal honesty. "She was taller than you are. I got used to her matching me stride for stride. But I wasn't comparing you. It was a comment on the differences and a reminder that I need to be more aware of how I treat you."

"I know." She bit her lip and looked up at him. "I know I can't compare to Fiona, and I'm not trying to. I've seen the photos, and we're nothing alike. She was beautiful. Like a model on a runway." She gave him a shaky smile. "Hence the height. I know I'm not her, and I'm not trying to replace her. This is just one date. It's that, I've never heard you talk like that before. It was obvious you cared deeply for her, but you didn't sound broken. If you know what I mean."

"Aye, I think I do." But it was something else she'd said that bothered him more. He reached out and cupped her cheek, feeling the satin-soft smoothness of the skin beneath the roughness of his palm. "She was beautiful, Angel, but you're beautiful too. There's no comparing you, because you're both unique."

She looked away, embarrassed. "You don't have to say that. I understand."

He frowned as he gently turned her face back to him. "I don't think you do. Do you know why I call you *angel*?"

"Because slave sounds wrong?" she quipped.

"No, it's because that's what you look like to me." She shook her head, and he stopped her. "Listen. There's been many a time you've stepped into a sunbeam, and your hair has shone around your head like a halo. No, I'm saying this wrong, it was more like the otherworldly glow that the Pre-Raphaelite painters used on their models. Your skin sparkles in the light and your hair fills with a million colours that blend and shimmer. The sight brings a grown man to his knees." He scoffed at himself. "I should know. It's done it to me often enough."

"Duncan, it's okay—"

"Shh, let me tell you how I see you." He stroked her silken hair. "You're all curves and softness. The kindness in your heart just radiates from you and pulls everyone around you in closer. I dream about your skin—its colour, its softness. I wonder if the colour of your lips appears anywhere else on your body, and I itch to find out."

She blushed, and it made him groan.

"And that blush, Angel. I want to fill a canvas with the colour, but only after I've stripped you naked to lie on the couch in my living room, with the warm evening sun bathing your mouth-watering curves and making your hair dance with a million colours."

Wide, green eyes looked up at him, holding such vulnerability, it ripped him in two.

"You're not Fiona," he told her. "And I don't want you to

be. You are perfect just as you are. Beautiful. Unique. Just. As. You. Are."

He closed the distance between them, sipping at her lips as though she held the most precious of nectars. The wild side of him that Fiona's death had freed wanted to take over, to press her back against the wall, flip up her dress, and plunge into her warm, welcoming depths. But he was strong enough to keep the instinct caged because he wanted her to know how beautiful she was and what she did to him. He didn't want there to be any doubt. Taking her in a fury of desire would make her think that this was only about his needs, and he wouldn't do that to her.

With a strength he didn't know he possessed, he broke their gentle kiss. "Come on, let's go eat this tiramisu before it goes off."

Looking dazed, Donna grasped his hand, and he led her to the orangery. This time, he remembered to shorten his stride.

Donna had been in the orangery many times—after all, she'd been the one to oversee its renovations—but the beauty of the room still took her breath away. The large solarium, or conservatory, on the south side of the house, had once been used to grow exotic fruit, such as oranges. Hence the name of the building.

The builder had told her that the wall between the house and the orangery was three times thicker than in the rest of the house, to insulate the room from the cold northerly winds. The rest of the room was built with stone and metal, rising up to the second floor of the mansion, to give enough height for the trees. Long glass windows filled the southern wall, to maximise the sun, and the roof was made of smaller glass panels, fitted into the domed shapes that formed the apex of the room. She knew it had been one of the first buildings to design an orangery with a glass roof, and it was one of the things that made the mansion special.

They passed the raised beds, filled with exotic flowers, and rounded the fountain that was not only ornate but gave the air the humidity the plants needed to survive. Tall ferns rose up around them. In the centre, where the roof was highest, were fruit trees and palms.

Outside, a mixture of grey-hued clouds and sparkling stars filled the sky above them. Donna knew where they were headed. There was a seating area hidden in the middle of the room. It held a small ironwork table and two chairs, and behind it was a rattan daybed, with plump, cream coloured cushions. If you lay on the sofa on a clear night, it felt like you were floating amongst the stars overhead.

All that could be heard was the running water of the fountain and her heels clacking on the terracotta-tiled path beneath them.

"I love this room," Donna said as she breathed the heady, green scent of the plants into her lungs.

Duncan looked around, as though seeing it for the first time. "It's the best part of this house."

"You don't like the mansion?"

"It was never my thing. It was Fiona's dream, but I don't mind it." Now that was interesting.

"If you could live anywhere, where would it be?"

"Glasgow," he said without hesitation.

"I'm not talking only in Scotland, I mean in the world."

He grinned at her. "The answer's still Glasgow."

"Well, that's just sad."

He burst out laughing as he placed the takeaway bag on the ornate table and pulled a chair out for her, before taking a seat facing her. "Spoken like a person who's never seen the good parts of the city."

"Are there good parts?" She wasn't convinced.

"Aye."

"Name one."

"The art school building. Built by Charles Rennie Mackintosh at the turn of the century—twentieth," he amended. "It's the most beautiful building in the world."

She was unconvinced. "Better than the Taj Mahal?"

"Way better. You've never been?"

"No." Just the thought of setting foot in a building dedicated to serious artists made her break out in hives. If she actually did it, she would spend the rest of her life comparing herself and coming up short as usual.

"I'll take you some time." His face grew wistful. "I still remember the first day I walked into the place. Up those stone steps, the gold brick looming in front of you, with the massive studio windows either side of the entrance. You pushed through the white double doors, making sure you used the one with 'In' on it, and into the foyer. There were Art Nouveau details everywhere you looked. From the carved wooden staircase up to the first floor to the emblems high in the walls. But it was the atmosphere that sucked you right in. It smelled of oil paint, turps and creative obsession. There was a buzz about the place. An energy I've never come across anywhere else. It was as though you'd stepped into a magical world when you walked through those doors."

Her throat felt tight as she swallowed. "You taught there too."

"For a time."

"You should go back. Take them up on the offer to lecture. It would do you good." She wanted to see him do something he loved, and for a moment, she forgot that the whole reason she'd set it up was to get him out of the way. Shame hit her and made her look away.

"That part of my life is over," he told her, but his tone wasn't harsh.

"I've seen the new paintings. I think you might be wrong."

Uncertainty flashed in his eyes before he turned his attention to their dessert. He reached into the bag and came out with two boxes. He placed one in front of her and she opened it to find a perfect piece of tiramisu, a plastic spoon, and a napkin. It wasn't chocolate cake, but it was still pretty damn good.

"I'll get some drinks." Donna made to stand, but Duncan stopped her.

"I'll get them. Don't go anywhere."

"No faith," she muttered as she eyed her dessert. If she was fast, she could eat hers and get into his before he got back.

He must have guessed what she was thinking because he swiped up his dessert box. "I'll just take this with me for safe-keeping."

"Whatever." She rolled her eyes at him, making him chuckle.

As soon as he disappeared into the foliage, the hordes descended.

Didn't I tell you that this evening was a mistake? Hermione appeared beside the pot-bellied stove that was used to keep the room warm in winter. *Just what do you think you're doing?*

"Having dessert." She spooned some into her mouth and tried to ignore the figures only she could see. "And wondering if I should see a psychiatrist," she said around her food.

Hermione rolled her eyes. *You don't need a psychiatrist. You need to listen to me.*

Really, there was nothing to say to that, so she took another bite of her pudding.

Mark my words, Gandalf the White boomed, *no good will come of this.*

"I miss Gandalf the Grey," Donna told him. "At least he knew how to have fun."

Is that what you're doing? Hermione said.

Harry Potter's mother appeared. *Of course she's having fun.* She waved a hand around. *Look at this. She has the stars, the moon, a beautiful setting and wonderful food. I hope you enjoy every minute of it, darling.*

He's going to crush her heart. Katniss Everdeen walked out from amongst the trees to join them. *Don't worry. When he does, I'll deal with him.* She patted her bow.

Do you really think violence is the answer? Molly Weasley said as she fussed with the stove. What she thought she would make on it, Donna didn't know.

Belle, from *Beauty and the Beast*, twirled through the room. *What a magical place! How romantic! This is the perfect place to fall in love.*

Donna glared at her. "Why are you here? I've never drawn you."

Belle looked sad as she tugged at her voluminous yellow dress. *Yes, you have. It was a long time ago. You loved my story. You thought that Beast should have stayed the way he was and never turned back into a prince.* She gave Donna a chiding look. *Do you have any idea how much hair he shed everywhere? I was so pleased when he lost that look. He's so handsome. It makes a girl swoon.*

I prefer books to boys. Hermione stuck her nose in the air.

Belle's eyes went wide. *Have you read Wuthering Heights? I adore that book. What about Pride and Prejudice?*

I love Pride and Prejudice. It's wonderful to meet another reader.

Belle hooked her hand through Hermione's arm. *I must show you Beast's library. Between you and me, it was a big selling point in our relationship.*

They walked off into the trees.

Are you going to have sex with him? Molly Weasley asked.

Mum! Ron appeared beside his mother, looking humiliated.

Hush, she told him. *If she's going to have sex, she needs to make sure it's safe. Don't forget about protection.* She rooted around in her apron pocket while Ron's whole head turned red. *Here it is.* She put a piece of paper on the table in front of Donna. *That's the best protection spell out there. Say that three times before you get busy, and you'll be fine.*

"I think a condom might be a better idea," Donna said. "But I have no intention of having sex, so it's all good."

I feel sick, Ron whined.

Donna, my girl, Gandalf said. *Get up to your room now, before you get yourself into trouble you can't get out of.*

I agree with him, Katniss said. *You don't look like you have any survival skills. It would be better if you ran.*

"That's it!" Donna shot to her feet and pointed towards the exit. "Everyone, out now. I've had it with your interference and advice. Go!"

"Uh, Donna," a very real voice came from behind her. "Should I be worried? Maybe call someone? Like a doctor?"

She groaned as she turned to Duncan who was scanning the room to see who she was talking to.

"Would you believe me if I said I was talking to the moths?" There were two fluttering around the light overhead.

"No."

"That's what I thought." She sank back into her seat.

"Spill," he ordered, placing a bottle of wine on the table in front of her, along with a glass. He opened a bottle of water for himself and sipped at it. "I won't give up until you tell me. I can be really tenacious about these things."

"No kidding." She eyed his untouched dessert. "I'll do it if you share."

He chuckled and pushed the food into the middle of the table. When she reached for it, he snatched it back. "Start talking before you take a bite."

"No trust." She sighed. "Okay, this will sound a little nutty."

He cocked an eyebrow at her. "Remember who you're talking to, Angel. I've been holed up here for over two years, bouncing off the walls."

"Fine. You know I read a lot." He nodded. "I tend to read kids' and teens' books, and I like fantasy—*Lord of the Rings, Harry Potter*—that sort of thing. The characters become real to me when I read, and sometimes they pop out of the books and talk to me."

"Like Dobby?"

She beamed at him. "Yes, exactly like Dobby."

Duncan looked around. "Was he here just now?"

"No, it was other characters." She tugged on the box. "Can I have dessert now?"

He held it tight. "In a minute. How often do these characters pop up?"

She shrugged. "I don't know."

"And you know they aren't real, right?"

She hoped her look was scathing. "Yes, Duncan. I know that when I talk to Gandalf that he is only in my head and the pages of a Tolkien book."

"Okay, then, have at it." He pushed the tiramisu towards her and sat back in his seat.

"That's it? You aren't worried that you hired a lunatic?"

"Nope. Everybody talks to themselves. You just prefer it when your inner voice has a fictional face." His smile was pure sexual invitation, and the temperature in the room suddenly seemed to shoot up. "Want to tell me what they were saying about me?"

She felt herself flush. "What makes you think they were talking about you?"

"So that's how we're playing it. I'll make you a deal, you tell me what they were saying, and I'll..." He searched around for something to offer.

Donna jumped in when he hesitated. "You'll give the lecture at Glasgow School of Art, just this once."

He frowned at her, and she thought he'd tell her to stop interfering. "Okay, I'll do it. Just this once. But you have to come with me so that I can show you around."

A surge of pure longing made her knees go weak, and she was glad she was already sitting down. "I can't. It's Mairi's birthday that weekend," she lied, hating herself for it at the same time. She looked up at him through her lashes. "Does that mean the deal's off?" She tried to sound hopeful so that he would think she wanted to back out.

"No, the deal's on. I'll take you another time."

"So, you're really going to lecture, just to hear what my imaginary friends told me about you?"

"Aye." His jaw firmed with determination.

"I'll be mad if I embarrass myself and you back out."

"You have my word that I won't."

Donna almost pumped the air in victory. "Fine. Then I'll tell you. Hermione says I should make my apologies, go to my room and forget all about tonight."

"I don't know who she is, but I don't like her," Duncan rumbled. "What about the rest?"

She swallowed hard and reached for her wine. "Molly Weasley told me to use protection if we sleep together."

"Did she now?" He leaned forwards and rested his arms on the table. "What did you tell her?"

"That I didn't think the spell she gave me would work." Her voice had become a husky croak.

His lips quirked, and his eyes sparkled. "No, I don't imagine it would."

They held each other's gaze for what seemed like hours as the air between them became charged with desire. At some point, Duncan had taken off his jacket, and the material of his white shirt pulled across his chest. She licked her lips as her eyes hungrily ate up the contours of the muscles she'd felt every time she'd touched him. Underneath that shirt were six-pack abs that would turn any woman into a blubbering mess.

Every move he made oozed strength and confidence. He had the air of a marauder. A pirate. A Viking. Sexy, dangerous, completely in charge. She placed a shaky hand over her heart as she felt it race out of control. Images she'd never dared to let into her mind, flooded in from every quarter, but one in particular rose to the fore.

Duncan behind her, bending her over the daybed behind her.

"Put your forearms on the cushions," he'd order. *"Don't move."*

Slowly, he'd inch her dress up her thighs, until it was over her hips. He'd groan at the sight of the thong she'd dared to buy after Mairi had goaded her. It was pink and matched the balconette bra that made her feel sexy and wanton.

"Spread those legs for me, Angel."

She'd inch them apart, aware that the heels she wore pushed her backside higher. The cool glow of the moon above them would bathe them in light. The sound of the fountain would become sensual background music, as the humidity inside the glasshouse coated her sensitive skin, and the cool night air soothed in its wake.

"I have your permission to do as I please?" her Neanderthal *would say.*

"Yes."

His hands would squeeze the globes of her behind. "Anything *I* please?"

"Yes." The word would tremble out of her.

"Donna?" A very real voice broke into her dream.

Donna shot to her feet. "I need to go." And then she ran.

The last thing she saw was Duncan standing at the table, staring after her, a frown on his face.

CHAPTER 19

It was mid-morning, the day after Donna had run out on her date. The ball was in three short days. Duncan was holed up in his office, preparing for the lecture he was to give at Glasgow School of Art. Not that she'd spoken to him. This information came from the cook. The Women's Institute committee members were sneaking in and out to make arrangements under Grace's watchful eye. The renovation of the carriage house was coming to an end.

And Donna had fallen in love with her boss.

She let out a strangled scream as she lay on her floor in the middle of her living room and stared up at the ceiling.

"I'm such an idiot," she said, and for the first time in years, no imaginary characters answered.

Her phone buzzed on the floor beside her, and she picked it up to read the screen. *On our way to the mansion,* Agnes had written.

Donna didn't move. Her sisters would come looking for her anyway, and she didn't particularly care if they found her having a breakdown in the middle of her floor. She'd found them in worse positions more than once.

A few minutes later, a key scraped in the door before it opened wide. Agnes and Mairi looked down at her.

"What happened?" Agnes said. "Who do I have to hurt?"

"Don't get up," Mairi said. "I need to take a picture for Isobel." She lifted her phone.

Donna was past caring. Her life had imploded. She stared at the ceiling some more as she heard the door click shut. Agnes sat on the edge of the sofa beside her.

"Did he hurt you?" she demanded.

"No, of course not. Why is that always the first conclusion you jump to?"

"The man is unstable. Sue me for expecting him to blow and take us all out with him when he does."

"FYI," Mairi said. "I'm recording this for Izzy." She kept her camera trained on them.

"Turn the damn thing off," Agnes ordered.

"Fine, be like that." Mairi put it back in her pocket and folded to sit tailor-style beside Donna on the floor. "What's up, Donnie?"

She took a deep breath and let it all out. "I've fallen in love with Duncan," she wailed.

Her torturous confession didn't get the response she'd expected. Mairi was staring at Agnes with confusion.

"She didn't know?" she said.

"Know what?" Donna snapped.

Mairi looked back at her. "That you've been in love with Duncan almost from the day you started here."

"That's not true!" She would have noticed.

The sisters shared a look, and Mairi's face softened. She patted Donna's arm. "Donnie, it's the reason you're still here. You love the man."

She swung her gaze between them. "Why didn't someone say something?"

"Because we thought you didn't want to talk about it,"

Mairi said. "And it didn't seem like Duncan was going to come out of his funk anytime soon."

Her eyes narrowed at her little sister. "It wasn't a funk. He was grieving."

"Yeah, that." Mairi nodded.

Donna let her head thump back to the floor. "What am I going to do?"

Her sisters spoke at the same time.

"Have sex with him," Mairi said.

"Get a new job," Agnes said.

Donna groaned. She would have been better off talking to Hermione and Gandalf.

"Have sex with him?" Agnes snapped at Mairi. "Are you out of your mind? She can't sleep with him."

"Why not?" That Mairi looked genuinely confused did not bode well for the IQ range of any children she might have. "She loves him, and that's what people do when they're in love, they have sex."

Agnes pinched the bridge of her nose before answering. "Exactly. *She* loves *him*. And Duncan loves?" Her eyebrows rose as she willed Mairi to join the dots for herself.

Donna couldn't wait for her. "He loves his wife," she wailed again.

Mairi's face was blank. "I still don't understand why that means she can't sleep with him. Fiona isn't here, and she is. Why can't she bonk his brains out so that she'll never regret not having sex with the man she loves?"

"You are deeply disturbed." Agnes pointed at Mairi.

Donna had to agree. "I'm not having sex with him. In fact, I don't even want to see him again. I think Agnes' idea about changing jobs is a good one." Although it would hurt to move on, she figured it would still hurt less than knowing she'd never have a place in Duncan's heart.

"I hate to break it to you," Agnes said. "But as much as I

agree that you need to move on and get away from him, you still have to see him every day until you do."

She groaned again. This was agony. "I'll talk to him. Tell him this isn't working for me and that I want to go back to the way things were."

There was silence for a beat before her sisters laughed.

"*You're* going to set him straight?" Mairi wiped her eyes.

"Yes. Is that so hard to believe?" Now they were really annoying her. Whatever happened to having the support of her sisters?

"You do that," Agnes said, clearly humouring her. "And while you're telling him all about how you want things to be between you, you can keep him away from the mansion too. This afternoon would be the best time to get him out of here and have your talk."

Donna ignored Agnes' tone. There was no point arguing. Her sisters would see for themselves afterwards that she was more than capable of putting some distance between her and Duncan until she could find another job. Although, she'd needed to get over feeling nauseous every time she even thought about leaving the mansion.

"What's wrong now?" she said.

"There's a problem with the sound system for the ball," Agnes told her. "The technicians need access. We can't use the varnishing excuse again to keep him out of there, so you have to come up with a reason to get him out of the building for a couple of hours."

"Why can't we tell him there's a problem with the varnish?" Mairi asked.

"Because," Agnes said with forced patience, "he's an artist. He knows about varnish. He'll want to go in there and see what the problem is for himself. Won't he?" she asked Donna.

"Probably," she admitted. "I think you two should keep him occupied and out of the way. I don't think it's a good idea for me to spend time with him until I've prepared what I want to say to him." Or possibly written it down and pinned it to his office door.

Agnes was shaking her head. "You're the only one he listens to. You need to get him out of here." She looked at her watch. "In an hour."

"How? It took two weeks to get him to agree to go to Glasgow. How am I supposed to get him out of the building in an hour?"

"Ask him to go play pool," Mairi said.

"I can't. I'm banned from playing. Remember?" She was banned from a lot of things at the local pub. The owner was a stick-in-the-mud.

"You're only banned from playing for money. You can still play for fun."

"Plus," Agnes added, "it's the only idea we've come up with."

"It's a stupid one. I need to distance myself from Duncan, not spend more time alone with him. What if he figures out I'm in love with him? What then?"

Again, they spoke at the same time.

"Jump his bones," Mairi said.

"Tell him he's mistaken," Agnes said, then glared at Mairi. "Is sex all you think about?"

She considered that for a moment. "Yeah," she said with a nod.

"Okay." Agnes stood before bending over to give Donna a hand up. "Let's ignore her and get you ready to take Duncan out."

"What's wrong with the way I am now?" Apart from the fact she was still lying on the floor that is. She wore her usual work clothes—black trousers, white blouse, flat shoes.

"Everything," Mairi said. "Come on. I'll help."

"Oh great," Agnes drawled. "With your help, we'll have her dressed like a stripper in no time at all."

* * *

DUNCAN SHOULD HAVE BEEN PREPARING his art college lecture, instead he was flicking through the copy of *The Hobbit* he'd found and marvelling again at the quality of the drawings. He traced the outline of the dragon with his fingertip. Maybe it wouldn't be so bad to mentor someone again. It would be a shame for talent like this to go to waste.

He made a mental note to find the book's owner after he came back from Glasgow, then slipped the book into the bag containing his lecture notes—what there was of them. If he got the chance, he'd have a word with the Fine Arts dean about the illustrations. Maybe she could give him some pointers on how best to encourage this kind of talent.

A knock on his door had him holding his breath. He'd kept his distance from Donna after she'd run out the night before because he was hoping she'd make her own way to him. She had until dinner to get her act together and then he planned to hunt her down.

When her head appeared around his door, he felt a wave of relief, quickly followed by something he hadn't felt in years—hope. She'd come to him.

"Got a minute?" she said, not looking him in the eye.

"Sure. What's up?" He came around to perch against his desk, playing it cool.

That lasted until she stepped into the room, and then everything changed. Because Donna wasn't wearing her usual workwear. Instead, she wore the fern green Snoopy T-shirt he loved and faded blue jeans that hugged her curves like loving hands. Her hair sat tousled around her shoulder,

188

her lips were painted a subtle shade of pink, and sexy beige suede boots peeked out from under her jeans.

She was talking, but he couldn't hear a word she was saying over the buzzing in his ears. He had to touch her. It felt as though he might die if he didn't. All the sexual frustration from the evening before came rushing back, and all he could think about was getting his hands on those sexy curves.

His eyes zeroed in on her lips, watching their lush fullness move as she spoke. If he didn't taste them, he was going to explode. She gestured, and the wide neck of her shirt slipped off her shoulder, exposing all that luscious creamy skin and one violet coloured bra strap. The sight was like a tractor beam locking onto him and pulling him in.

Before he'd made a conscious decision to do so, he was on his feet and moving. He stalked towards her, watching the green of her eyes deepen as those perfect pinks spread like an ink blot over her skin.

He followed her as she backed up against the wall, his hands going to her hips.

"Stop talking," was all he said before his mouth took hers.

And it was a taking. A frantic, desperate taking—from them both. He groaned when her hands slid up over his shoulders and her fingers threaded into his hair. Their bodies pressed tightly together, and he could feel every soft, voluptuous curves against him.

She tasted like paradise. Or maybe hot, sensual sin. Aye. On the outside, Donna was all angel, but inside, she was molten sin. Perfect. He slid his hand down her outer thigh and tucked it under her knee, intent on pulling her leg up around his hip so he could grind their bodies together. Too short. She couldn't reach. He tore his lips from hers, clutched her waist and lifted her off her feet.

"Legs around me, now."

Deep green, slumberous eyes met his as she did as he ordered, hooking her ankles behind him. Her swollen lips parted, but Duncan didn't give her time to say anything. He leaned forwards and nipped her bottom lip. She moaned into his mouth. *Hot. So bloody hot.*

He pressed his hard length against her, feeling the heat of her entrance against him, wishing they didn't have two pairs of jeans between them. The sounds she made drove him wild: little whimpers of need, deep moans of protest when he moved his head away from hers, gasping whines when he pressed into her.

"Angel, you're noisy," he said against her lips.

"Is that bad?" Green eyes searched his.

"No, I'm just not used to it. But I love it." He kissed her again. Tangling their tongues, desperate for more. She didn't disappoint, letting him know what worked for her with every little sound she made.

"Do you scream when you come?" he whispered as he kissed his way across her jaw to her ear.

"Yes," she gasped.

One word and he almost came in his pants. He felt like he was a teenager all over again, losing control with the first girl who drove him wild. He felt her back arch and her breasts push into him.

"What is it?" he whispered against the shell of her ear.

She made a needy little sound, pressing her lush breasts against him again.

"You want me to touch your breasts, Angel?"

She shivered. "Yes," she breathed the word.

It seemed his Donna was shy about asking for what she needed, and somehow that made him hotter than hell. He covered her breast with his hand as he nuzzled her throat, feeling her fingernails digging into his shoulders. She fit his hand and more, spilling over his hold, her hard, little nipple poking into his palm as he massaged her. By the sound of it, she liked what he was doing. A lot. The noises were fantastic. They took the guesswork out of pleasing her.

The scent of her skin made his knees go weak. Vanilla and cinnamon were his new favourite flavours. She arched her back, baring her throat to his teeth, and he took the invitation, nipping, sucking, licking.

"Duncan." She panted, rocking against his hard cock.

He moved back to her ear. "Do you think you can make yourself come like this, Angel? Can you rock your way to the finish line?"

His answer was a deep moan, and he smiled against her throat as his fingers teased her hard nipple through her top. Was it the same colour as her lips? Darker? Did the skin over her chest flush when she was turned on? He was suddenly desperate for the answers to his questions.

Her gasps were coming faster now. He ground his hips against her as he pinched her nipple. Fingers clutched at him as her head fell back against the wall. Duncan took her earlobe into his mouth and bit.

Donna's back bowed, and a long, explosive cry filled the air. As she writhed against him, he held her tight, reciting lists of Renaissance painters to keep himself from following her over the edge. He'd never seen a woman come so fast from so little. It blew his mind.

As she relaxed in his hold, and her breathing slowed, Duncan found himself smiling. His Donna was easy. And he bloody loved it.

"That was humiliating," Donna said when she came back down to earth.

"You mean because you came all over me and we're both still fully dressed?" He beamed at her. She had the tousled look of a well-satisfied woman, and he couldn't help the stab of pride he felt at the sight.

She narrowed her eyes at him. "Stop looking so smug."

"I think I have a right to, don't you?"

She made a strangled little cry. This time it was more irritated than sexy. "Put me down."

He did as she ordered, adjusting himself in the tight confines of his jeans while she righted her top. Through the window, movement in the grounds caught his eye.

Two men were hefting a large black box across his lawn. "Are they carrying a speaker?"

"What?" Her eyes jerked to the window. "Don't be daft," she said before taking his arm and steering him to the door. "So, are you going to answer my question?" She batted her eyelashes at him, mesmerising him.

"What question?"

"I knew you weren't listening." She opened the door and pushed him into the corridor. "I asked you if you'd like to come to the pub with me this afternoon for a game of pool and a chat."

He stopped dead. "You want to go play pool?"

"Yes. *And* chat."

Obviously, the chat part was important to her. He hoped to hell she wasn't going to bang on about their confusing work relationship again. Not after what had just happened. "You want to go play now?"

"Yes."

"In the middle of the day. When you have work?"

She narrowed her eyes at him, and he got the impression he was treading on thin ice. "I can make up the hours tonight."

He studied her face to see if he could figure out what she was up to. There were no clues in those sparkling emerald eyes of hers.

"Why do you want to play pool?"

"I like the game, Duncan. It isn't rocket science. Now, do you want to go or not?"

"Aye, we can go play pool, if you're that desperate for a game."

She muttered about Dementors again as she stalked down the corridor in front of him. As she went, all he could do was watch the roll of her hips in awe. Her backside in those jeans was a work of art, worthy of a place in the Louvre.

"Are you coming?" she said, casting an irritated look over her shoulder.

"I wish," he muttered as he followed her.

CHAPTER 20

Well, that was embarrassing.

She'd gone to Duncan's office with the intention of getting him out of the building and telling him that they needed to go back to being employee and employer—if that's even what they'd been in the first place. Instead, all she'd done was make him think her libido was equipped with a hair trigger. Had any woman in the history of the planet ever orgasmed over so little? She was an embarrassment to her gender.

And to make matters worse, judging by the smug smile on Duncan's face, it seemed he now thought he was God's gift to women. He glanced her way as he drove thought the back roads to Campbeltown.

"Wouldn't you rather spend the afternoon in the mansion?"

"No."

"We could spend some time in the studio. I wouldn't say no if you wanted to pose naked for me."

"Good to know."

"Is that a yes?"

"No."

He sat in silence until the town came into view. "I thought you had a problem saying no."

"Seems you've become an exception to the rule."

If he looked smug before, now he seemed ready to take a bow and accept an award. "Guess that makes me special then."

She pressed her lips together to stop herself from describing all the many ways he was truly special—from his antisocial attitude to his penchant for firing staff. He had to be the most annoying man in Scotland. Which begged the question, was she really in love with him, or just sad, lonely and deluded?

"Not a-bloody-gain." The car screeched to a halt beside the drystane wall that circled the old Church of Scotland building.

Donna watched as he stalked over to stand under the boy who was halfway to the top of the wall, clinging on to the stones for dear life.

"What did I tell you about this?" he snapped up at the child.

"Sorry, Mr Stewart," little Cameron said.

Duncan shook his head, held out his arms and gave the order, "Jump."

Without even a second's hesitation, the wee boy launched himself off the wall and into Duncan's waiting arms. He put him down on the grass and held his shoulders as he looked him in the eye.

"Stop climbing that damn wall. If I catch you at it again, I'm taking you to the police and they can deal with you."

The five-year-old nodded solemnly. "I won't." And then he ran off down the road to his house.

Duncan climbed back into the car. "He'll break his neck one day. That's the fourth time I've got him off that wall this year. It's his pure luck that I'm here whenever he gets stuck."

"Or," Donna said as he drove back onto the road, "it could be that from his house he can see your car as it comes into town, and he runs for the wall."

He slammed on the brakes and looked between Cameron's house and the road. The wee boy had a good view of oncoming cars for miles, and Duncan's silver SUV was distinctive.

"I'm going to wring his neck." He started the car again. "Next time I'm no' stopping. He can bloody well fall, for all I care."

It was a wasted threat. They both knew he'd stop.

"Maybe you should try talking to his mother?" Donna said.

"Ah cannae." Duncan's face turned a deep shade of red. "She flirts with me."

Donna covered her mouth in an attempt to smother her laughter. It didn't work. Duncan glared at her as he rounded the pub building and parked behind it.

"I feel I should warn you," he said as they walked into the pub. "I'm very good at pool."

She cocked an eyebrow at him. "Is that your way of telling me you don't plan on letting me win?"

"I'm also very competitive."

"And short-tempered."

He frowned at her as he held the door to the Highland Pub open for her. "Are you sure you want to prod the bear? He's very horny, and it's making him grumpy. Unlike some people, the bear's no' had any relief today."

It was Donna's turn to blush. "Talking about yourself in third person, and as a bear, is weird—even for you."

"Are you sure you wouldn't rather go home than play

pool? I have other games in mind that would keep us occupied this afternoon."

The promise in his eyes made her want to rub herself all over again.

She tore her gaze from his. "Let's get on with it."

"Okay, but don't say I didn't warn you. Don't go crying to me when you lose."

Men and their fragile little egos. "I'll keep that in mind."

It was midweek, which meant the bar wasn't as busy as it could have been. There were fifteen or so regulars dotted around the place, having a quiet afternoon. Until they walked in.

"No," Ewan McKenzie called out from behind the bar as soon as he spotted her. "No. Just no."

Duncan looked at her askance, and she shrugged like she didn't have a clue what he was going on about. When Duncan turned back to the bar, Donna made a slicing gesture across her throat to tell Ewan to stop talking. He didn't read it right because he glared and pointed at her.

"Don't even think about threatening me! I'll take you outside and skelp your arse."

"No, you bloody well won't." Duncan's chest puffed up as he confronted Ewan. "Nobody touches her arse but me."

Donna groaned, and she felt her face burn. She scanned the room to see that everyone had heard Duncan's declaration.

"He isn't touching my backside either," she announced to them, but could tell from the smiles that no one believed her.

Ewan pointed at her again. "If you go anywhere near the karaoke machine, you're barred for life."

That got Duncan's attention. "This is about karaoke?"

"Pathetic, right?" She gave Ewan a look of disgust, but he stood his ground.

"You sing?" Duncan's look of shock was becoming offensive.

"No, she doesn't," Ewan snapped, "and that's the problem. We had two bloody hours straight of her wailing like a banshee to Madonna. She doesn't go near that machine ever again." He looked around the pub. "We took a vote. Nobody wants her near it."

There were nods of agreement.

"Bunch of drama llamas," she muttered. "It's not like I come in here all the time. I haven't been to a karaoke night for months."

"And we're still suffering," Ewan said.

"You sing?" Duncan said again, obviously stuck on that nugget of information.

"Let it go," Donna told him before grinning. She should have sung her answer.

He gave her a confused look before he turned to Ewan. "We're playing pool. No singing, I promise. Now"—he turned back to her—"what do you want to drink?"

She would have answered, but Ewan wasn't listening anyway, he was too busy laughing.

"You're playing pool?" He slapped the bar. "With her?"

Some of the regulars joined in the laughter, and Donna gave them her dirtiest look. It had no impact. Agnes would have shut that crap down already.

"Maybe this is a bad idea," Duncan said. "I wouldn't want you to embarrass yourself in front of everyone like you did with your singing."

"Hey." She poked him in the ribs, coming up against a solid wall of muscle that left her strangely fascinated and a little breathless. "I can sing. I'm just underappreciated. And I can play pool too."

"Then what's up with your pool game that has Ewan in stitches?"

"Nothing."

He turned to the pub owner, who held up his hands. "There are some things a man needs to experience for himself. I'll bring your drinks over."

"We haven't ordered them yet." Duncan was losing his limited patience.

"You both get Coke." Ewan reached for the glasses. "Agnes told me you don't drink anymore, and Donna's only allowed soft drinks."

Duncan gave her a bewildered look, which made her think that coming to the pub wasn't the best idea the Sinclair sisters had ever come up with.

"It's a family thing. Ewan thinks we fight if we drink too much." She glared at the pub owner. "Which. I. Don't."

"Better safe than sorry." Ewan was unrepentant. "If your sisters are anything to go by, we'd better not risk it."

"I'm telling Agnes you said that."

Ewan paled. "Do you want a wine? You can have one if you really want it."

"I don't...now." And she was still telling Aggie.

It seemed Duncan had reached the limit of his tolerance for social interaction, because he tugged on her hand. "Let's go," he said.

And then he dragged her behind him again, making her wonder if he'd remember her *wee* legs if she kicked his ankles a time or two.

* * *

As Duncan racked up the balls, he tried to get his head around Donna being banned from singing. The fact she'd gotten up in front of people to sing in the first place stunned him enough without thinking about how bad she had to be to deserve Ewan's reaction.

"Will you sing for me when we get home?" he asked, even though he expected her to refuse.

"Yes." She examined the cues. "But you have to buy me a microphone first. I saw one in town that has a built-in speaker and Bluetooth, so you can send your music to it." She batted her eyelashes at him.

"I know what Bluetooth is. I'm not *that* old."

"It's pink and sparkly," she said solemnly.

"Bluetooth?" There was a ripple of laughter, and he looked over to find that most of the pub regulars had moved their chairs closer to the pool table.

"No," Donna said. "The microphone."

He wasn't looking at her when she spoke, but he would still have sworn she'd rolled her eyes at him. "Why do we have an audience?" Was Donna that bad they'd come to watch?

"There's nothing else to do in Campbeltown," she said. "Now, can we get started? I want to talk about some stuff as soon as we're finished this game."

"That sounds ominous."

"Let's just play," she snapped.

He smiled at her, hoping she was terrible at pool. He had visions of him leaning over her and sensually coaching her on how to play the game. Oh, aye, this wasn't such a bad idea after all.

"You can break first," he offered, being a gentleman.

There were loud groans from the peanut gallery.

"Don't do that!" an old man shouted.

Donna ignored their audience and gave him a sweet smile. "Are you sure? I don't mind if you want to break."

"Aye, Angel, you go ahead. Don't worry about anybody watching you—they'll keep their opinions to themselves." He glared at their audience, making it clear what would happen if they didn't.

It was cute that Donna had invited him to play pool. Clearly, she'd put some time into thinking of an activity they could do that would give them something to talk about. And after last night's disastrous date, he was very grateful. Even to the point that he planned to only win by a few points so as not to dent her spirits.

"Okay then, if you're sure." She smiled before she placed her hand on his shoulder, rose on tiptoe and kissed his jaw. He felt the heat from her palm rush through his veins, making his blood boil. Her sweet, soft lips made him want to wrap his arm around her waist and pull her closer.

He felt her tremble as she moved away from him and felt a deep satisfaction in knowing he wasn't the only one affected by the touch. Although, it bothered him that she'd given the same chaste kiss to the restaurant owner the night before. It made him want to go back there and punch him all over again. Those kisses belonged to him, and no one else.

She glanced at him as she headed around the table to line up her shot. "One game and then we talk, right?"

"Aye."

"Uh-oh," one of their watchers said, "when a woman says she wants to talk, it's time to run."

There was laughter, but Duncan ignored it, keeping his eyes glued to Donna. She bent over the table, giving him a perfect view right down her top. His mouth watered at the sight of all that soft, creamy skin encased in violet lace. His hand tingled at the memory of how her breast had felt in his hold, and he shifted uncomfortably as he wondered again why they were playing pool instead of spending their time in bed.

"Duncan? Are you looking down my top?"

"Aye," he said hoarsely. There was no point denying it.

Her position didn't change as she looked up at him. "Did I give you permission?"

It took a few seconds for the words to sink in. He threw his hands in the air as he moved to the side of the table. "Damn it to hell! I hate dating."

"Trust me," Donna said. "It's no fun for me either."

He heard more laughter at her dry comment and was about to deal with their onlookers when Donna took her shot. His jaw dropped, and he stilled. His woman was no novice at the game. She flashed a knowing smile at him as she sashayed around the table in those jeans that made him want to beg for mercy. She didn't miss one shot after that, and all he could do was stand there gaping while she wiped the floor with him. He never even got a chance to play. Ten minutes after the game had started, Donna had cleared the table and finished her Coke.

She placed her cue on the rack and nodded at Ewan. "Can I have another Coke? Is that allowed?"

"Smart arse," the man muttered as he reached for a glass.

Duncan was still staring at the table, wondering what had happened, when she took his arm. "Let's go sit down."

"But." He pointed at the table. "But."

All around him, people whooped with delight. He glared at Ewan. "You knew she was a pool shark. Why didn't you warn me?"

"And miss out on all the fun?"

He didn't get a chance to argue back because Donna was dragging him for a change—right towards a high-backed booth at the rear of the room. Obviously, she needed privacy for their 'talk.'

Lord help him.

CHAPTER 21

She probably should have told him she could play pool. In her experience, men didn't like it when they were humiliated in public, especially when it came to sport. But to be honest, it had been too much fun to ruin with a confession.

"Where did you learn to play like that?" Duncan said as he —thankfully—slid into the booth facing her instead of beside her. She needed whatever distance she could get for their conversation.

"Church youth group." She smiled at his shocked expression. "They had a pool table, and I discovered I had a knack for the game. I used my skill to make some extra cash for us when we needed it." She didn't tell him about the many hair-raising times she'd had to run from Glasgow pubs after fleecing the customers. She'd been lucky to escape with her life.

Of course, Duncan heard the things she didn't say. As he was wont to do. "Who was watching your back in the pubs?"

"Aggie." Mairi had been too young and Isobel had the kids.

He shook his head. "It's a miracle the four of you are still in one piece."

"Or, you could say it's wonderful the way we have each other's backs."

"That too." His lips quirked, and when he looked over at her, his eyes were sparkling. "Next time we play, I want you to teach me that trick shot of yours."

"The one that bounces behind the other balls?"

"That's the one. It was a thing of beauty."

She blushed at the compliment as Ewan came over and placed her drink in front of her. "Don't get any ideas that I'm your waitress for the night. Next time get your arse to the bar."

"You know," Donna said. "I think people would be hard-pressed to decide who was the most bad-tempered between the two of you."

"Him," both men said at the same time as they pointed at each other.

Donna laughed at the looks of horror on their faces. With a huff of irritation, Ewan stomped back behind his bar.

"What is it you want to talk to me about?" Duncan's eyes were on hers as he sipped his Coke.

His hair was tousled from running his hand through it, his shirt was a tad too tight across his wide shoulders, and his jeans were moulded to thighs that made her mouth water. This was part of the problem. If Duncan had looked like Danny DeVito, they wouldn't be sitting here right now. Sure, she would have cared for him, and worried about him, but she wouldn't be lusting after him with every cell in her body.

"Well, then?" He leaned back in his seat, folded his arms and gave her a look that practically dared her to say something he didn't like.

There was no getting around it. Things had to be stopped between them before they both got hurt. She rubbed her temples. Who was she kidding? They had to be stopped before *she* got hurt.

Donna stared down at the table, knowing she couldn't say what she had to while looking at him. "I don't think we should do this."

"Play pool? Drink Coke?"

She frowned at him, knowing full well he was being deliberately obtuse. *"This."* She motioned between them. "The physical stuff."

Relaxed, he reached out to pick up his drink. Of course, he wasn't bothered. She meant nothing to him.

Stop feeling sorry for yourself, Hermione appeared beside Duncan to admonish her. *You knew he was still in love with his wife before you ever touched him. You have only yourself to blame for this mess.* She stuck her nose in the air. *You should have listened to me in the first place.*

"Go away," Donna hissed.

Her eyes shot to Duncan, and she turned red. There was just no end to her humiliation.

"Who was it this time?" Duncan asked as though they were talking about the weather.

Donna drew patterns in the condensation her glass had left on the tabletop. "Hermione. She's a know-it-all who constantly sticks her nose in where it isn't wanted."

"In other words, she thinks you're an idiot for breaking up with me too."

"What?" She sat up straight. "I'm not breaking up with you. We don't have a relationship. We have one kiss and... what happened earlier, between us. That doesn't constitute a relationship."

"The words you're looking for are *screaming orgasm.*"

Ewan walked past their table as Duncan spoke. "Neither one of you is getting anything with alcohol in it, so you can put those fancy cocktails right out of your heads."

He carried on, leaving Donna's face burning as she looked into Duncan's amused eyes.

Duncan leaned forwards, resting his forearms on the table. "You seemed to enjoy your orgasm, Angel. Is there a reason you want to stop at one? Because I have a hankering to see how many I can wring out of you before you pass out from exhaustion."

There were no words. All she could do was stare at him as her mouth opened and closed and her body screamed at her to take him up on his offer.

"There you are." A voice cut into her shock, and she turned to see Flora and Joyce heading straight for them. "Grace said we'd find you here."

They charged at her, a look of determination in their eyes. From the direction they were approaching, they couldn't see Duncan, as he sat facing her with his back to them, shielded by the high booth partition. All they could see was Donna and the look of utter panic she knew must have been on her face.

"We need to talk to you about—" Joyce said, slamming her walker down on the floor as she made her way towards them.

"Duncan!" Donna pointed at him.

Joyce missed the gesture, too busy concentrating on her walker. "Not about him. You deal with him. We need to talk about—"

It was Flora who spotted Duncan first, and she put a hand on Joyce's arm to stop her. "About the chickens," she said over the top of whatever her partner in crime was about to say.

"Chickens?" Donna's voice went up an octave and her palms began to sweat. She slid them under the table and tried to wipe them on her jeans without Duncan noticing.

Flora came to a stop beside their table, her back was

straight, and she wore a peach coloured twinset over a grey skirt. Her grey hair was perfectly styled and her smooth cheeks were rosy. She looked like she'd walked straight off a Christmas card.

"Hello." She smiled at Duncan. "You must be Mr Stewart. I've heard so much about you. You're a wonderful artist. The community is lucky to have you here."

She held out a hand to Duncan, and Donna held her breath as she waited to see if he'd shake it. She let out a quiet sigh of relief when he did.

"You look familiar," he said to Flora.

She patted her hair and gave him a benevolent smile. "You've probably seen me around the place. I do a lot of volunteer work. It can take me to the strangest places."

Duncan studied her, and Donna began to panic. The man's mind was like a vault. He remembered most things he saw.

"So, ladies," she said a little too loudly. "What about the chickens?"

Joyce glared at Duncan for a minute before narrowing her eyes at him. "I'm Joyce MacDonald. My husband died ten months ago, and I'm over it already."

Donna lifted her eyes to heaven. *Please just hit me with lightning,* she prayed.

Flora elbowed Joyce.

"Elbows!" Joyce snapped as she rubbed her side.

This situation was quickly deteriorating. Donna pushed out of the booth, making the women back up. "Duncan and I were just leaving. What did you need to tell me about the chickens?" She cast a glance at Duncan, who was studying the three of them intently.

"Um." Flora and Joyce shared a look before Flora turned back to Donna. "Well, you know how we ordered eighty chickens?"

Donna nodded, she well remembered that they'd sworn there would be eighty people maximum coming to the ball. The room would hold seventy comfortably. Eighty was pushing it, but they'd make it work.

"Well," Flora licked her lips. "It seems there was a mix-up with the order. We have almost one hundred and twenty chickens being delivered this Saturday, and we don't have the fridge space for them. We need your help to squeeze them in."

Donna felt the blood rush from her head and had to put a hand on the table to steady herself. One hundred and twenty? She tried to stare holes through the heads of the women who were giving her an ulcer. They didn't notice. Or if they did, they didn't care. She suspected it was the latter.

"Aye," Joyce nodded, looking at Duncan. "We've started a new charity called Chickens for Old People, and Donna's been helping us with it." She looked around, obviously searching for something else to say. "Donna likes chicken," was what she came up with.

"I thought Donna was a vegetarian," Duncan drawled.

"She likes *live* chickens," Joyce amended. "She pets them."

"You can't fit *live* chickens into your fridges?" Duncan said.

"Don't be daft," Joyce snapped. "It would be cruel to put live chickens in a fridge. We'll kill them first. But don't worry. Donna won't be around for that part. She'll just cuddle them first. Flora catches the chickens and I, you know, *dispose* of them." She leaned towards Duncan. "You can't chase a chicken when you're using a walker—they're fast wee buggers."

"Stop talking," Flora hissed through a fake smile.

"What?" Joyce demanded. "We ordered live instead of frozen because they're cheaper that way," she told Duncan. "A charity has to watch its pennies."

Donna held up a hand. It took all of her self-control not to slap it over Joyce's mouth to stop the drivel pouring out.

"A hundred and twenty chickens? Really?" She glared at them. "We talked about this, and we agreed you only needed eighty—at most. We can't fit any more in the fridges, so you need to cut the numbers."

"But we can't." Flora cast a nervous glance Duncan's way. "People are expecting their chicken. We can't disappoint them. We just have to figure out how to get the other forty into the fridges."

"It isn't possible," Donna said through clenched teeth. If they had one hundred and twenty in the ballroom, it wouldn't be a ball, because there would be no space to dance.

"We have an idea for that," Flora said, casting a glance at Duncan. "That's why we were looking for you. To talk about the idea."

"You didn't answer your phone," Joyce reprimanded.

"I was playing pool."

"Did you win?" Flora said.

Donna just looked at them. She wasn't going to answer any stupid questions.

"Of course she won." Joyce rolled her eyes. "Anyway, we need to talk about the chickens." She looked at Duncan, then back at Donna. "When's a good time? And remember, we're on a tight schedule here. Chicken goes off easily."

"Live chickens go off?" Duncan said.

"Did I say *go* off? I meant *run* off. We need to get them in the fridges before they escape. Isn't that right, Flora?"

Flora looked at the ceiling. Donna thought she might be praying.

CHAPTER 22

"You want to tell me what that whole chicken conversation was about?" Duncan said as he drove them back to the house. "Because there's no way it was about chickens."

"It was about…none of your business." She flushed a deep red and looked at him with a mixture of defiance and trepidation that made him feel kind of proud. This new Donna wasn't a woman you could walk over easily, which meant she'd be much safer around the conmen in town.

"Then do you want to tell me what all that crap about breaking up with me was?"

Her hands trembled as she wedged them between her knees. "You and I are a bad idea."

"No, we're an excellent idea." One he liked better every minute he was around her.

"When it all goes wrong, I'll be out of a job and a home, and I'll have to buy a car."

He shrugged. "That's assuming it goes wrong. In the meantime, you're welcome to sign the contract. The whole point of adding all the extra clauses was to stop you from freaking out about the future."

"What do you mean 'assuming it goes wrong'? Of course it's going to go wrong. There's nowhere else for this to go!"

"And I thought you were the more positive one out of the two of us."

He turned in to a quiet road that had Donna looking around them. "Where are we going? The mansion's back that way."

"I need a break from the mansion. Sometimes I feel more like the crypt keeper than the owner. I thought we'd sit at the viewpoint overlooking the bluff and have this talk."

That seemed to agitate her. "Aren't you hungry? It's nearly dinnertime. We should get back, or whatever cook is making will spoil."

"She can hold dinner for an hour."

Donna sank back into her seat, defeated. The sight tugged at the heart he thought had died along with Fiona.

"You can cope with an hour in my company, can't you?" To his surprise, he found he was nervous about her answer.

"I suppose," she huffed out ungraciously, making him grin.

"I love the enthusiasm. Makes me feel warm inside."

That earned him a glare, which ironically, made him beam at her. She was adorable and sexy as hell. It was an unusual combination, but one that seemed to work for her, and definitely did something for him.

He pulled the car to a stop in the small parking area at the edge of the bluff. There was no one else there, and all that was between them and the Firth of Clyde was a weathered bench.

The sky was cloudy, and the water had turned a murky green. Duncan unfastened his seatbelt. "Come on, let's sit outside."

"It's cold and I don't have a jacket with me."

"Don't worry, Angel, I'll keep you warm."

As she reached for her door, he heard her mutter, "That's what I'm worried about."

By the time he reached the other side of the car, she was already climbing out to meet him. He took her hand and slowly walked—*not* dragged—her to the bench.

She sat down facing the water and Duncan straddled the bench beside her. He tugged her into the V of his legs, hooking her legs over one of his, and wrapping his arms around her. "Is that better? You're no' too cold?"

"No." She hesitated for a second before she snuggled into him.

She fit perfectly in his arms. Fiona had been a tall, slender woman, whereas Donna was a tiny, curved bundle. Her size brought out the protective streak in him—that and the way her kind heart made her a target for everyone around her.

Fiona had been totally different in that respect, her big-city upbringing meant she could see through a liar within seconds, and she'd had no problem dealing with them either. She'd toss her hair, look down her nose and shut them down with an icy word or two. And she'd been spectacular when she did it. Donna, on the other hand, needed a keeper, preferably someone who could scare away anyone who'd take advantage of her—and he was just the man for the job.

"Are you going to tell me what's bothering you?" he asked as he nuzzled the top of her head with his chin.

She was silent for a while and then said, "No."

He burst out laughing, his arms tightening around her as she scowled up at him.

"I've created a monster," he said. "One who has no trouble saying no to me."

Her look of shock was quickly followed by a smug little smile. It warmed his soul to see her so pleased with herself. They sat quietly, watching the waves as the sky darkened with the threat of rain.

"If you're no' going to tell me what's wrong, how about you sing me a song?"

She arched an eyebrow at him as her eyes sparkled with mischief. "I'm not sure you're sophisticated enough to appreciate my musical stylings."

"That can't be right. I'm a well-respected artist, top of my field. I've got culture coming out of my a—" She slapped a hand over his mouth, and he laughed behind it.

"I'll sing for you, if you'll do something for me," she said as she dropped her hand.

"A trade. I can do that. What do you want? Another orgasm? I'd be happy to provide one for you." He waited for the familiar blush to paint her cheeks pink.

"You're terrible," she admonished as her eyelashes lowered, taking her eyes from his.

That was something else that was different from Fiona. His wife had been hard to shock, and she'd had no problem talking about sex. But his Donna was shy.

He kissed her head. "Tell me what you want then."

"You have to answer whatever question I ask."

"Okay then."

Her eyebrows shot up. "Aren't you worried what I might ask you?"

"If you didnae blush at the mere thought of sex, then aye, I might be worried, but I think whatever you ask me will probably be tame."

She smacked him on the chest.

"First you start telling me no, now you're hitting me. What's next? Imprisoning me in a tower?"

"You'd deserve it." She stuck her wee nose in the air. "You're hell to live with."

There was no arguing with that. "Where's my song?"

"Fine." She let out a sigh and pushed away from him to sit up straight.

He expected her to look around to see if anyone was nearby, but she didn't. She just opened her mouth and belted out a tune. Well, that's what he assumed it was supposed to be. It was kind of hard to tell because it was nothing like any other music he'd heard in his lifetime. The notes seemed to be on a sliding scale only Donna understood, and every time she sang the chorus, the tune was different. It was painfully bad. The kind of bad that could be used to torture terrorists into surrendering.

When she'd finished, she looked at him expectantly as he tried to decide whether to react honestly or to go for something vague and neutral that wouldn't get him killed in his sleep.

"Well?" she demanded. "What did you think?"

"I can honestly say that I've never heard anything like that before."

She narrowed her eyes at him. "And is that good, or bad?"

"Well, it was an experience, that's for sure." He paused before throwing caution to the wind. "That high note you hit was almost out of human range. I'm fairly certain there are dogs in Campbeltown howling right now, trying to get to you. I especially liked the Middle Eastern, Indian, Martian thing you had going on with the scales. Most people stick to do, ri, me, but you had the guts to try something different, and I applaud it."

"That is just mean." She frowned at him, but her eyes were dancing. "I have a good mind to—"

"What? Beat me with your teeny-tiny baby fists?"

"That's it!"

She shoved him hard, right in the middle of his chest. He presumed she was trying to topple him back off the bench. All she did was make him laugh.

"Stop laughing when I'm attacking you," she snapped, which made him laugh harder.

Before he realised what she was doing, her fingers latched onto his nipple and she twisted.

"Argh! That hurts. Stop it." He grabbed her hands.

"How's that for a wee tiny baby hand?" she said triumphantly.

It was like wrestling with a kitten. "How would you like it if I twisted your nipple?"

As soon as the words were out of his mouth, they both stilled. Donna's eyes darkened, and the tip of her tongue flicked out to wet her lips.

"You drive me crazy," he told her.

He didn't wait for an answer, he just cupped the back of her head and pulled her mouth to his.

* * *

KISSING DUNCAN WAS EVEN BETTER than eating bacon. Her two vices had a lot in common: they were hard to resist and bad for her heart. Unfortunately, when she was indulging, she found she didn't care about the consequences. She only cared about how wonderful it felt right then, and she never wanted it to end.

Duncan's kiss wasn't timid, and there was no hesitation. He held her firmly, moved her where he needed her to be, and took what he wanted—while giving far more in return. With previous men, there had always been a part of her that she held back, worrying about what she should be doing and if she was doing things right. Not with Duncan. With him, there was no anxiety about the act—he made it very clear what he wanted—and all she had to do was relax and let him take her where he wanted her to go.

It was bliss.

She wrapped her arms around his neck, and his fingers grasped her hair, using it to angle her mouth the way he wanted. She moaned against his lips, deciding confidence was sexier than looks any day of the year. Although, God hadn't skimped with looks when it came to Duncan either, which meant she got the best of everything.

"You taste like heaven," he said against her mouth, before his tongue delved deep—tasting, learning, teasing, dominating.

Her bones turned to jelly in his arms as her mind spiralled in a tornado of desire. She felt light-headed. Her skin ultra-sensitive. The world around them faded until it was just the two of them, locked in a sensual cocoon.

A hand slid under her top and skimmed up her back, sending shivers of sensation in its wake. She moaned and pressed closer to him, feeling the strength of his chest and arms enfold her. Feeling safe and protected. As though he'd made a place for her where she could let go completely, never fearing, because he would be there to watch over her. It was a heady delight that captured her senses.

She felt like she was falling into him, losing herself in him. The mundane details of life that forced her to attend to them, to focus on them, and the things that kept her chained to the world—they all disappeared, leaving only sensation. The sound of their breaths merging, the taste of his lips and tongue, and the rasp of his teeth. The scent of musk, and hunger, and need.

Her skin felt hot. Like she was flying too close to the sun. She was soaring, losing herself in his kiss. In the touch on her back. In the pressure of his hand in her hair. She was losing herself in Duncan.

"If you two don't stop it, I'm gonna fetch a bucket of water and pour it over you."

The words jerked Donna out of her daze, and she clung to Duncan. Feeling confused and vulnerable. His arms tightened around her as his body tensed and surrounded her, protecting her from whoever had spoken.

"This is not the place for that sort of thing," a woman said. "Get yourselves away from here and do that in the privacy of your own bedroom."

"Aye," a man snapped. "You're setting a bad example for the weans."

"What weans?" Duncan said. "There's only the two of you standing around gawking at us."

"Connie," the man said. "Get your phone out and call the grandkids. We'll have them up here in no time, then we'll see who thinks there are no weans around."

Donna giggled as she peeked out of Duncan's hold to see two tiny old people, wrapped up in winter coats, scarves and hats. She guessed they hadn't got the memo that it was spring either. The man had puffed out his chest and was glaring at Duncan. Donna giggled again. Even if the couple stood on each other's shoulders, they still wouldn't be big enough to take him on.

"Come on," Duncan said on a sigh. "Let's go home."

He lifted her and placed her on her feet before swinging his leg over the bench and standing beside her. He wrapped an arm around Donna's shoulders and walked her to the car.

When he passed the old couple, he paused. "The bench is all yours. See if you can beat our record." He glanced at his watch. "Over half an hour. Good luck."

The man started to bluster as Duncan opened the car for Donna and helped her in.

"The grandkids are coming," the woman said as she put her phone back in her pocket. "Now what?" She'd obviously missed Duncan's comment.

Her husband turned to her, and his face went beetroot red. "We're no' kissing like teenagers if that's what you're thinking. That necking stuff isn't contagious."

Duncan slammed her door shut, and Donna missed his wife's reply. Which was a shame, because the look on her face promised something priceless.

With a shake of his head, Duncan put the car in gear and took off down the road. Donna was still smiling about the old couple when he spoke.

"What was the question I had to answer in exchange for the song?"

A dull pain settled in her heart. "I'll ask you later." And she reached for his hand and held it tight.

When he pulled up in front of the mansion, Duncan turned off the engine, then leaned forwards to rest his arms over the steering wheel. He looked at the building he'd come to view more as a prison than a home, and part of him didn't want to go inside. Out on the bluff, with Donna in his arms, he'd felt light and carefree. He knew that as soon as he walked through that door, he'd feel the weight of his responsibilities to Fiona bear down on him.

He felt Donna's timid touch on his thigh and looked over to see compassion on her face. There were moments, times like this, when he could have sworn she was able to read his mind.

"Have you been inside the carriage house yet?" she said. "The builders finished it yesterday."

"No, I can't say that I have."

"Why don't we go have a look?"

He nodded and restarted the car, driving past the mansion around to the back and out to where the carriage house sat. The small building was built in the same style as the main house, so it was basically a smaller grey cube with windows. Except, the three old wooden doors on the front of the building had been replaced by glass, turning them into large arched windows.

Duncan parked by the side door and followed Donna. She smiled at him before letting them into the house.

"All Fiona's plans stated for the carriage house was that she wanted it turned into guest accommodation," Donna said as she led him into the large open-plan space. "Since it was an empty shell, there weren't any original features to work with, so we kept it simple."

Duncan walked into the middle of the room. The arched windows sat at the front of the building, with the living area, kitchen and dining in front of them. Behind that were three doors, leading to the back of the building. The walls were painted a pale yellow, and the furnishings were dark wood with white accents and yellow cushions. The space was bright, airy and—although still classical—much more modern than the main house.

Donna walked over to one of the doors. "There are two bedrooms, each with its own bathroom." She opened the door wide for him to look inside. The room was decorated in white and sailor blue. She pointed to the middle door. "That's a small bathroom and laundry."

Her shy gaze met his. "What do you think?"

He could tell by the stiffness of her shoulders that she was nervous about his reaction. He didn't know why as she'd gone over the basic plans with him and he'd told her to do what she liked. The result was something Fiona would have approved of, and something that also appealed to him. She'd managed to find the perfect middle ground between his and his wife's tastes.

"I think it's perfect." He reached for her hand. "Truth be told, I'd rather live here than in the mansion."

Her cheeks flushed at his praise.

"Do *you* like it?"

She nodded. "I love it." She gave him a wicked look. "I was going to try to talk you into letting me move out of the housekeeper's apartment and into here."

He cocked an eyebrow at her.

"Yeah, I didn't think it would work."

He tugged her to him. "Oh, I don't know. I think I could be persuaded." His eyes caught hers, and he spotted the moment when she became aware that there was a large bed in the room behind her.

She nervously bit at her lip. "Cook made dinner. You must be hungry."

"Aye." He backed her into the room. "I'm starving." He closed the door gently behind him. "But not for food."

Her cheeks were glowing now, and her lips were berry-red from the kisses they'd shared on the bluff. He smoothed her hair away from her face, aware that his girl was shy when it came to anything sexual.

"Would you like to get into that bed with me, Donna?" he asked.

Sparkling eyes looked up at him. "I'm not very tired, Duncan."

He fought back his smile. "Neither am I, but I'm thinking there might be other things we could do in that bed."

She cocked her head at him, her eyes going wide with feigned innocence. "Massage? Read? Watch TV?"

He hooked a finger into the neck of her top and pulled her closer. "Those are good too. We can do those later."

"Well, what would you like to do in the meantime?" Her hands flattened on his chest and the look she gave him almost brought him to his knees.

"What I really want to do"—he reached for the bottom of her shirt—"is get you out of these clothes and make you more comfortable."

"You think I'm uncomfortable?"

He slowly peeled the top over her head and tossed it onto a blue-and-white-striped armchair that sat nearby. The sight before him was a feast for a hungry man. Plump, ripe globes encased in violet lace.

He traced a finger over the curve of her breasts. "Is it a matching set?"

"Why don't you have a look?" Her hands curled on his arms.

"I think that's a rare idea." He unhooked the button of her jeans and slid the zip down. All day long those jeans had been driving him crazy. It would give him great pleasure to peel them from her.

"My boots," she reminded him as he slid her jeans over her hips.

"I think this would work better if you sat on the bed." Not giving her time to reply, he just swept her up into his arms and sat her down, dropping to his knees in front of her. "That's better."

He found the zippers and dispensed with her boots. Sparkly purple toenails rewarded him for his efforts, and he smiled.

"Why am I the only one getting undressed here?" Donna said on a pout. It was cute, and she couldn't quite pull it off, but he appreciated the effort.

"You don't expect me to undress myself, do you? I mean, I'm helping you. The least you can do is return the favour."

With a wide smile, she reached for the buttons on his shirt then stilled. His heart missed a beat with the fear that she'd changed her mind.

"Duncan? How many tartan shirts do you own?"

He looked at her, figuring she would know better than he did. "A lot." He tended to find one thing that worked and then stick to it, and that way he didn't have to think about what to wear.

"Then you won't miss this one, will you?" She grabbed each side of his shirt and tugged.

The buttons flew off, pinging around the room, and Donna grinned at him. "I've always wanted to do that."

He could do nothing other than laugh. "Well, I'm pleased I could help."

With her eyes on his, she opened each one of the buttons on his Levi's.

"Don't you want to check to see whether I'm a boxers or a briefs man?"

"Duncan, I do your laundry. The cleaners are too scared to go into your rooms."

"Well, that just takes the mystery out of this relationship."

Something dark flickered in her eyes before she smiled again. "Kick off your shoes for me."

"My pleasure." He stood, his eyes eating her up as he did as she'd asked. "My turn now." Things were going far too slowly for his liking.

Placing a hand in the middle of her chest, he pressed her back until she was lying on the bed looking up at him. His hands went to her hips, he hooked his thumbs into the waistband of her jeans and pulled them down. And lost the ability to speak. A small triangle of matching violet lace barely covered her mound.

He fell to his knees in front of her as he finished removing her jeans and tossed them to the side. His hands slid up her creamy thighs, feeling the tremors he left in his wake. Her breath hitched, and she began to squirm.

"Lie still now," he commanded her.

Her eyes darkened, and the pink blush of her cheeks spread down to her upper chest. He clasped the thin straps of lace that curved over her hips and slid his fingers under them, shimmying her underwear down to her ankles.

"Duncan?" She was already panting, and he hadn't even touched her yet.

Donna Sinclair could make a man feel like he was ten feet tall.

"Hush now," he said as he clasped the inside of her thighs and spread her legs. "A man needs to eat to keep up his strength."

"Oh crap, I'm never going to survive this."

He looked his fill, taking in her plump, pink, wet and ready flesh. He'd been right, the colour of her lips was an accent throughout her body. Slowly, he lowered his head and licked her length. She arched off the bed with a long wail, and his hands clasped onto her hips to keep her in place.

"I was wrong," he said. "I thought your kisses were the most addictive thing I'd ever taste." And then he licked her again.

As he listened to her moans and pleas and felt her fingers tugging at his hair, Duncan took his time enjoying her. He never wanted it to end.

* * *

SHE WAS GOING to pass out. Seriously. She'd heard it could happen, but she'd thought it was an urban myth. Until Duncan and his wonder tongue. Within seconds he'd delivered the screaming orgasm he'd promised in the pub.

"I bloody love the sounds you make," he muttered, before starting all over again.

"I can't take any more," she wailed.

"Oh, aye, you can. I have a hankering to find out just how many times I can make you come in one night." He kissed her inner thigh. "Buckle in, Angel, this is going to be fun."

She just groaned. And then she felt his fingers slip inside of her as his tongue went to work on her clit. Stars exploded inside her mind as her breath came out in desperate pants.

Don't come, don't come, don't come...

"Chanting won't help you," he said with a smile against her sensitive nub.

She hadn't realised she'd been saying it out loud. All she wanted was to hold out for as long as possible, or Duncan's ego would be impossible to live with.

"I'm not going to come," she shouted.

"We'll see about that." And then his fingers found the turbo button inside of her, and she went off like a rocket.

She came back to earth to see a naked, grinning Duncan poised above her.

"You were saying?" he said.

"I hate you," she complained as she ran her hands over his hips, up his sides and around to his pecs. She played with the smattering of hair in the middle of his chest before running her fingertips over his abs. "Never stop working out," she said in wonder at the sight before her.

The chuckling brought her attention back to his face.

"Damn, you're beautiful," he said before his mouth met hers in a kiss that stole what little breath she had left.

She kneaded his back, working her way down until she reached his backside. A groan of ecstasy escaped her at the feel of his taut behind in her hands.

"I need you," she whispered against his mouth.

"I need you too." But she saw hesitation in his dark gaze. Trepidation. And then it hit her, and her ardour cooled. As far as she knew, he hadn't been with anyone since his wife. This was a big step for him. Giving up another part of himself that he'd kept just for Fiona. Her heart split in two at the thought. He truly did still belong to his wife. His heart, his body, his soul.

"You don't need to do this, Duncan. I understand."

He brushed her hair back from her face. "You are a mystery to me, with that soft heart of yours. You can't help but worry about everyone around you, can you?"

"I won't be upset if we stop." She wanted him to see the truth in her eyes. She wouldn't hurt him for anything. And if that meant he couldn't give himself to her physically, then she was okay with that.

His lips captured hers, sipping at them softly before his tongue snuck out to trace the outline of her mouth. Her fingers tightened on his backside, pulling him to her.

"I'm sorry." She moved her hands up to his shoulders.

"Never, Angel. Never be sorry for wanting me." His kiss was ferocious in its intensity this time, sweeping her away in a maelstrom of desire.

And then she felt the soft crown of his shaft press into her, and she sucked in a breath. "Duncan, condom."

He stilled. "I forgot. I never used them…" He looked away from her.

She cupped his cheek and brought his face back around. "With Fiona. You never used them with your wife. You can talk about her." She smiled, although her heart was shattering. "I've been living with her memory these past few years too, and I don't resent the comparison. She must have been a wonderful woman for you to have loved her so very much."

"Hell," he hissed as his forehead met hers. "You humble me."

"I don't want to humble you, Duncan. I want to…" *Love you.* She wanted to love him, but those were words she would never be able to say. "I want to make you feel good, the way you've made me feel. That's all. We can stop if you like. I really do understand."

He kissed the tip of her nose. "I don't want to stop. Let me get something to protect you." He twisted away from her and climbed from the bed.

"The protection charm Molly gave me is in my pocket," she said.

He shook his head with a smile, which was exactly what she'd intended. A few seconds later, he was sheathed and walking towards her.

"Brace yourself," he said with a smile. "I'm going in."

She spread her legs wide and closed her eyes. "Do what you must. I'll just lie here and think of England."

His laughter poured into her heart and made it feel like it would overflow with love for him.

"You do that," he said. "Because I need to spend a minute or two warming you up again."

"A minute or two?" That seemed a bit scant.

"You're right. With the way you go off, we'll only need thirty seconds."

She smacked his shoulder as he bent over and sucked her nipple.

"Oh!" She gasped, threading her fingers through his hair and holding him to her. Her legs bent, and her knees clutched his hips, as though trying to pull him closer.

His tongue made circles around her nipple and she couldn't help but moan. He sucked her hard before releasing her with a pop. "I'd better do the other one too. We wouldn't want you to be uneven."

She couldn't speak. All she could do was push her breasts out towards him. With a chuckle, he gave her other breast the same attention.

"I could play with these for hours," he said reverently. "I wonder if I could make you come just by teasing these wee nipples. I bet I could."

"Duncan!" He was taking far too long, and she needed

him inside her. She felt empty without him and more than a little desperate to feel his hard length filling her.

"Shh, it's okay. I know what you need."

She felt him press against her entrance, and her eyes flew open to find him staring down at her.

"You are amazing," he told her before taking her lips.

He kissed her deep as he surged inside her. She ripped her mouth from his. "Yes!"

"Aye," he agreed.

And then he raised up on his arms above her and started to move. "Perfect. So. Damn. Perfect." He ground the words out.

Donna was lost to him. And although she knew she was gasping in air, she felt as though she was holding her breath to the point of becoming light-headed.

"More?" he growled.

"More. More. More. More. More."

He leaned down and bit her bottom lip. She curled her legs around him, pushing him deeper.

"You goin' tae come with me, Angel?"

All she could do was gasp.

"Aye, I think you are."

He changed the angle of his thrusts and hit the spot that made her body melt and then burst into flames. She screamed his name as she came, clenching down on his hard length. Needing all of him, she held him tight—never wanting to let him go.

With a groan, he found his own release and slumped on top of her. "I'll move in a second. I don't want to crush you."

"Stay," she whispered. She liked his weight pressing her into the bed.

She could feel their hearts racing against each other and hear their breaths as they mingled. His skin felt hot against hers, and his scent engulfed her. He felt wonderful. He felt like home.

His lips found her throat, and he kissed her. "Let me deal with this."

She couldn't help but moan as he slid out of her.

"I like that sound," he said. "I have a hankering to hear a lot more of it."

He headed for the bathroom, and Donna stayed where she was. There was no energy to move. He chuckled at the sight of her when he came back into the room.

"My wee Angel is spent." He climbed onto the bed, tugging her to his side before pulling the duvet up over them. "Time for a nap before round two." He gave her a cocky smile. "Or in your case, is it round four hundred?"

She managed to find the energy to poke him in the ribs. "You're just jealous because you're a 'once and done' man."

"I'm too old and tired to take issue with that right now, but after a rest, I'll show you who's once and done."

Donna smiled and then pressed a kiss to his chest. She loved seeing him like this: funny, self-effacing, and sexy as hell. He'd come a long way from the man she'd rescued from the driveway.

But, he still wasn't hers.

When she looked up at him, he'd closed his eyes. A little voice in her head told her not to do what she planned, to let sleeping dogs lie and enjoy the present, the future would bring enough trouble when it came. But she couldn't do it. She had to ask the question that had been eating her up.

"Duncan, can you answer my question now?"

"Mmm," he said sleepily, "it had better not be how long a thirty-eight-year-old man takes to recover for round two."

"No." She propped herself up on her elbow to look at him, memorising every line on his face and the strong cut of his jaw. Her stomach lurched as she opened her mouth to speak.

"What I want to know is, do you think you could ever love someone other than Fiona?"

He went taut beneath her touch and his eyes flew open. "Why would you ask me something like that? Ask me another question—one I can answer."

Donna forced a smile as a dull ache spread like a fungus through her body, contaminating everything it touched. "You're right. That was a dumb question." And he'd already given her his answer in telling her to pick another. "I'm too tired to think of another one right now. Can I have a rain check on my side of the deal?"

"Aye." He sank back into the bed, wrapped an arm around her back and pulled her into his side. "Let's get some sleep. You've knackered me out."

She could hear the smile in his voice as she pressed her cheek to his chest. "I'm exhausted too, sleep sounds good."

"No' for too long, mind. I have plans for you."

She tried to keep her voice light as her throat tightened around her words. "I thought you were leaving early for Glasgow. You need to be rested for the drive."

"I'm heading out late morning, so we've plenty of time left for round two. Now go to sleep."

His thumb stroked her side until he fell asleep. Donna lay there, listening to his steady breathing and feeling the beat of his heart under her cheek. She felt as though her own heart had been weighed down with standing stones. The dull, low throb of agony made her feel like she could sink through the floor and into the very earth beneath her, where it would press in on her until she lost the ability to breathe. The relentless pressure against her heart and soul crushing her into dust.

With his refusal to answer her question, Duncan had confirmed that there was no space in his heart for anyone but his wife. All he would ever be able to offer her was affection, and a touch to ease the lonely nights. She suspected it might have been enough for her—if she hadn't already fallen in love with him. Now, it felt like exactly what it was: Fiona's leftovers.

As she stared out at the night sky, she realised that her fate was sealed. Agnes was right, there was no way she could stay at the mansion, pining after a man who was constrained in what he was able to give her. A relationship with Duncan, of any kind, would always be unequal. She would always want more, and he would always be unable to give it to her.

It would be agony.

She had to leave and find another job. And it was clear she couldn't stay to work out her notice. As soon as the ball was over, she'd pack up and move in with Agnes. It would be best for both her and Duncan. Then, maybe, he could find another woman that would sleep with him and enjoy his friendship, without ever wanting his heart. She knew one thing for certain: she wasn't that woman.

She angled her head to look up at him. Even in sleep, he was formidable. So beautiful, and yet so broken. She could only imagine the agony of having your soulmate and then losing them, leaving you ripped in two and forever yearning.

Tomorrow, he would leave for Glasgow, and he wouldn't come back until after the ball. By then, she'd be gone. It didn't matter whether she spent the rest of the night touching him or not, either way, it would tear her apart to leave.

But she would take the few hours she had left with him. Because, even though she knew it was the foolish thing to do, she wanted to sleep in the arms of the man she loved. Before she left him forever.

CHAPTER 24

"Has he gone then?" Grace asked Donna as she came into the kitchen for lunch the following day.

"He just left, and he won't be back until late on Saturday. He's having dinner with the dean tomorrow night, after he teaches." Which was good, because as he sat down to eat in Glasgow, his house in Kintyre would be full of strangers.

She slipped into the booth and looked out the window to the immaculate estate grounds. There was no doubt she'd miss the place, but her sisters were right, she hadn't stayed in the job because she loved the mansion, she'd stayed because she loved Duncan.

Holding two mugs of tea, Grace slipped into the seat facing her. "Food will be ready in five minutes. We've got time for a cuppa."

Donna accepted the drink gratefully. "We might as well enjoy the peace while we can. The institute women will be here after lunch to set up."

"It's not the set-up I'm worried about. It's the clean-up afterwards."

"I've hired a cleaning crew," Donna said. "They'll be here first thing Saturday morning."

Grace's eyes narrowed. "Who's paying? I know the money can't come out of the mansion accounts, or Duncan will notice. You'd better be charging the Women's Institute to clean up their mess."

Donna felt her cheeks heat as she sipped her tea. "I can't, Grace, then it would come out of the amount raised for the cancer charity."

"So you're paying for it yourself." She let out a sigh. "You need a keeper, lassie."

The timer went off on the oven, and Grace went over to dish up their food. She returned with two steaming bowls of cock-a-leekie soup and a freshly baked loaf of walnut bread.

"Perfect." Donna's mouth watered.

"You need to get your strength up for dealing with Flora, Joyce and Ann."

"No kidding." The soup was delicious, with leeks that melted on her tongue and chicken that was tender and tasty.

"I saw you saying goodbye to Duncan," Grace said as she buttered her bread.

Donna focused on her soup, aware that she must have witnessed the kiss they'd shared when Duncan had backed her up against his car. Her body was still vibrating from it. She felt a hand curl around hers and looked up to find Grace's understanding smile.

"Are you okay?" she said.

"Yeah." She had no choice but to be otherwise. She reached for the bread, as an excuse to retreat, and cleared her throat. "I'm leaving the mansion after the ball. I'll be staying with Agnes while I look for a new job."

"Are you sure?"

Donna nodded and focused on her soup. It was hard to look Grace in the eye when all she saw was sympathy there.

"He doesn't need me anymore. He's a changed man—he's smiling and laughing and working again. I don't think he'll ever be the man he was before he lost his wife, but he's ready to get on with his life."

"But not with you?"

"No." She looked back out of the window. "His love for Fiona is too big to allow room for someone else."

"That's not how love works, my darling. Love is never-ending. The bigger it is, the more it can encompass. And if you have learned to love well, and deeply, as Duncan has, then there will always be the space and resources to love more."

Her words were like needles jabbing her skin. "I asked him, Grace. He said there wouldn't be another."

She let out a sigh. "What did I tell you about listening to men? No good ever comes of it. You have to pay attention to his actions, and that boy loves you."

Donna shook her head. Grace was wrong. Duncan felt affection for her, and he liked her, but there was nothing more. Fiona had taken it all when she'd left.

"Will you stay and look after him once I'm gone? For a wee while, anyway?"

"You mean until he fires me?" Grace smiled ruefully. "Aye, I'll stay, but I think you should too."

"I can't, Grace. I'm sorry if that disappoints you."

"You numpty." Grace stood and came round the table to enfold Donna in a hug. "Don't you know by now that there's nothing you could do that would ever disappoint me?" She straightened and wiped her eyes. "Now, it just so happens that I made cake for pudding."

With that, she turned and strode towards the pantry, leaving Donna to finish her food in silence.

* * *

"ARE YOU SURE ABOUT THIS?" Mairi asked as they loaded the last of Donna's boxes into the back of a van Keir had borrowed to help her move.

She'd spent the afternoon and early evening dealing with the many people there to set up for the ball and then packing up her things in the housekeeper's apartment.

"It's the right thing to do."

She watched as Agnes shut the doors to the van, with most of her belongings inside. All that was left were the clothes and toiletries to get her through the next two days and a few things she had to pick up from around the house—like her copy of *The Hobbit* from Duncan's office, and the painting he'd given her, which hung facing her desk. Once these things were gone, there would be nothing left of her in the mansion.

"I think you're making a sensible decision," Agnes said as she came to stand beside them.

"Of course you do." Mairi frowned. "Your heart is a block of ice."

"Thank you," Agnes said with pride. "Do you want to come back to the apartment and stay there tonight?" she asked Donna.

"No, I need to be here early tomorrow to make sure the caterers can get in." Although, the thought of sleeping in her empty flat, and empty bed, made her ache.

"Okay, if you change your mind, just drive on over and let yourself in."

"I will." She gave her sisters a hug and watched as they climbed into the van beside Keir. Sean and his friends, who'd turned up to help carry boxes, honked the horn of their car as they followed.

She watched them head down the drive until they were out of sight before turning back to the building that had been her home these past two years. The sun was setting over

Kintyre, and the warm glow made the grey stone seem almost welcoming. There was no denying that it was a lovely building, if a little on the sterile side. Still, she'd cared for it, and its owner, with everything she had to give. But neither the house nor the man had ever truly belonged to her.

"Watch over him," she whispered. Unsure if she was talking to the house or the spectre of Fiona's memory that clung to it.

She lifted the small bag she'd brought downstairs with the last load and walked around the building, following the path to the carriage house. Cook had already stocked the fridge for her, and she'd left the lamps on so that she wouldn't walk into a dark house.

Donna had decided to spend her last nights, not in the mansion, but in the one place she felt belonged to her and Duncan—if only a little. She placed her bag on the table, smiling at the covered chocolate cake that sat there with a note stuck to the top: *Don't eat it all in one go, or you'll be sick.*

After taking a can of Irn-Bru out of the fridge and her book out of her bag, she curled into the corner of the sofa, facing the windows that looked out at the trees between the carriage house and the mansion. The builders had suggested chopping down the trees so that the guests had a view of the house, but she hadn't agreed with them. Somehow the wooded area made the retreat seem more secluded. Now, she was grateful for her decision because she didn't want to look at the building that had taken over her life these past two years. The one that owned the man she loved, just as much as the memory of his dead wife did.

* * *

DUNCAN HAD DECLINED an invitation to meet up with the art college faculty when he arrived in Glasgow. He wanted to wander the city on his own, and he had a visit he needed to make.

As he walked up to the cemetery on the hill overlooking Glasgow's city centre, he remembered the last time he'd taken this route—the day he'd laid Fiona to rest. He hadn't been back since because that had felt too much like admitting she was gone forever.

The day they buried his wife, the sun had been shining, and the breeze had been brisk. He couldn't remember how he'd gotten to the funeral, or if he'd said anything when he was there. Nor could he remember who else had attended, or even who took the service. But he did recall the way the sun filtered through the leaves to form patterns that danced on Fiona's grave. And he remembered the birds singing in the trees, the smell of the flowers all around her grave, and the colour of the sky.

Most of all, he remembered wishing he had been in the hole alongside his wife.

The sun was setting as he wended his way along the paths between the graves. He watched as the markers became less ornate and more modern. There was something comforting about the moss-covered headstones that were worn with time. As though the earth was welcoming the person resting there back inside of it.

Fiona had picked out her own headstone. The same way she'd planned her funeral before she'd left him. All Duncan had done was stand guard over her wishes and make sure they were carried out to the letter.

He spotted the stone as he rounded the corner into a small clearing beside some trees. It was a block of soft pink marble that was rough and unpolished at the bottom but smooth and perfect at the top. She'd told him it symbolised the things she'd left unfinished. The inscription was simple: her name and the dates of her short life, with the words *Well*

Loved beneath them. She'd joked that the words could be taken several ways, one of them being that he'd taken excellent care of her in bed.

Duncan stopped beside the stone and rested his hand on top, feeling the smooth marble under his touch. There were fresh flowers on her grave: pink roses like the ones she'd loved. He knew they were from her parents, two more people he'd cut from his life when he'd lost her.

He sank to the grass beside the stone and, bringing his knees up to rest his arms, he looked out over Glasgow. Dusk brought a flicker of lights, springing up throughout the city, as the place finally came to life.

He wasn't sure how long he sat there, or even what went through his mind while he did. But it was time spent remembering, instead of wishing for something different. He wasn't a man for flowery words—Fiona used to say that he saved that sentiment for his art, and she always knew how he felt by looking at his paintings. He smiled at the memory but didn't say a word. Some might find comfort in talking to the graves of their loved ones, but Duncan knew she wasn't really there. Her soul had gone home, and her body had returned to the earth. All that remained was a pink stone and the memory of something that had been beyond description in its perfection.

As the sky turned black over the city, he got to his feet and wiped off his jeans. He wouldn't be back, visiting graves wasn't something he did, not with his parents and not with his wife. There were other ways to pay respect to the dead, and Duncan preferred to do it through his art. Fiona would live on in every painting he made. His love for her would sneak into the work through the colours and the brushstrokes. He wouldn't be able to keep it out, because Duncan painted everything he loved.

This visit had been a chance to lay to rest the vows he'd

made. It was time to move on with his life—without Fiona. Slowly, he tugged off the ring that sat on his wedding finger and looked at the weathered gold. There was no inscription inside—there hadn't seemed any need when they could look into each other's eyes and say what they felt.

He crouched down and dug a small hole at the foot of the pink stone, placing the ring inside and covering it over before patting the dirt down firm. It belonged with Fiona. He'd taken the ring from her as a symbol of the promises he'd made to her, and now, those were fulfilled. He'd loved her until she died, and then beyond. He'd loved her in sickness and in health. In wealth and poverty. He'd loved her with all of him and cherished everything she'd had to give.

Until death they did part.

He stood and headed back down the path to the city, never once looking back.

CHAPTER 25

"I say we play rock, paper, scissors to see who's going to kill those three old bats," Agnes said as she stalked into the mansion's kitchen.

"Nobody's killing anyone," Grace said from where she was talking to the caterer, as waitstaff scurried around them.

"Can we at least add Metamucil to their food?" Mairi asked as she followed Agnes into the room.

"That, I'll think about," Grace conceded.

"What have they done now?" Donna was going over her list of things that still needed to be done before the ball started in ten hours.

Agnes put her hands on her hips. "I caught them trying to pick the lock on Duncan's studio door."

That was it. Donna was on her feet. "No need to play games for the privilege, I'm going to wring their necks." She stormed towards the door.

"Stop her," cook shouted, but her sisters were smart enough to step out of her way. "Did you hear me?" Grace snapped, and two huge waiters stepped in front of the door to block her exit.

"Get out of my way," she told them.

"I can't," said one who couldn't have been older than their nephew Jack. "Cook promised us we could take the leftovers home if we did what we were told."

"I never get haggis," the other one said.

"For goodness' sake." Donna spun back around to look at her sisters. "Tell me they didn't get into the room."

Agnes huffed in disgust. "I can't believe you said that. Of course they didn't. I was there and nothing gets past me."

"You." Donna pointed at one of the teenagers. "Go stand guard at Duncan's studio door. You can take turns. If no one gets in there, I'll make sure Grace feeds you and your flat-mates for a week."

They whooped and ran off.

"And there goes two of my waitstaff," the caterer complained. "What am I going to do now?"

Donna looked at her sisters.

"Hell no!" Mairi said.

"Please," Donna begged.

"You owe me big time." Mairi walked over to the caterer. "Give me an apron."

"Aggie?" Donna batted her lashes at her older sister.

She glared back as she walked over to join Mairi. "I cannot wait for the day when I have to stop bailing you lot out of trouble."

"When will that be?" Mairi asked.

"On the same day I pencil in for every important task, isn't that right, Aggie?" Donna said. "The twelfth of never."

Her phone rang, and she dug it out of her pocket to look at the screen. "It's Duncan," she shouted, and there was instant silence as everyone froze in place. "Hello," she said into the phone. "How are things going?" She turned away from everyone and walked to the window.

"I'm just about to start my lecture." The sound of his deep, rumbling voice made her eyes well up.

She forced a smile so that she'd sound normal when she answered. "Are you nervous?"

"No, but there are an awful lot of people out there. It's standing room only." He sounded bewildered.

"Duncan, you're Scotland's most famous living artist. Of course people want to hear you talk about your work."

"My *old* work," he amended in irritation.

"Tell them there's new stuff, but you're not ready to show it or talk about it yet."

He paused for a second. "I can do that. How are things at the mansion?"

"Oh, you know"—she glanced around the room at the people quietly staring at her—"same old, same old. What time will you be back tomorrow?"

"I don't know, late I think. After my lecture, I've got one-on-one tutorials for the rest of the day, and then I'm having dinner with Zoe and her husband." He lowered his voice. "I couldn't get out of it."

"You'll survive." And he would be nicely busy while the ball was on.

"I'd better go. They want to get started."

"Good luck." She hung up and turned to see that everyone had started moving and talking again.

"Wait," he called. "I'm no' done."

"What?" she said.

"Think about me in bed tonight, Angel. I know I'll be thinking about you." The line went dead and Donna's hand clenched around the phone.

"Are you okay?" Mairi said as she came up beside her.

"Why wouldn't I be?"

"No reason." She gave her a tight hug. "What's next on the list?"

"Setting up tables in the foyer and the orangery for people who want to get away from the music or don't fit into the ballroom." That had been Flora and Joyce's bright idea for squeezing in forty more people. "And I want to string up ropes on the staircases and corridors that are off limits during the ball."

"I'm not sure that will stop people," Mairi said.

"I need more teens to stand guard." Donna looked down at her iPad.

"Now that I can sort. Leave it to me," Mairi said with a grin as she pulled out her phone.

Donna wasn't sure leaving anything to Mairi was a good idea, but honestly, she was desperate, so she did just that.

* * *

"Are you nervous?" Zoe, the dean of Fine Arts, asked Duncan as he eyed the crowded auditorium.

"No," he answered honestly. As soon as he'd walked up the grey steps at the front of the building and stopped to look at the warm golden stone that made up the Mac, he'd felt like he'd come home.

"That's good to hear," Zoe said. "We've got an eager crowd this morning. And the tutorial slots filled up faster than they've ever done before. Within minutes of posting the signup sheet."

"I don't recall offering to do one-on-one tutorials." Duncan cocked an eyebrow at her.

"Now, isn't that strange?" she said without cracking a smile.

They were in the lecture theatre in the basement of the Mackintosh building. It was the same room he'd sat in on many occasions during the four years he'd spent studying there, and he well remembered how hard those old benches were on your backside when a talk droned on.

The room was square and high-ceilinged, with the stage area down in one corner facing three stacks of black benches that formed a semi-circle in front. High in the corner opposite the stage, was the tiny technician's closet, where his old lecturers used to get a student to load up their slides for them. Times had changed, and Duncan had a laptop on the stand beside him, rigged to the projector overhead.

The blinds on the windows to his right were drawn, and overhead, the small golden drop lanterns were lit. High on the walls, at the top of the thin dark wood panels, was one of Mackintosh's signature motifs—four squares, arranged two by two.

"It brings back memories, doesn't it?" Zoe said softly.

"Last time I was here, I got into an argument with Thomas Joshua Cooper in this exact spot." He gave her a wry look. "I seem to remember him winning."

She laughed. Thomas was a world-renowned photographer who, although American, had been around The Glasgow School of Art for decades. What he didn't know about photography wasn't worth knowing, and he was always up for a discussion with someone who needed some schooling on the topic.

"I met my wife in this room," Duncan said. "During a piss-poor lecture on German Expressionism. She was studying textile design not painting, so she wasn't even supposed to be in there. She told me later, over lunch in the bar, that she'd followed me into the room and shoved another girl out of the way to sit beside me." He smiled at the memory. "She wasn't known for being shy." Not like another woman who had stitched his heart back together again.

"That sounds like Fiona." Zoe grinned at him before putting her hand on his arm. "You can't imagine how pleased

I was when you emailed with the offer to lecture. I've been worried about you ever since we lost Fiona."

"My offer t—" He was cut off as the lights dimmed.

Zoe squeezed his arm. "We'll talk tonight. I can't wait to see this illustrator's work you've found. It must be something special to have caught your eye."

All Duncan could do was nod as those alarm bells that usually went off around his sneaky housekeeper sounded in his head. As Zoe introduced him, he thought back to all those other times he'd felt his hairs stand on end around Donna. Something was up, and he intended to get to the bottom of it as soon as he got back to Kintyre.

As the crowd applauded, he stepped forward and looked out at all the eager faces.

"As Zoe said, I'm Duncan Stewart, and I learned to paint in this building. More than that, I learned how to *see* my own work with a clarity and honesty that has stood me in good stead over the years. Today, I'm going to share with you my thought process when I paint, to prove I was listening when I was a student here." There was laughter. "And to encourage you to soak up as much as you can from this place before you leave. No matter what you choose to do in life, the things you learn here will help you make the most of it. So pay attention."

With that, he brought up the image of the first painting he wanted to talk about, and a sense of peace swept through him the likes of which he hadn't felt since losing Fiona. No, that wasn't quite right, he'd felt that same soul-deep peace with Donna.

The same Donna who was up to something back home in Kintyre. He'd bet his last painting on it.

CHAPTER 26

The invitation for the ball had specified the dress code as 'fancy,' which, it turned out, left a lot of room for interpretation. One elderly couple arrived in topcoat and tails for him while her silver gown wouldn't have looked out of place on Princess Margaret.

"Are those real diamonds around her neck?" Mairi asked as they watched the couple enter through the mansion's main doors.

"I think so," Donna said. "If she handed over her bracelet, we could sell it and raise more than enough money to call this ball off."

Her sister snorted. "Too late for that. You know, if you can afford vintage Chanel couture and enough ice to freeze your husband's balls off, surely you could invest in some Botox? She looks like someone's dressed up a Shar-Pei dog."

"Mairi!" Donna frowned at her.

She shrugged. "I call them as I see them." Her eyes widened. "Holy flying fairies, is that a tutu?"

Donna looked back at the line of people making their way inside the mansion. And yes, it was a tutu—on Joyce. It looked like someone had dipped the Sugar Plum Fairy in Pepto-Bismol. She'd even wrapped pink tinsel around her walker.

"I like the matching Reeboks," Mairi said. "I didn't know they came in that colour."

"Her hair looks like candy floss," Donna said in awe.

"I see Ann's made an effort," Mairi said.

Sure enough, Ann Dunbar was dressed in grey—but it shimmered. "I like her lipstick, and her shoes are pretty. Oh, look at Flora. She's the fairy godmother from Cinderella."

"Holy Nutella, here comes the pumpkin!"

Donna twisted her head to see through the crowd, and she gasped. A short, round man had arrived—wearing an orange suit.

"I freaking *love* this ball," Mairi said with glee. "If only I was still taking photos to show my online boyfriends, I could have milked this event for months. Oh, wait, I'm *definitely* taking photos of those guys." She whipped out her phone. "For personal use."

Donna's jaw dropped at the sight of a group of six men who'd arrived wearing traditional Scottish dress. Built like rugby players with their shoulders straining against their shirts, they towered over the crowd.

"Is it wrong that I really want to see their thighs?" Donna muttered. "I bet they would be tree trunks."

"Forget the thighs." Mairi snapped pictures. "I want to see what else is under those kilts."

They watched as an assortment of people came through the doors, from the elegantly dressed to the quirky. As different as they all were, they had one thing in common— they all gaped at the mansion, snapping photos like a busload of tourists on a trip to Big Ben.

Donna glanced at her wristwatch. It was only seven o'clock. The music hadn't even started, the food wasn't due to be served until eight, and the Women's Institute had promised to start winding things down at eleven. It was going to be a long, long night.

"I didn't know there was a bucking bronco," Sean said as he approached in an ill-fitting suit. "Can't wait to give that a go."

"What do you mean?" Donna looked around as though it would appear.

"The mechanical bull in the library. I saw it when I passed." He jerked a thumb over his shoulder. "Very cool."

"Mechanical bull?" Donna felt the colour drain from her face.

"Aye." Sean was oblivious to her reaction. "And I can't wait to try my hand in the casino."

"Casino?" she squeaked.

He gave her a strange look. "You know, the one in the dining room?"

She grasped Mairi's arm and held on tight. "There's a casino in the dining room?"

Sean looked between the two of them. "Didn't you organise this thing?"

"I'm going to kill them," Donna muttered. "We talked about setting up tables in the orangery, and the buffet tables in the ballroom. We didn't talk about a mechanical bull and a casino."

"Take a deep breath," Mairi said to her before looking up at Keir's brother. "Please tell me there isn't a bouncy castle in the garden."

"No, but some old men are running a game of boules on the front lawn."

"There's no point in screaming," Mairi said as Donna opened her mouth. "There's Flora, let's go talk to her."

They didn't bother saying goodbye to Sean. They just ran across the entrance to cut off Flora.

"Hello girls," she said. "My you look pretty, Donna."

"There's a casino in the dining room. A bull in the library and men playing a boules tournament on the front lawn." Donna's eye twitched.

"To be fair," Flora said as Joyce came up beside her, "the bull isn't real."

"What. Were. You. Thinking?" The words were squeezed from between clenched teeth.

"That we needed to keep people occupied and get the crowd circling so that the ballroom didn't become too over-crowded."

"That's why we set up tables in the orangery."

"Aye," Flora said with a smile. "But we might have under-estimated the numbers we expected tonight. Turns out there may be a wee bit more than a hundred and twenty in attendance."

"How many more?" Donna said through clenched teeth.

"We don't exactly know," Flora said. "Joyce put out an open invitation. But don't worry. There's someone on the door making sure people pay to get in."

Donna's eye began to twitch.

"With all the extra people," Joyce said, "we needed to provide some decent entertainment. Not to mention, we had to liven the place up. What sounds like more fun to you? Having tea in the greenhouse or seeing how long you can sit on a bucking bull?" She gave Flora a disgusted look. "I'm no' allowed on it because I had a hip replacement last year. Apparently I'm a liability."

"Group B," a voice called. "Group B, assemble here."

Donna's head snapped around to see a woman standing at the bottom of the staircase holding up a placard with the letter B on it. People around them checked pieces of paper in their hands before some headed towards her.

"What is she doing?" Donna snapped.

"Guided tours," Joyce said. "Everyone wanted to get a look around the mansion. Which reminds me, could you call off your guard dogs outside the studio, so we can get in? People want to see what Duncan's working on."

"No, I can't call them off." She was about to lose her mind. Right after she killed three old women and buried them under the bloody rose bushes.

"If it made you feel better, we could charge an entrance fee to the studio," Joyce said. "It would raise a lot more money for the wee sick babies."

"That's it! I'm going to kill her!" Donna launched herself at Joyce, but Mairi held her back.

"Witnesses," her sister hissed. "Nothing happening here," she said loudly, through a fake smile.

"Duncan's going to kill me," she wailed.

Flora scoffed. "He won't find out."

"Eh," Mairi said. "I think he might."

Donna turned to see what she was looking at. A group of women were posing for a photo in front of the staircase.

"Don't forget to use the right hashtag," one of them called. "Kintyre Mansion Ball."

"I'm dead," Donna said.

* * *

DUNCAN WAS SURPRISED to find a young woman sitting at the table in the restaurant that Zoe led him to.

"This is Madeline," she said. "Gordon's niece."

The woman shot to her feet, holding out a hand for Duncan. "I'm a big fan. I can't believe I'm meeting you in person. It's so exciting."

He shook her hand and mumbled something with the word pleased in it. As he went to sit down facing the woman,

Zoe stopped him. "No, you sit over there beside her." She pushed him in the right direction.

He caught Zoe's husband, Gordon's eye as he sat down and the man, "sorry," he mouthed.

That's when Duncan knew he had been set up. He'd walked right into the middle of his own blind date. With a frown, he rounded the table to sit with Madeline. He supposed she was pretty, in her own way, with her long black hair and her trim figure, but she was no Donna. There were no curves to entice a man, and her smile didn't light up the room. It was on the tip of his tongue to tell Zoe that he was already seeing someone, but he didn't want to make his personal business public. His only option was to suffer through the evening and get back home to Donna as fast as he could.

He stilled at the thought. Once, home had meant Fiona, but now it meant Donna, and instead of being upset at the thought, all he felt was a warmth around his heart and a longing to get back to her.

Once he'd sat down beside the woman, she curled both of her hands around his arm. "I'm so sorry to hear that you lost your wife."

"Eh…thanks?" He glared at Zoe. It was wasted on her.

Thankfully, the waiter arrived with menus and the strange woman let go of his arm.

"I have something to show you," Duncan said to Zoe as he rooted around in the small backpack he'd brought with him from the college. He handed her the paperback copy of *The Hobbit*.

"Thanks, but I've read it." Zoe handed it back.

"Look inside."

With an indulgent smile, she did just that. Duncan watched her carefully and smiled at the shocked expression on her face once she'd opened the book.

"Gordon," she said in awe.

"What?" Her husband dragged his eyes away from the menu and sucked in a breath when he looked at the book.

Zoe looked over at Duncan. "This is the illustrator you mentioned. Where did you get this?"

"Found it at the mansion. I don't know who it belongs to, but I wanted to check with you before I tracked down the owner. I'm no' imagining things, am I?"

She shook her head. "No, you definitely aren't. These are sublime. When was the last time you saw illustrations like these, Gordon?"

The older man rubbed his chin. "I honestly can't recall."

"Oh"—Madeline bounced in her seat—"is it like a picture book? I love those. Don't you?" She held up her phone at arm's length as she leaned into Duncan's side. "Smile," she said. He didn't. She took the photo anyway, then started to type with her thumbs. "Out for dinner with art royalty," she read aloud as she typed. "Hashtag blessed." She beamed at him.

He blinked at her before turning back to the art school dean. "What do you think then?"

Zoe gave him a serious look. "I think, if you can find the owner, I can offer them a place on the illustration course. If they want it."

"Without a portfolio?" That was a standard requirement for applying for entry.

"This *is* a portfolio, Duncan. Are you planning to mentor this person?"

"I don't do that anymore." But the words sounded false to his ears.

Zoe heard it too. "The same way you don't teach anymore?" She gave him a smug smile. "I knew you wouldn't stay in your enforced retirement forever. You have no idea how pleased I was to get your email. You need to share your talent with the world, not only through your paintings but through your teaching too."

"Which reminds me, I'm confused. You asked me to come lecture. I didn't ask you."

"Initially, yes. But you were the one who contacted me about today."

Just then, Madeline distracted him by getting up from the table to take a photo of them all from halfway across the room. When she came back, she read her caption aloud again, "Great food. Great company. Hashtag happy."

Gordon rolled his eyes, and before Duncan could pursue the matter of who had asked whom to lecture, the waiter came to take their order.

"Are you on Instagram?" Madeline asked as the waiter poured her wine.

"No." Duncan shook his head when it was his turn to have his glass filled.

"Oh, but you have to be," she gushed. "You can't get anywhere these days without a social media presence. I can help you if you'd like."

"That's what Maddie does," Zoe said. "She's a social media consultant."

Madeline pointed at her own face. "Hashtag connected," she said, then laughed like that was hilarious.

"I don't need a social media presence," Duncan said, hoping to shut her down. Reminding himself of the times Donna had drummed into him that he had to be polite, he added a "thanks" to his statement.

"Oh, but you do." She flicked her black hair over her shoulder. "How will people hear about you if you don't? It's the only way to increase your profile."

"Maddie," Zoe said patiently, "Duncan's in every modern art book they publish. His profile is as good as it gets."

"I forgot." She laughed. "Still, the consumer likes to feel connected to a brand. You should interact with your fans."

Consumer? Brand? Fans? Duncan looked at Gordon for help, but the man was just chugging back the wine. He wished Donna were with them. She would have found the humour in the situation and helped him to find it too. Without her, he just wanted to be rude and get up and leave. But he didn't. Because he knew she would be disappointed in him. Although, he was tempted to get Madeline to send her some 'hashtag' messages to include her in the irritation he felt.

The starters arrived, and Madeline promptly took photos of everything and posted the pictures online.

"Do you ever Google yourself, Duncan?" she asked as she nibbled at her salad.

The sight of her eating reminded him that Donna would never have ordered a salad. She would have gone straight for the deep-fried mozzarella sticks and bread. Then she would have talked him into sharing his food too if he hadn't eaten it all before she'd finished.

"Google yourself?" Gordon said with a laugh. "That sounds rude."

"That's enough wine for you, dear." Zoe confiscated the bottle.

"No," Duncan said. "I don't. I already know who I am."

"Oh, but you should." She tapped at her phone. "Look, there's lots about you on here." She scrolled. "There's your work. Your past relationships. Your home. Gosh, it looks pretty! It's so nice of you to let all those people use it for their fundraiser."

He stilled then slowly turned to her, but she wasn't paying attention.

"I'll send a message from you, shall I? Telling them to have fun. It will make people think you're a generous man, prone to philanthropy. That's always good for your image."

"What people?" Duncan said evenly.

Zoe stopped with her wine glass halfway to her mouth, before placing it back on the table.

The tense atmosphere went over Madeline's head, mainly because she didn't look up from her phone. "The ones at the ball. Hashtag Kintyre Mansion Ball. Hashtag have a great one! Oh, look, there's a ceilidh band."

Those alarm bells that had been sounding for weeks suddenly made sense. "Who's running the fundraiser?"

"Don't you know?" Madeline was busy thumb typing.

"No, I don't know, so I wouldnae mind if you told me." Duncan clasped her hand to stop her typing. "Who's running it?"

She licked her lips nervously. "The local branch of the Scottish Women's Institute."

A flash of the woman he'd met at the pub came to mind. Flora Reid. It came to him where he'd seen her before—she'd been walking across his lawn with a wheelbarrow full of glitter. The chickens—they were the number of people attending the ball! His heart missed a beat. There were a hundred and twenty strangers in his house.

And his housekeeper had let them in.

He was going to wring her neck. Then work his way through her sisters.

He shot to his feet. "I need to get to the airport. There's a flight to Campbeltown at eight. I have to be on it." Without waiting for a reply, he jogged from the restaurant and straight into one of the taxis waiting outside.

Donna had lost control of the mansion. It was now in the hands of hundreds of rabid party goers and three old women who were stirring everyone up.

"Any ideas?" she asked the women at her side.

"Call the police and have them thrown out?" Grace suggested.

They were standing at the back of the ballroom, watching as a swarm of locusts dressed in formal attire decimated the buffet.

"They won't do anything," Donna said. "I spoke to the police officer who came with the ambulance to pick up Flora's father." She gave them a bewildered look. "What was a ninety-five-year-old man doing on a mechanical bull?" She shook her head to clear it. "Anyway, the police told me that there was nothing they could do because I'd given permission for the Women's Institute to use the mansion for the fundraiser. He said that if they were still here after the cut-off time, he could help us evict them. Until then, we're on our own."

"Is anyone else wondering how Flora's dad is still alive?"

Mairi said. "I mean, Flora's ancient. And she has a father? That seems wrong."

"Focus." Agnes smacked Mairi on the back of the head.

She rubbed the spot. "Every time you do that, I lose brain cells."

"Can we concentrate? I need a plan to…contain this." Donna pointed at the chaos in front of them.

"It's like every American teen movie I've ever seen," Mairi said. "The parents are away, and the kids have a party that gets out of hand. Only, the twist is that Duncan is the parent. We should sell this concept to Hollywood. We'd make a mint."

As they watched, the band stopped playing. "We're going to take a wee break," the lead singer said. "No doubt you'll miss us, but not too much because the Women's Institute have organised a halftime show for you. Hit it, boys!"

Coloured spotlights flitted across the dancefloor as music with a heavy beat blasted from the speakers. A voice boomed out as the group of six men wearing traditional Scottish dress sauntered into the middle of the room.

"What's happening?" Grace said.

"Oh, no," Donna moaned.

"Ladies and gentlemen," a voice shouted out. "Please put your hands together and welcome Scotland's answer to the Chippendales—the Highland Hotties!"

The men started to gyrate to the music and Donna's jaw dropped.

"Oh good," Mairi said gleefully. "I wanted to know what was under those kilts."

All Donna could do was stare at the strip show taking place in the middle of the Georgian ballroom. Fiona must be turning in her grave. She blinked several times as one of the men whipped off his sporran and tossed it into the crowd.

"Aggie," she said. "I'm going to my office to see if there's a clause in that agreement I signed that will get us out of this."

"I'll stay here and keep an eye on them—I mean, on *things*. I'll keep an eye on things." Agnes had her eyes glued to the men.

"Is this even legal?" Grace asked in bewilderment.

"Oh aye," Mairi said. "Women and men are equal opportunity perverts these days."

Donna groaned and headed for the door. If she couldn't find something in the contract to get her out of this mess, she'd set off the fire alarm and blame it on Joyce, because she would bet the balance in her bank account that the male dancers were her idea.

* * *

DUNCAN CLIMBED out of the taxi in front of the mansion to find a group of men in suits playing boules on his lawn. He ran a hand down his face and told himself that at least they weren't in the building—unlike the rest of Kintyre.

The noise coming from the house was loud enough to wake the dead. He wouldn't be surprised if the whole of the peninsular was vibrating with it. As he walked up his driveway, a woman carrying a placard with the letter D on it came around the corner of the building, with a crowd in tow.

"This is the northern face of the building. Here you can see the windows to Duncan's studio, where the masterpieces that reside in New York's Museum of Modern Art and London's Tate Modern were created. Unfortunately, we are currently unable to enter the room, due to the two feral teenagers guarding it in return for pizza. If you follow me, we can get a look at the renovated carriage house."

The group crossed his path on their way to the back of the property.

"Hey," one of the women said. "Isn't that Duncan Stewart?"

"Don't be daft," her friend chided. "He's in Glasgow for the weekend."

Duncan walked past the tour group and up the steps to his wide-open front door. There were people everywhere, but his eyes went to the banner spanning the balcony that read: *The Fiona Stewart Memorial Ball*. Underneath it, in smaller letters, were the words: *Raising Money for Families with Children Fighting Cancer.*

Now he knew how Donna had been talked into this fiasco. The bloody Women's Institute had used his dead wife and sick children against her. She never stood a chance. He walked down the corridor towards the music, passing the dining room where a pop-up casino was making a killing, and then the library where—he stopped in his tracks.

They'd pushed the furniture back to the edge of the room and rolled up the rugs, and in the middle of the floor, sat a mechanical bull. There was a wee woman dressed in a silver ballgown sitting on its back. She looked to be about a hundred and was being cheered on by an elderly man in a top hat and tails. He closed his eyes for a second or two before opening them again. Nope. They were still there.

He backed out of the room, dodged a group taking selfies in the hallway, and continued to the ballroom, his anger growing with every step. She'd told him the room was off limits because the floor was being varnished, while all along, they'd been setting up to have a party in his absence. She'd lied to him about everything—posing and playing pool to get him out of the house, telling him Zoe had invited him to Glasgow when she'd sent the email...the list went on. And the most annoying thing was that he'd known something was up, but he'd ignored the warning signs because he'd been too busy chasing after her to think straight.

He stepped into the ballroom, only to be confronted by six topless men in kilts dancing to a room full of clapping women and bored-looking men. Everything Fiona had hoped to achieve had been reduced to a backdrop for people letting off steam. He wasn't even sure who he was angrier at —the Women's Institute for conning Donna, Donna for not coming to him instead of organising things behind his back, or himself for ignoring the signs that something was up. He's been in Kintyre long enough to know that, where the Sinclair sisters were concerned, you *never* ignored any warning signs. He'd been slack. He'd left his woman without protection—from con artists and from her sisters.

As he scanned the room, he spotted Agnes, Mairi and Grace standing near the buffet tables. Clearly they were as captivated by the dancers as the rest of the women in the room. He headed straight for them, pushing his way through the crowd.

Mairi spotted him first. "Oh hey, Duncan, how's it going?" She smiled and it froze on her face. "Duncan!" She elbowed her sister.

Agnes' eyes shot to him. "It wasn't her fault," she said in a rush. "She was conned. The Women's Institute told her it would be a sedate ceilidh using only the ballroom. Then they upped the numbers and asked to use the orangery too. Donna knew nothing about the guided tours or the bull or the strippers—"

"Or the casino," Mairi added.

"Aye." Agnes nodded. "None of us knew what they'd planned until it happened. She's trying to figure out a way to shut it down earlier. She's really upset about it, Duncan."

"Funny, so am I." He cocked his head towards the corridor. "Out there. Now."

The three women made their way towards the door

without protest. As Grace passed him, she looked him straight in the eye. "You don't have to say it. I already know I'm fired."

Damn right she was fired, just as soon as he'd cleared up this mess and dealt with his housekeeper.

* * *

DONNA HEARD noises from the linen closet as she passed the door. As soon as she opened it, she deeply regretted it. There was a couple, who looked to be on the ripe side of middle-aged, getting it on amongst the bedding. She slammed the door shut, wishing she could take out her eyeballs and roll them in bleach.

She made a quick detour past the studio, only to see the teenage boys standing shoulder to shoulder to keep out the hordes. They spotted her at the back of the crowd and saluted her, grins on their faces. They deserved two weeks' worth of Grace's cooking instead of one.

Her office door was slightly ajar as she approached it, and her heart sank. The wildlife that had infected the mansion had even made it into her workspace. With a fortifying breath, she pushed open the door then gasped.

Because Bill, the gardener they'd fired, was helping himself to the painting Duncan had given her.

"What do you think you're doing?" she snapped.

He didn't even hesitate. "Taking what's owed to me, that's what. I told that bastard you work for I'd get my severance pay, one way or another."

"Put that back, right now." Donna's voice shook and her hand trembled as she pointed at him. "That painting doesn't belong to Duncan. It belongs to me."

He shrugged. "Can't say that I care."

She stepped towards him, blocking his path out of the room. "Take your hands off it. It doesn't belong to you."

"It does now."

He tried to step around her, but she blocked him, aware that he was a good head taller than her and had a lot more bulk. And from the vicious look in his eyes, she didn't think he would have any problem hurting her to get his way. If it had been anything else he was stealing, she would have let him walk out of the building and then have called the cops, but this was *her* painting. The one thing she owned that was a piece of Duncan. The only piece she would ever have, and she wasn't going to let anyone steal it from her.

"Get out of my way," he ordered as he crowded her, pushing at her with the painting.

"No! It's mine. Put it back."

"Well, look at that." He sneered. "The tiny mouse has finally learned to say no. Does it make you cry at night, knowing that the whole of Kintyre sees you as a soft touch? We'd sit in the pub and discuss whose turn it was next to come work at the mansion, just to get the handout when we left. It was my turn this time, and there's no way in hell I'm leaving without my money." He glanced at the painting she loved. "This piece of crap should be worth a penny or two."

"Help!" Donna screamed. "Thief!"

It was no use—the band had started playing again, and the music drowned out her words.

He shoved into her, using the delicate canvas as a battering ram. "The whole of Campbeltown is laughing at you. Donna Sinclair can't say no, she'll give money to anybody with a sob story. She's probably bending over for her boss while she's at it, giving him a pity fuck because she's too timid to refuse. Look around you—three old women walked all over you to take over the building. You're the laughing stock of Kintyre. You always have been."

"No," she forced out the word, but his aim had been true with the barbed arrows he'd shot. They ripped through what remained of her pride.

"Aye." He stepped into her. "Now get out of my way."

CHAPTER 28

"Where is she?" Duncan demanded of the three women in front of him. Mairi tried to look innocent while Grace looked resigned and Agnes looked like she wanted to hit him. "I'll no' ask again. Where is she?"

"She went to her office to see if she could find a way out of the contract she signed with the Women's Institute," Grace said.

Agnes glared at him. "You'd better not lay a finger on her."

"I would never lift my hand to a woman." And he was insulted that she thought he might.

"Don't make her cry either," Agnes said.

Now that, he couldn't promise. Although, the thought of Donna crying made him want to take a knife to his own heart.

"She was only trying to please everybody," Grace said. "The things she did weren't just about getting you out of the mansion. She wanted you to enjoy yourself and to step back into the art world."

Aye, he wasn't buying that. "So this ball was just an

unlucky by-product of Donna trying to get me to back into the world?"

"Oh no," Mairi said. "We planned the whole thing. Donna wanted to ask you for permission, but she was scared you would shoot the messenger, then say no." She smiled at him as though it was all perfectly logical.

"I would definitely have said no to this."

"To be fair," Grace said. "Donna thought she was hosting a gentile charity ball, not a bacchanal for the depraved."

"The women from the institute conned her," Agnes said.

"Walked all over her," Mairi added.

"Took advantage of her kind and loving heart," Grace said.

"Aye. I get it." He'd come to that conclusion all by himself. Although, he was sure the women in front of him hadn't been much of a help in protecting Donna from those who wanted to take advantage. No, it looked like they'd encouraged her wild plans instead. "Clear the building out while I deal with my housekeeper."

"Haven't you been listening?" Agnes snapped. "We've been trying to clear the building out. Nobody pays any attention to us."

"Is that right?" He turned on his heels, stalked back into the ballroom and headed straight for the stage. When he climbed up and snatched the mic from the lead singer's hand, the band behind him stopped playing, plunging the room into silence. "This ball is over. Get your stuff and clear out."

"Hey, who do you think you are?" A young guy in a three-piece suit got to his feet. "We paid good money for this ball. We're not leaving until we get what we were promised—a party until midnight."

He glared at the young man, ensuring he could see that Duncan had run out of patience. "Who do I think I am? I'm Duncan Stewart, the mansion's owner, and this ball ends when I say it does. If you want your money back, see the women from the institute. This is their problem." He looked around at everyone else. "Get your stuff and leave. Now!"

As people jerked to their feet and rushed towards the door, Duncan strode back to the three women who'd helped Donna get into this mess. "Grab every member of staff you can find, including the waiters, and get them to sweep the building to herd people out." He looked at Agnes. "Tell the guy in the library he has ten minutes to pack up and get his bull outside, or I'll take an axe to it." He looked at Grace. "Inform the casino that if they're not gone in the same time, the house is going to confiscate their takings."

"What about me?" Mairi said. "What should I do?"

He turned to the youngest Sinclair sister, who was prone to causing more damage than good with any task she was given. "Take photos of every bastard who gives us trouble. We'll hand them over to the cops later." She nodded happily, making him wonder, yet again, what planet she lived on.

"What are you going to do?" Grace said.

"I'm going for my woman."

He walked away from the shocked look on the three women's faces and stalked down the corridors to Donna's office, telling everyone he met to get their arses out of his house.

He heard voices through her open door as he approached, and he slowed his stride to listen.

"The whole of Campbeltown is laughing at you," a callous male voice said. "Donna Sinclair can't say no, she'll give money to anybody with a sob story. She's probably bending over for her boss while she's at it, giving him a pity fuck because she's too timid to refuse. Look around you—three old women walked all over you to take over the building. You're the laughing stock of Kintyre. You always have been."

"No." Donna's voice trembled.

"Aye," the man snapped. "Now get out of my way."

"No!" she shouted. "I'm not going to let you take that painting. It's mine. Duncan gave it to me."

"For services rendered, no doubt. Now back up or I'll make you."

Duncan had heard enough. He rushed to the open doorway. Donna stood with her back to him and her arms spread, trying to stop their ex-gardener from leaving with her painting. The one he'd given to her. The one that belonged to her.

Hell no!

"Put that down, you bastard," Duncan roared.

"Duncan!" Donna screeched, and the colour drained from her face.

"Go to hell, cheapskate," Bill snapped. "I'm leaving with this, and neither one of you can stop me." He pushed Donna aside, making her stumble and fall into the desk.

She cried out, and Duncan saw red.

"We'll see about that." His fist reared back before he launched it at the gardener's head.

At the last second, Bill lifted the painting to use as a shield. Duncan's fist ripped through the canvas, hitting the man on the jaw, and he crumpled to the floor, taking the ruined painting with him.

"No!" Donna's wail cut through his anger.

She fell to her knees beside the man, and for a second Duncan thought she was checking to see if the gardener was still alive rather than out cold. Instead, she lifted the ruined artwork and cradled it to her like a child. Tears streamed down her face as she looked up at him.

"It's ruined," she whispered, the torment in those big eyes ripping right through his anger, leaving him just as broken as the painting in her hand. "It's gone. The only thing I have of you is gone."

What the...? His anger fled at the sight of her. He crouched beside her, brushing the tears from her cheek. "What are you talking about, Angel?"

The pain that twisted her face was one of the worst things he'd ever had to witness. He never wanted to see her beautiful features that tormented again.

"This was all I had that was yours." She sobbed like her heart had been broken in two.

"I'll give you another painting." Hell, he'd make a houseful of them just for her, if she would only stop breaking his heart. The heart she had revived and that now belonged to her and her alone. "It's okay."

"It's not okay." She dissolved into sobs, still rocking as she held the trashed painting.

He might not have been the most sensitive man on the planet, but even he could see she'd reached the end of her tether. On top of weeks of scheming behind his back, the chaos of the evening had taken its toll. Donna wasn't cut out for subterfuge—her heart was far too soft to cope with the guilt that went with it—and the strain had worn her out.

"Come on." He scooped her, and the painting she wouldn't release, into his arms. "It'll be fine."

"It won't be fine. I've messed everything up." The resignation in her tearful voice made him want to hit more people, in the hopes it would make everything better for her.

She turned her face into him as she sobbed, curling her hand into his shirt. As he strode through the kitchen to the stairs at the back of the house, he found Grace helping the caterer pack everything up. She rushed to his side.

"What happened?" The cook reached for Donna, stroking her hair as she continued sobbing.

It raised his opinion of the woman that she didn't even entertain the thought that Donna might be crying because of him. "The gardener I fired broke into her office and tried to steal her painting. He was bullying her when I walked in on them." He looked down at Donna, tightening his grip on her as he watched her fall apart. "Can you call the police and send a couple of the men to stand guard until they get here? I don't want that arse to run off."

"I'll see to it."

Duncan nodded as he listened to Donna cry. She seemed to be lost in her own misery, oblivious to what was going on around her. "I think she's reached the end."

"It's been a tough couple of weeks," Grace said softly. "Unlike her sisters, she's not cut out for these shenanigans."

"I figured that out for myself. I wish she'd resisted the Women's Institute."

Grace gave him a pitying look. "Do you see her saying no to a ball for cancer patients? One given in your wife's name?"

"If she'd told me, I would have stood up to them for her."

"Next time, Duncan. Do that for her the next time they come at her."

He nodded. Making that promise to himself. "Make sure you get everyone out. Get the cops on to that as well. Tell them I didn't sign the bloody contract, and as far as I'm concerned, everybody is trespassing. I'm taking her up to her room and putting her to bed. We'll deal with this in the morning."

"I'll bring up some hot chocolate, just in case."

Duncan nodded his thanks as he held his woman tight. Her tears seemed never-ending, and she'd folded in on herself. "You take care of the mansion," he said. "I'll take care of Donna."

"I know you will." Grace gave his shoulder a squeeze before turning back into the room.

He ignored everyone else as he took the stairs two at a time to the housekeeper's apartment. Her door was as she usually left it, unlocked, which wasn't sensible in a house full of strangers. Something else to add to the list of things to talk about in the morning.

He swung her apartment door open, took two steps inside, and stopped dead.

"What the hell?" She'd been robbed. The whole place had been cleaned out. There was nothing of hers left. "Donna, Angel." He kept his voice soft so as not to upset her further. "I'm sorry, but you've been robbed. I'll get you settled on the couch, and then I'll let the police know. Don't worry. I'll take care of it."

She lifted her head, tears still rolling down her cheeks as she looked around the room. "I haven't been robbed. I've moved out, and I'm quitting my job." And then she started sobbing all over again.

Duncan stood in the middle of the empty room, unsure of what to say or do. She'd moved out? She was leaving him? Was it because she'd been frightened of how he might react when he found out about the ball? Surely not. He'd never hurt Donna. But one thing was for sure—she was in no fit state to answer his questions right now.

Taking care not to hit her head off the doorjamb, he took her through to the bedroom and settled her on the bed. There was nothing of hers in the room, except one lone book on the bedside table.

He took off her black shoes and considered stripping her of the plain black dress she'd worn to the party, but then thought better of it. He didn't want her to feel any more vulnerable.

"I need to take this," he said as he gently prised the painting from her hands. "You have to get some sleep. I'll leave it on the floor beside the bed and you can decide what to do about it tomorrow." She reluctantly let go of the canvas. Duncan tucked the duvet around her and pressed a kiss to her forehead. "Everything's going to be okay," he told her.

"No, it's not." She curled into a ball on her side, facing away from him.

He sat on the floor beside her bed, guarding her as she cried herself to sleep. Outside, voices called to one another and car doors slammed. People were leaving the building. Strangely, he felt no sense of invasion at them being there in the first place. Probably because the mansion had never really been his home.

He ran a hand through his hair before letting his head fall back to the bed behind him. Tomorrow was soon enough to deal with Donna and the manipulations that had gone on behind his back. Right now, he needed to make sure everyone was gone, and that the police dealt with the gardener.

He looked over at the bedside table and reached for the book, the only thing in the room that belonged to Donna, seeking some comfort in touching something that was hers. He smiled at the title—*Peter Pan*—another kid's book. He shook his head at yet another sign of her soft heart. And then he flicked the book open.

CHAPTER 29

Donna woke to the early morning sun streaming through her bedroom window. She'd forgotten to close the blind. She rolled to her back and groaned at the thought of getting up to face the day, but someone had to be there to deal with the cleaning crew so that the house would be in pristine shape when Duncan came home.

"Duncan!" She sat up in bed with a squeal.

"Good morning, Donna." He was sitting on the armchair in the corner of her room, facing her bed.

Although he was dressed in fresh clothes, and had obviously showered and shaved, he didn't look like he'd gotten very much sleep. Her mind raced over the events of the night before, and her stomach sank. She was in so much trouble.

Who knew what state the mansion was in, and then there was the gardener to deal with…

"My painting!" She leaned over the side of the bed to find the ruined canvas still on the floor where Duncan had left it.

"I haven't touched it." His low, rumbling voice was a warning. Unfortunately, it was also the same tone that acted like a tuning fork for her libido.

She plastered on a fake smile. "How did the lecture go? Did you have a good time in Glasgow?"

"Aye." His dark eyes captured hers. "It was 'hashtag awesome.'"

She blinked at him, unsure of what to make of his response. "That's great. I need to get ready."

"No, you don't. I've already dealt with the cleaning crew. We've got a lot to talk about, and I think it's best if you stay where you are. We both know how good you are at avoiding things you don't want to deal with."

"At least let me use the bathroom."

He inclined his head in permission. "But no running. I'll just catch you."

She swallowed hard and dashed for the bathroom, where she did her business, then washed her face and brushed her teeth.

"Don't think you can hide in there all day." Duncan's voice came through the door.

There was nothing else to do but face him—and the mess she'd made of things. With a sense of dread, she left the safety of the bathroom and returned to the bed.

He eyed her coolly. "Let's start with the ball."

She winced. There really had been nowhere else to start. "I'm sorry." There was nothing else to say. It had been a screw-up from beginning to end.

"You should have asked me if you could hold it here."

It was hard to look him in the eye. "You would have said no."

"Damn right, I would. I'd also have stood by you while you dealt with those women. They walked all over you. And you let them."

"I know." She stared out at the green vista for a minute. "But it was for cancer patients. How could I say no to that?"

He ran a hand over his face. "That's exactly why you

should have told me. They played you. They wanted to hold the party here, and they knew they needed a cause that you couldn't say no to."

Donna snorted. "They didn't have to look far—there isn't much I'd turn down."

"Which is why you should have let me stand up for you. I would have protected you, and this wouldn't have happened."

"Or would you have shot the messenger?"

"No' this week." His lips twitched, and she could have sworn he was about to smile. "From now on, I'll deal with the Women's Institute."

Donna didn't argue. She hadn't planned on being there to deal with them anyway. Her mouth felt dry, and she licked her lips to wet them.

"There's water on the bedside table," Duncan said.

Grateful, she took it and drank her fill.

His eyes never left her. "There's also the matter of you lying to me."

She took another sip of water, wishing it was wine. She could have done with some fortification for this conversation. "Are you firing me?"

"Oh, no, Angel. I have other punishments in mind."

She wasn't sure she liked the sound of that. "If it's any consolation, I hated lying to you. I was sick over it."

"I know."

"How?"

"Because I know you. Although, you don't seem to think I do," he said ominously. "We'll deal with the issue of you lying to me later. There are other things we need to get sorted first. Like this."

He tossed a book onto her bed, and she grimaced. "I don't suppose you're just upset because you don't like *Peter Pan?*"

He wasn't amused. "Why didn't you tell me you could draw?"

She almost choked on her water. "Because I can't. *You* can draw. I doodle."

He stared at her for so long, she started to squirm. "You really believe that, don't you?" He didn't wait for an answer, he just leaned forward, resting his forearms on his thighs. "Those are some of the best illustrations I've ever seen."

The blood drained from her head so fast she felt dizzy and had to curl a hand into the bedding to stop from falling over. "You don't mean that."

"Aye, I do. And the dean of the Fine Arts school thought the same thing when I showed her your copy of *The Hobbit* last night."

"I'm going to be sick." She swung her legs over the side of the bed.

Duncan was there in a flash, pressing a gentle hand to the back of her neck. "Lean over and breathe slowly until it passes. You'll be fine."

She didn't think so, but she did as he told her. When she sat back up, he was on the bed beside her.

"Okay," he said. "We'll deal with that topic later too. There's something more important to discuss first. Why are you moving out of the mansion and quitting your job?"

"Oh." Donna had forgotten about the state of her apartment.

"Aye, *oh*. I'd like an explanation."

She eyed the bedroom door.

"Don't even think about running," Duncan said. "I've locked us in and taken your key."

"Do you realise how wrong that is?"

He narrowed his eyes at her. "As wrong as running out on me when I wasn't here to stop it happening?"

There was no other option but to brazen it out. "We both know this situation is going nowhere."

"What situation?"

"You and me. Our…romance. The sensible decision was to cut ties and let us both start anew."

"Sensible?" A muscle on his jaw ticked.

"Yes."

"Did you no' think it might be a good idea to ask me if I thought this thing between us was going nowhere too?"

The water bottle shook in her hands, and she couldn't look at him. "I did."

* * *

DUNCAN TOOK the bottle from her and placed it back on the bedside table. She was trembling hard, and it took all his willpower not to pull her into his arms. What a mess she'd gotten herself into.

"When did you ask me this?"

She flicked an agony-filled glance in his direction. "The night before you left."

He went over their conversation in his mind, finding the point where he'd messed up.

What I want to know is, do you think you could ever love someone other than Fiona?

Why would you ask me something like that? Ask another question—one I can answer.

He's been an idiot. Again.

"Oh, Donna," he said on a sigh. "Will I ever get things right with you?"

Her face turned back to his, but she didn't ask the question in her eyes.

"When I told you not to ask me if I could love again, it was because I was worried about scaring you off."

"What?" she whispered as her eyes went wide.

He tucked her bed-tousled hair behind her ear. "I knew I

was falling in love with you, and I wanted to give you time to, maybe, fall in love with me too before I told you." He snorted. "I'm under no illusions that I'm any sort of catch. I come with a boatload of issues, a house that sucks money and needs to be maintained for eternity, and a reputation in the art world that can sometimes make demands on me and gets in the way of life. I thought that after you'd seen the way I struggled to get over Fiona's death, you would think I wasn't worth the effort. And the truth is, Angel, I'm not. But I wanted you for myself anyway."

He saw a whole gamut of emotions flash across her face—hope, joy, fear, worry. He stroked her cheek with his thumb. "What's going on in that head of yours?"

She took a deep breath. "You're over Fiona's death?"

It wasn't the first thing he'd expected her to ask. "Aye." He held up his bare left hand. "I gave her back her ring. Those promises were fulfilled. It's time to make new ones. With someone else. With you."

She gasped and searched his eyes. "You're falling in love with me?"

"No." He shook his head, quickly adding before she could misunderstand and do something else daft that he'd have to sort out, "I've *fallen* in love with you. It's already happened. It's a done deal as far as I'm concerned."

She trembled under his touch. "Duncan?"

"I don't know when it happened," he told her softly, wanting everything out in the open between them. "It came on me slowly, and it took me a while to realise what the feelings were. That was because it was different from what I'd experienced with Fiona."

"Oh," her whole body became taut and she looked away from him.

He was screwing it up again. "No. Not *oh*." He gently

clasped her chin and angled her face to make her look at him. "I said *different*, not *less*. The love I had for Fiona was a gentle thing. It's hard to describe, and I'm rubbish at this, but I'm going to try. So don't freak out if I get it wrong."

She nodded.

"Fiona didn't need me the way you do. She needed someone to support her decisions, to think they were as important as she did, and to indulge her dreams. She needed a man who shared the power with her, and who hung back when she was sorting things out for herself. I loved those things about her, and I loved that our sex life was always a battle of wills.

"With you, it's different, but more intense than it was with Fiona. I don't know if that's because her death changed me into a rougher man, or because we're just two different people who relate to each other in a way that's unique for us.

"You need a man who'll protect that soft heart of yours from those who'd take advantage of it, someone who'll give you the courage and self-confidence to see how truly amazing you are. You need a man to take control in the bedroom, and to step in when needed outside of it, to ensure that you don't get hurt. I can be that man for you. I know I can. If you'll give me a chance."

"Oh Duncan, I hear what you're saying, but I'm not Fiona. And you said it yourself, she's the love of your life."

"No, you're not Fiona," he told her. "You never will be—and listen carefully—I don't want you to be. Fiona wasn't the love of my life. She was the love of my youth, of the man I was. You are the love of my adulthood, of the man I've become. I thought my heart had been buried along with her, but I was wrong. It was still in there, being put back together, piece by piece, each day that you were patient with me. I know who you are, and I want you exactly the way you are." He smiled ruefully. "Although, if you could stop lying to me, that would be greatly appreciated."

Her eyes welled up and a tear slid down her cheek.

"Now you know how I feel. The question is"—Duncan took a deep breath—"can you love me back?"

* * *

THERE WAS ONLY one answer to that question. Duncan captured her heart the moment she'd held him on the driveway on that cold spring night. She wasn't a woman to second-guess people when they told her things, and she saw the truth in his eyes as he lay his feelings before her. If he could take a chance on having his heart broken again, then she could take a chance on him.

"Yes." Donna got up onto her knees, clasped Duncan's shocked face, and pressed a gentle kiss to his lips. "Yes," she said again. "I've loved you since that night on the drive. Maybe even before that."

He clasped her hips and frowned. "Are you sure? There's no taking it back mind. So make sure you're certain."

"I have never been more certain of anything in my life."

He let out a little growl, clasped the back of her head, and slammed his mouth over hers. The kiss was untamed, much like the man.

When he broke away, it left them both panting. "So," he said, "there'll be no more talk of you leaving me?"

"No." She kissed him again.

It took a little longer for him to stop this kiss and she moaned her complaint when he did. "No' so fast. You're still in trouble."

"You're kidding, right? Don't we have better things to do than talk about the past?"

"Nice try, Angel," he said.

She looked over his shoulder at the crowd of hand-drawn characters filling her bedroom. *Duncan loves me,* she told them in wonder.

I can't believe you didn't see it coming, Hermione said. *I've known for years.*

Gandalf the White nodded. *Any fool could see it in the man.*

I'm glad I don't have to kill him, Katniss said. *I might kill a lot of people, but I don't actually enjoy it.*

If you're really good, Master might give you your freedom, Dobby said.

Oh, I plan to be really, really good, Donna told the house-elf. But probably not in the way Dobby meant.

Eww! Hermione snapped. *Do you mind? We're PG-rated characters!*

Well done, darling, Harry Potter's mother said. *I knew it would all work out.*

We need cake! Molly beamed at her before running off. *I'll get one started,* she called over her shoulder.

"Donna? Are you listening to me?" Duncan said.

She looked into his handsome face and smiled. "No, I was telling my imaginary friends that you'd come to your senses."

His smile was a thing of beauty. "Aye, I might have at that, but that doesn't mean we don't still have to deal with the ball situation, and the lying, and the talent you've been hiding, and the fact you roped your sisters and the cook into conning me, and—"

"Shut up and kiss me," Donna demanded, then blushed at her audacity.

He grinned at her. "I can do better than that. You'd best tell your friends to leave, or they're going to get an eyeful."

"Is that right?" she asked as he lowered her back into the bed.

"Oh, that's definitely right."

As he took her mouth in a passionate kiss, Donna opened

one eye and peeked behind him. Everyone but Ron had gone. He stood grinning at her, taking it all in, until his mother appeared in a flash, hit him with a wooden spoon and dragged him off by his ear.

With their exit, Donna closed her eye again and lost herself in the kiss of the man who loved her.

EPILOGUE

Four months later

Fighting the urge to vomit, Donna paced their Glasgow apartment, her palm flat against her stomach. "I can't do it," she told her husband.

"Of course you can. You married me, so you can do anything." He winked at her from where he was sitting at the breakfast bar, waiting for Grace to dish up their food.

If Grace hadn't moved to the city with them, they would have died of starvation before the new school term even started.

"He's right," Grace said as she dished out bacon and omelettes.

"As usual," Duncan said into his coffee mug.

"I don't know about that, but he's right about you being able to do this. You have talent and passion, go make something of your life." Grace smiled encouragingly.

"I can't. Everyone will think the only reason I got a place

at the art school was that I married one of the tutors." It was mortifying. She pointed at Duncan. "I should never have let you talk me into a quickie wedding."

"Too late now." He was unrepentant as he dug into his food. "And don't think you can get out of the honeymoon either. I've paid for it, and as soon as the term ends, we're flying out of here."

"I didn't need to get married or have a honeymoon. You've done all that before, and I was happy to live in sin."

"But I wasn't. It's done. Suck it up."

That was her husband—oozing compassion and tact.

"Even if everyone does think you got the place because of Duncan," Grace said. "They'll soon change their minds once they see your drawings."

"That's what I told her," Duncan said.

"No"—Donna smacked him on the back of the head as she passed—"*you* said to pay no attention to what people said because you wouldn't have married someone with no talent."

"Same thing." He flashed that grin that made her melt inside.

"It will be a disaster," she said as she continued pacing. "I'm too old to be a student."

"There will be all ages there, plenty of them older than you," Duncan said.

"I need cake." She stalked towards the kitchen.

Grace smacked her away with her spatula. "You're not getting cake for breakfast. Sit down and eat your omelette."

Her phone rang on the coffee table. She picked it up and looked at the screen. "I can't deal with this right now." She tossed the phone to Duncan who snatched it out of the air.

"Duncan," he barked when he answered. "No. I won't tell the board they're being unreasonable about the ball. If you want to raise money for Fiona's cancer foundation, you must abide by the decisions of the mansion trust and board. They run the mansion and the charity." He paused and then burst out laughing. "That doesn't work on me. You can whine on about every sick kid and broken animal in Scotland, but it won't get you anywhere. You're talking to the wrong Stewart." He hung up. "Bloody Flora," he muttered.

He reached for his own phone and dialled. "Janine?" he said to his lawyer. "Shut that crap down with the Women's Institute. They either run a nice civilised ball that's overseen by the board of trustees or they don't get in at all." He paused to listen. "Aye, I'll tell her."

He hung up and smiled at Donna. "Janine said good luck for your first day."

Donna groaned as she stalked to the large bay window overlooking the city. They'd bought a large apartment at the top of a Victorian tenement on Garnet Hill, near the art school. She'd thought she would miss the countryside of Kintyre, but she loved being in the city. Of course, she had the best of both worlds because they'd kept the carriage house for their personal use and signed over the mansion to a trust that ran it as a charity to raise money for cancer patients in Fiona's name.

She wished she were in the carriage house right now, losing herself in a good book, instead of walking into art college for the first day of a degree course.

Strong arms wrapped around her waist, and Duncan's chin rested on her head. "You owe me," he said. "You're still paying off your debt for all that lying and scheming you did months ago."

Which reminded her. "When, exactly, is that debt going to be paid?"

"I'll let you know." He squeezed her tight. "Come on. I'll walk you to school."

"That sounds so wrong." She turned in his arms. "I'll only go if you give me a kiss."

"And that's my cue to leave," Grace announced. "I'll see you both at dinner."

As Grace left the room, Duncan pressed a gentle kiss to her lips while staring into her eyes. "Have I told you how much I like our new sofa?"

"No." She glanced at the huge, cream coloured sofa behind him.

"You would look great bent over the arm of it, while I took you from behind."

She sucked in a breath, her body rushing ahead of her brain, getting ready for him to do whatever he pleased. "Is that right? And what if I say no?"

His eyes darkened. "Angel, you know you can always say no to me."

And then he kissed her, taking away her first-day nerves once and for all.

Read on for a taste of Isobel Sinclair's story.

The village of Arness, Scotland

Isobel Sinclair should have contacted the authorities the first time she saw the boat sneaking into the cove. But she didn't. She should have called when there was a storm during the boat's third visit, and the crew lost some of their baggage on the rocky path up to Arness. But she didn't. Instead, she'd gathered their lost cargo, called it her own and sold it to help pay off her ex-husband's debts.

Which made her a thief, just like him.

And her thieving was the reason she still didn't call in the authorities the time the boat turned up in the dead of night, and there was shouting in the darkness. Or the time she'd seen evidence that someone had dragged something heavy over the beach.

No, she'd never called the authorities. Not once. Even though she knew the boat brought nothing but trouble each time it snuck into shore.

But she should have called, because the boat had come back.

And this time, they'd left a body behind.

"What are we going to do with him?" Isobel's youngest sister, Mairi, stared down at the man.

The dead man.

"I suppose we could bury him," Agnes, one of their middle sisters, said.

"We can't bury him here." Isobel gestured to the rock-strewn beach. "Even if we do manage to dig a hole, the tide will unearth him in a day or two."

Mairi looked up at the steep, rocky path behind them, the only route down from the bluff where the tiny town of Arness sat. "We'll never get him back up there. He looks like he weighs a ton."

"And he's wet." Agnes nodded. "That makes you heavier."

"Aye," Mairi said. "Water retention."

Isobel and Agnes stared at their sister.

"What?" Mairi said.

With shakes of their heads, Agnes and Isobel turned their attention back to the body.

"How do you think he died?" Agnes said.

"I suppose we should look him over and see if we can tell." Isobel didn't like the thought of touching the man, let alone examining him for clues as to his cause of death.

"Does it really matter how he died?" Mairi said. "I mean, it isn't going to change the fact that he's dead. Or that he was left here by the boat people."

"The boat people?" Agnes looked towards heaven and seemed to be counting to ten. Again.

Mairi shrugged, her long red hair shifting with the movement. "What else are we to call them? And he was left here by the boat crew. Isobel saw them while she was spying."

Isobel adopted her patented "haughty eldest sister" look—

it helped take her mind off her shaking hands and the fear gnawing at her stomach. "I wasn't spying. I was looking out of my window and saw them carry him off the boat and dump him here."

"You were looking out of your window with the aid of binoculars," Mairi reminded her.

She had a point. "What I don't get is if these boat people are so keen on going unnoticed, then why are they dumping bodies on the beach?" Isobel said. "I mean, they only come in the dead of night. And we know they're up to no good."

"Smuggling," Mairi said with a decisive nod.

Agnes walked around the prone man and looked back out at the choppy waters behind them, then up at the hill leading to town. "Do you think they meant for him to be swept out to sea? Or to be eaten by the crabs?"

"If they wanted him to be swept out to sea, why not dump him out there in the first place?" Isobel said. "And I don't think half a dozen crabs are enough to eat a full-grown body. At least not fast enough to get rid of the evidence."

"Even then," Mairi said, "there would still be the bones."

They nodded in agreement, and Isobel couldn't help but notice that her sisters were struggling to hide their shaking hands, just as she was doing.

"I think we should call the police." Seeing as Agnes wasn't the most law-abiding member of the family, it said a lot that she was the one to suggest calling them in.

"I can't." Isobel tugged at the sleeves of her oversized purple cardigan and wrapped her arms around herself. "They'll find out that I sold the stuff I found, rather than reporting it to them in the first place."

"I told you, you shouldn't have gone to the pawn shop in Campbeltown," Mairi said. "Too many people know us there."

"I wanted rid of it fast."

Plus, she'd needed the money to pay off the loan shark who was hounding her over her ex-husband's debt. Seeing as the man couldn't find Robert, he'd decided to make Isobel pay in his stead, with cash or her body, making it clear that her family would suffer if she didn't comply. That was the reason Isobel's moral judgment had been silenced when she'd found the stolen goods on the path—the thought of handing over her body to pay her ex-husband's debt made her ill. But she'd do it if she had to. She'd do just about anything to make sure her kids were safe.

"Enough of this." Agnes crouched down and turned the body over.

He flopped onto his back, and the cause of death was instantly clear. There was a wide, gaping slit where his throat used to be.

"I think I'm going to be sick." Mairi covered her mouth and turned her back on the body, making gagging sounds as she did so.

"Don't," Agnes ordered. "You know I'm a sympathetic puker. If you start vomiting, we'll both be doing it."

Isobel ignored her sisters as she stared at the body. It was the most horrifying thing she'd ever seen. She swallowed hard. "You can't accidentally slit your own throat, can you?"

"No," Agnes said firmly.

Aye, that would have been too much to hope for.

There was a scrambling noise from the bluff behind them. The women yelped and spun, to see their remaining sister coming down the rocky path.

Isobel put her hand to her chest. Her heart was racing hard. "You nearly gave me a heart attack," she told her sister.

Donna rushed up to them, her blonde hair flying out behind her. "Sorry. What's so urgent we had to meet in the dark on the beach? Did you find more bounty?"

It was then she saw the body. The colour drained from

her face, she turned and promptly vomited. Which, in turn, made Agnes vomit.

Mairi started making gagging noises. "I'm okay, I'm okay." She held one hand up, pressing the other to her stomach. "I can hold it."

"What a relief," Isobel told her.

Mairi shot her an irritated look. "I told you not to call Donna. She's vegetarian."

"I didn't expect her to eat him." Isobel glared back at her.

"That's just gross," Mairi said, and gagged again.

Isobel threw her hands up in disgust. "Why did I bother calling any of you? You're no use at all. We have a situation here and all you're doing is being sick."

"It's not like we can help it," Agnes said, looking decidedly green.

"Some warning would have been good." Donna swayed in place. Her eyes were on the water instead of the man.

"I did warn you when I called," Isobel said through gritted teeth. "I said, come quick, there's a dead body on the beach."

"I thought you were joking," Donna said.

"About a dead body?" Isobel practically shrieked.

"Right." Agnes held up her hands. "Everybody calm down. This isn't helping. It's getting light, and we need to deal with the body. It's not like people use this beach, but if someone did come down here, they'd call the police." She looked at Isobel. "And seeing as your house is the closest, you'd be first on their list to interview."

"That wouldn't go well," Mairi said. "Your whole face goes red when you lie, and you start stuttering."

"Then you just blab the truth and apologise for trying to lie," Donna added.

"Which means you'd get arrested for fencing stolen goods." Agnes nodded. "Something we're trying to avoid."

"Are you all about done?" Isobel put her hands on her hips

and glared at them. Was this really the time to bring up every single one of her flaws? "The kids will be awake soon. We need to deal with this now."

They all stared at the man.

"I've never seen a dead body before," Mairi said. "They look so lifeless."

"Idiot." Agnes smacked Mairi on the back of the head.

"What was that for?" Mairi rubbed her head.

"For being an idiot," Agnes said. "Now focus. Do we leave him here? Cover him and come back later to bury him? Bury him now? Or move him somewhere else while we think things over?"

"I think we need to move him. It would be too hard to bury him here, and we couldn't guarantee the tide wouldn't unearth him later." Isobel felt weary. She was sick of the stress in her life. Sick of dealing with other people's messes. Sick of struggling every single day just to survive. "Whatever we do, we need to do it fast, before the kids wake up. Either way, I want him off the beach. Jack sometimes comes down here with his friends after school, and I wouldn't want them to find the body."

"You could put him in the freezer in your garage," Donna said. "It still works, doesn't it?"

"Aye, but it's old, full of rust and smelly," Isobel said.

"I don't think he'll care," Donna said.

"What do we do with him once he's in the freezer? We can't leave him there forever." Isobel gnawed at her bottom lip and wondered how her life had come to this point.

She was a single mother of two, with two failed relationships behind her, a mountain of debt she hadn't personally accumulated, a minimum-wage job in the village shop and an ever-growing list of crimes under her belt. It was not how she'd imagined life would be at the grand old age of thirty-two.

"We need advice. We need someone who knows what to do with a dead body," Agnes said. "We need an expert."

"I'm not calling the police," Isobel said adamantly. She was the only stability her kids had. She couldn't even think of risking it.

"I wasn't thinking of the police," Agnes said. "I was thinking of an outlaw."

"Yes!" Mairi clapped her hands and grinned. "Great idea, Aggie."

"No." Isobel shook her head. "No. Just no."

Donna placed her hand on Isobel's arm. "Don't dismiss this idea just because you fancy the man. He used to be in the army. He's bound to have seen dead bodies during conflict. He must have an idea what to do with them."

"I-I don't f-fancy him," Isobel protested, but nobody was listening. No, she just dreamed about him every blooming night. What was it with her and bad boys? Hadn't she learned her lesson by now? Why couldn't she find a nice six-stone weakling of an accountant to fall in love with?

"It's well known he's dangerous," Agnes said. "Old man McKay used to tell everyone that his grandson was deadly. He was in the Special Forces. He knows about dead bodies."

"Plus," Mairi said, "there's a security company watching him—covertly." She whispered the last word as though it had special powers. "That must mean he's on the other side of the law now, which means he won't report us to the cops."

"I didn't know he was being watched." Donna's eyes went wide. "Maybe talking to him isn't such a good idea."

"I spoke to the woman who was setting up cameras," Isobel said. Of course she was going to grill a stranger who was setting up CCTV in the street, in the dark. "She showed me her ID and said he wasn't dangerous to the town. He isn't a criminal. She said he's only dangerous to bad guys." And then the blue-haired woman had laughed. It wasn't reassuring. Neither was the fact she was wearing a Wonder Woman T-shirt and a pair of pink, glittery Doc Marten boots. "She gave me her business card, in case I was ever worried about anything."

"Maybe we should call the security company instead?" Mairi said. "We can ask them what to do."

Agnes groaned. "I can just imagine that conversation— 'Hello, we have the body of a stranger in our freezer and we're looking for suggestions on what to do with it.' Aye, that would go well."

"It was only an idea." Mairi frowned at Agnes.

"Whatever," Agnes said. "I think our best bet is the outlaw. You said he's huge and there are weapons lying around in his house. He's obviously used to dangerous situations. I bet he'd know what to do with the body. You need to ask him for help."

"No."

Isobel had been delivering groceries to Callum McKay's house for almost four months, and she'd only seen the man three times. All three times, he'd scared the life out of her. Rage covered him like a shroud. But there was also something about him that made her heart ache. Maybe it was the utter desolation in his eyes, or the fact that the only people she'd seen near him had been from a security company that was hiding in the dark. She'd never met someone so completely alone. And so brutally raw. He was the embodiment of her own personal weakness—the tortured bad boy, with muscles like Thor. She didn't have to be massively self-aware to realise that he was the last person she should approach for help. No, for the sake of her sanity, it was best to keep far, far away from the man.

"Honey," Agnes said, "we don't have a lot of options here. Either you get help from someone who knows what to do with a body, or you keep the guy frozen in your old chest freezer for the foreseeable future."

"Aye," Donna said. "And what if this is just the beginning? What if the boat people dump more bodies? We need a plan. We need advice."

"Or we need to start our own crematorium business," Mairi said.

"Think of your kids," Agnes said. "This is getting worse every month. We're in way over our heads. We need help. If this guy can help, then great. If not, we'll try something else."

Isobel's heart sank. Agnes was right. They were out of options. Staying away from Callum McKay had become a luxury she couldn't afford. And it wasn't as if she wanted to start a relationship with him. No, she just wanted advice on what to do with the dead stranger who'd been dumped on her beach.

"You can do it," Donna said softly. "We have your back."

Isobel blinked back tears, as love for her sisters overwhelmed her. She didn't know how she'd survive without them. She needed to talk to Callum for their sakes. This situation with the mysterious boat was well past the point of being dangerous, and they were getting in deeper every month. No, they weren't —she was. And she was dragging her sisters down with her.

"Okay, I'll talk to him."

"You'll be okay, honey," Agnes said.

"Just keep your hands off him," Mairi said. "Maybe you could call him instead of talking to him face to face."

That caused Agnes to smack her again. "She isn't going to jump the man, idiot."

There was a pause as all three sisters gave her speculative looks. Isobel threw up her hands in disgust. "So I have a type. So what? It's not like I'm going to throw myself at him and offer to sleep with him in return for his help."

There was a shuffling of feet as her sisters cast sideward glances at each other.

"Thanks a lot," Isobel said. "Good to know you have so much faith in me."

"You tend to get physical without thinking it through," Donna said gently.

"I only did that once," Isobel protested. And ended up pregnant and alone at seventeen because of it.

Her sisters stared at her.

"Fine. Twice." And she had the ex-husband from hell to show for that little slip in self-control.

"If it's any consolation," Mairi said, "I've totally learned from your mistakes."

"No. It's no consolation. Now do you three think you could stop analysing my past mistakes long enough to help me get this body off the beach?" She looked at the sliver of light on the horizon. "Sun's coming. We need to get him to the garage and into the freezer before the kids wake up."

"This is going to be gross," Mairi said. "I'll need to burn my clothes after this."

"I might vomit again," Donna said.

"Get a grip," Agnes snapped, "and take an arm or a leg each."

With each of them clutching a limb, the four sisters carried the dead man up the hill to Isobel's house. Donna and Agnes were only sick twice.

Get Rage now to keep on reading!

ABOUT THE AUTHOR

I'm a Scot, living in New Zealand and married to a Dutch man. I write contemporary romance with a humorous bent – this is mainly due to the fact I have an odd sense of humour and can't keep it out of anything I do! If I wasn't a writer, I'd like to be Buffy the Vampire Slayer, or Indiana Jones. Unfortunately, both these roles have already been filled. Which may be a good thing as I have no fighting skills, wouldn't know a precious relic if it hit me in the face and have an aversion to blood. When I'm not living in my head, I'm a mother to two kids, several pet sheep, one dog, four cats, three alpacas, two miniature horses, eight guinea pigs and an escape artist chicken.